Prescription for Murder

Prescription for Murder

David Williams

St. Martin's Press
New York

PRESCRIPTION FOR MURDER. Copyright © 1990 by David Williams. All rights reserved.
Printed in the United States of America. No part of this book may be used
or reproduced in any manner whatsoever without written permission except
in the case of brief quotations embodied in critical articles or reviews. For
information, address St. Martin's Press, 175 Fifth Avenue, New York, N.Y. 10010.

Library of Congress Cataloging-in-Publication Data

Williams, David.
    Prescription for murder / David Williams.
        p.   cm.
    ISBN 0-312-05009-7
    I. Title.
    PR6073.I42583P74   1991
    823'.914—dc20   90-15549
                                                                  CIP

First published in Great Britain by Macmillan London Limited.

First U.S. Edition: March 1991
10 9 8 7 6 5 4 3 2 1

This one for
Frank and Polly Muir

Prescription for Murder

Chapter One

'Should I buy shares in Closter Drug?' asked Sir James Crib-Cranton before blowing his nose. It was a large nose on a craggy, imperious face topped by snow-white hair in plenty. He thrust the linen handkerchief deep into a side pocket of the double-breasted pin-stripe jacket, then pushed a fragment of Stilton cheese on to a biscuit. The speaker's searching gaze stayed on his lunch guest through most of these small manoeuvres. Crib-Cranton was after inside information and wasn't about to miss a reaction.

'What's your stockbroker say?' Mark Treasure responded easily, before consuming the last bit of his lemon pancakes.

It was a Thursday in early May. The two were at a window table in the panelled first-floor dining room of Crib-Cranton's club at the top of St James's Street in London.

'My stockbroker says yes to anything that earns him commission, including bets on horses, I shouldn't wonder. All stockbrokers are the same these days. Not an objective thought between the lot of them. Too hard up, I expect,' Crib-Cranton continued loudly. He turned the distinguished head in a token, defiant searching of the room for stockbroker members of the club, of whom there were several – all of them quite as affluent as he was. 'I'm asking about Closter Drug because it says in the prospectus that you're the Chairman. I'd forgotten that.'

'Non-executive Chairman,' replied the forty-four year old Treasure, Chief Executive of Grenwood, Phipps, the merchant bankers.

Crib-Cranton – known as Jumbo to his intimates since international rugby-playing days – was considerably older than his companion, and the autocratic head of CCB, one of Britain's largest construction groups. He was a corporate customer of Grenwood, Phipps, and an old friend of Treasure's. His private portfolio of shares was handled by stockbrokers and not managed by the bank: this was because the self-made Jumbo begrudged paying the bank a management fee when he could have Treasure's advice for nothing.

'I'm a simple sort of chap, of course,' he said next, without in the least meaning it. 'But I'd have thought you needed to know a bit about pharmaceuticals to be chairman of a drug manufacturer. Even a non-executive chairman,' he said, the tone speculative not disparaging.

'I rub along.' Treasure leaned back in his chair, wiping his mouth with his napkin. 'I took it on for a special reason five years ago. When we agreed to finance the company.'

'Management buy-out wasn't it?'

'That's right. Closter was a subsidiary of Philer International. Philer bought it eight years before that, but it never really fitted. They needed to sell it to help fund something else.'

'Philer are in sweets and soft drinks?'

'And convenience foods,' Treasure supplied.

'Exactly. So why dabble in pharmaceuticals in the first place?' Jumbo Crib-Cranton disapproved of what he termed over-diversification – meaning any diversification. He was in the construction business, and when he acquired other companies they were always in that business too. 'People should stick with what they're good at,' he went on. 'So the Closter managers came to you five years ago, did they?'

'To the bank, yes. They wanted to go it alone. Rather than have the company sold over their heads to another drug manu-facturer.'

'And they've done well? Since they're going public next Wednesday. The prospectus in the paper yesterday looked healthy enough. The shares aren't cheap, of course. Ah, *gracias*, my dear. *Muchas gracias*,' Jumbo's big frame straightened, and he was pulling in his stomach. The look he was directing at the pretty, dark-haired waitress was shallowly benign but deeply lascivious. The girl, in a tight-fitting black dress, had brought the celery he had asked for earlier. His eyes followed the neat figure as she retreated. 'Been here a week. Doesn't speak English. Spanish,' he assured Treasure in a confidential sort of tone. 'I can always tell by the bearing. Did I mention it earlier?' He had, though his companion thought the supposition wrong. 'Delicious creature.'

Treasure worried some breadcrumbs on the table with his finger. 'But not cheap, you said?'

'Good God, how should I know?' Jumbo's eyes narrowed speculatively. 'Why? D'you suppose she'd er— ?'

'I mean the Closter Drug shares. You think they're expensive at a hundred and ten?' said the banker. The appearance of a pretty girl regularly distracted Jumbo from any business on hand. Treasure usually overcame such lapses by ignoring them. 'The *Financial Times* also says we've pitched the offer price too high.'

After supporting the managers of Closter Drug when they had taken over the business, Grenwood, Phipps were now handling the public flotation of the company on the stock market. The prospectus Jumbo had referred to had been in four national newspapers a day earlier. It contained an offer to the public at large to buy shares in Closter Drug at a hundred and ten pence each, along with the ponderous information every such prospectus must carry by law, and covering four pages of newsprint.

'I saw the comment in the *FT*. But you don't usually get these things wrong,' said Jumbo, abandoning his Spanish interest. 'The Closter forecast looked tempting enough. Bit speculative still, is it? Four and a half million pre-tax profit on a turnover of twenty million? That's reasonable in anyone's language. Less debt than you'd expect, too. I read a good deal of the small print,' he added, as if the action was deserving of credit.

'It's projected profit, yes. The company's not hit those kind of figures yet. But when we've paid off the loan-stock holders— '

'Which you'll do with the flotation money. That's fair enough.' Jumbo circled the air with a stick of celery. 'I suppose the full-time Closter directors will be millionaires overnight?'

'Directors who took a big holding at the time of the buy-out, they'll do well, certainly. Ordinary members of staff will too. It's why they've all been working their heads off for five years. There'll be a few paper millionaires. The Managing Director for one. He'd staked everything he had. Mortgaged himself to the eyeballs to own a sizeable piece of the action.'

'Wise man,' Jumbo scented a fellow entrepreneur.

The banker nodded. 'He ends up with ten per cent of the company. Eight million shares.'

'Worth eight point eight million pounds.' Jumbo did the easy arithmetic, his bushy eyebrows arching briefly as he spoke. 'And the other directors?'

'A bit over six per cent between the five of them. Not equally

9

spread. The figures are in the prospectus. Incidentally, nearly half the staff became shareholders at the time of the management buy-out.'

Jumbo beamed, while chomping on the celery. 'How many people employed?'

'Three hundred and twenty.'

'Hmm. Wish half my staff was keen enough to own company shares. Different kind of animal, of course,' The CCB payroll of mostly semi-skilled workers topped thirty thousand in Britain alone. 'By the sound of it, Closter Drug is really a one man show,' Jumbo went on. 'This Managing Director – what's his name?'

'Larden. Bob Larden. Mid-fifties. He's a chemist by training.'

'And the driving force with the most at stake in the business. Thruster, who believes in himself?'

Treasure frowned. 'Maybe, but that's not the impression he fosters.'

'Which is why he got you to be Chairman. The special reason you mentioned.'

'Larden doesn't care to be in the spotlight.'

'And while there are plenty of lesser directors of Grenwood, Phipps who could have taken the chair, he wanted the man with the biggest reputation and got him. Smart chap.'

'That's overstating it. But it may have helped the credibility of the outfit for me to be involved. We wouldn't have put a director on the board at all unless they'd asked.'

'Even though the bank's been staking them?'

'Not our policy. Anyway, Bob Larden wanted to look like a member of a successful team, not its indispensable leader.'

'Because that makes a small company look vulnerable? He's wrong there.' Jumbo was pontificating again. 'People like an obvious leader, and leaders hardly ever get run over by those proverbial buses.' He'd been avoiding buses for years, along with all other forms of public transport. 'Was Closter Drug a loser when the management bought it?'

'More or less, yes. That wasn't the fault of the present management team though. Larden and his right-hand man, a much younger chap called Hackle, they'd been brought in from another pharmaceutical company about a year before. There really hadn't been time for them to turn the situation round.'

'And Closter hasn't got a real wonder drug of its own yet?' Jumbo put the bull question as casually as he could.

10

Treasure hesitated. 'Not quite yet. The recent success has been with me-too products. Our own versions of formulas just out of patent.'

'At lower prices?'

'That's about it.'

'Sounds too simple.'

'It's not really. You need a lot of finesse to do it profitably. There's a great deal of competition. And the Department of Health is red hot about safety.'

'But it's still work for marketing people, not chemists?'

'No. For both. Some of the products are identical to the ones first patented. Others are . . . well, refinements.'

'Reworkings of other people's discoveries. I've heard of that,' Jumbo commented dismissively. 'I'd have thought the lifeblood of a pharmaceutical company should be in dramatic discoveries made by dedicated researchers.' He was a romantic on plenty of subjects in addition to pretty women – and definitely on the subject of how other people should run their businesses. 'Isn't that where the real profit is?' he pressed.

'The first part of your premise is true. The lifeblood ought to be in discovery. Innovation. Unfortunately the bit about profit doesn't always follow,' Treasure replied, thinking that if the same applied in the construction industry, the profit-oriented Jumbo Crib-Cranton would long since have moved to pastures new. 'It's estimated nowadays that it takes nineteen years of sales, world-wide, to cover the development cost of a new drug.'

'Astonishing.' Jumbo fixed the celery jug with an accusing stare, as if the fault might lie inside it.

'More so when you know that new drugs can only be patented for twenty years. And that includes the ten years or more they'll stay in the testing stages.'

'Ten?' The speaker extracted a short piece of celery from the jug and salted the end.

'And that's less than the average, before a new drug is approved. It's sometimes as much as fifteen.'

Jumbo shook his head as he chewed. 'So companies like Closter could stand to do better with their me-too products than the real innovators?'

'It could happen, yes.'

'Which is why Closter don't do any serious research?'

Treasure shook his head. 'I didn't say that. I was— '

11

'I see. What about coffee?' Jumbo had interrupted after looking at the time. 'We'll go downstairs.'

While his host was signing the bill at the cashier's desk near the door, Treasure fell in with a mutual friend of theirs at the top of the carved mahogany staircase. The man's name was Starch, a member of the club who had been lunching alone. He was an orthopaedic surgeon of some eminence and close to retirement. He and Treasure knew each other because both were trustees of one of the opera companies.

'Mind if I join you?' asked the amiable Starch later, as the three entered the coffee room on the ground floor, with its celebrated bow-front on to St James's.

The surgeon was tall, slim, and stooped, with a high-pitched, dry voice – in contrast to the thickset, straight-backed Jumbo with his penetrating bass grumble.

'Delighted,' Jumbo replied, but with a signal lack of enthusiasm. As it happened, this had nothing to do with the newcomer. On enquiry from the dining-room manager upstairs, Jumbo had learned that the new waitress was a Turkish-speaking Cypriot. It wasn't something he intended telling Treasure, but the error rankled.

'I'm much taken with this flotation of yours, Mark,' Starch volunteered as they settled themselves in deep leather armchairs.

'So's Jumbo,' said Treasure. 'I'm glad there's so much interest. Bodes well for the success of the issue.'

'Oh, I've already put in for a modest stake,' Starch affirmed. 'It's a good little company. With er . . . with promise of even better to come it seems.'

'In your line, of course,' said Jumbo, waving for the steward. 'Port, anyone?' The others shook their heads. 'Just coffee for three then, please, Cyril,' he ordered.

'Not really my line,' said Starch, as the steward went away. 'You could say almost the opposite. All this progress in chemotherapy is rapidly destroying the future for the honest saw-bones.'

'Nonsense,' said Treasure with a chuckle.

'Good thing if it does, too,' said Jumbo, still irritated enough with himself to be taking it out on others.

'Oh? But you were telling us the other day what a success your prostatectomy has been,' the surgeon observed, a touch of amusement showing on the edges of the slim mouth.

'Er, yes, it has. Bloody painful though,' Jumbo re-acknowledged with reservation. 'Till they put me on to a new painkiller. Chemicals

12

again, you see?' he added. 'Anyway, I've been pumping Mark for privileged information. Except so far he hasn't told me anything I couldn't have read in the papers.'

'I'll send you our Investment Division's analysis of Closter prospects if you like,' said Treasure with a sly grin. 'No charge.'

'You've both seen the lunchtime edition of the *Evening Standard* I expect?' enquired the surgeon. And because the others said they hadn't, he went on. 'There's a report in the City section about Closter's new drug.'

'Is there now,' said Treasure, his face clouding. 'That's supposed to be under wraps— '

'Hidden, it seems, even from close friends and valued customers,' Jumbo interrupted with a glower.

'Until the news conference tomorrow,' the banker completed. While his host had been speaking he had reached for a copy of the paper from the table behind them. Now he rustled through the pages to the City news. 'I was just about to mention the fact when you said we should come down for coffee, Jumbo. Ah, here it is.' He studied the item for a moment. 'Yes, they've jumped the gun. Pity. It's given the subject a dramatic importance it really doesn't require.'

'I'll decide that when one of you tells me what the subject is,' said Jumbo, still affecting hurt feelings.

'It's a new drug for migraine. Not before time either,' said Starch. 'One of my sons is a martyr to migraine.'

'It's not such a common malady, is it?' said Jumbo, who happened never to have suffered from it himself. Treasure passed him the paper.

'Very common indeed,' the surgeon supplied. 'And one of the oldest ever recorded. Hippocrates gave us an account of it in about 400 BC. Approximately one person in ten gets it. It has many manifestations.'

'So a cure would be profitable?' Jumbo's interest had measurably heightened.

'Very much so. A lot of drug companies have been researching more effective treatments for years.'

'That's true,' said Treasure, 'Closter being one of them. We patented a formula six years ago. There's no secret about that.'

'So why does the *Standard* suggest there is?' demanded Jumbo, taking off his gold-framed half-spectacles after reading the report.

'It doesn't exactly. It simply assumes the news conference

tomorrow is to announce further progress on that particular Closter project. And as it happens that's perfectly correct.'

'You have other projects like that one?' asked Jumbo, scratching the hairy orifice of one ear with the end of his spectacles.

'Several. But none as advanced as this one.'

'Why isn't all this in the prospectus?'

'It is,' said Starch.

'It is,' said Treasure, almost at the same time. Both speakers smiled as the banker went on. 'You didn't read enough of the small print, Jumbo. There are details on three research projects at various stages of development. All involving formulas we've patented. Curiously, till now the media haven't shown interest in any of them.'

'Because they don't sound at all exciting the way they're covered in the prospectus,' said Starch. 'Difficult subject to handle in that way, I suppose. I expect there are legal restraints on a company being over enthusiastic about anything in a prospectus.'

'Very much so,' the banker replied seriously.

'Good thing too, of course,' Starch accepted, tweaking the end of his aquiline nose. 'Anyway, you've decided to give the migraine project an airing tomorrow? Any special reason?'

'Yes. Though I'm not sure it's an adequate one,' said Treasure. 'There's been a positive development since the prospectus was drafted. The results of the first clinical trials. They'll be formally reported in an article in one of the medical weeklies next Monday.'

The surgeon frowned. 'But Closter have decided to give a news conference about them now. Handy for the flotation of course, but pre-empting the medical journal report. Hmm. Quite sensible, I expect.' But there was a detectable degree of professional diffidence in the tone. Such information, the speaker seemed to infer, was best disseminated with restraint. A responsible learned journal provided just that. One didn't give advance grounds for revelation in the tabloids.

'It was a recommendation from the company's public relations consultants,' said Treasure uneasily. 'The report should have been published last Monday. It was delayed for some reason.'

'Pity,' said Starch quietly, dropping his gaze to study the fingertips of one hand.

'Parasitical breed, PR consultants,' Jumbo thundered, even more loudly than his comment in the dining room about stockbrokers – but with less likelihood of giving offence. There were no members of the club in the public relations business.

'I'm afraid the news conference was arranged without enough consultation.' Treasure rearranged a glass ashtray on the occasional table beside him.

'You mean they didn't ask you, and you don't approve?' Jumbo challenged, metaphorically twisting the knife to confirm his prejudice. He leaned forward in his chair to deal with the coffee that had just arrived. 'Typical.'

'Let's say the decision may have been taken too lightly,' said Treasure, without directly answering the question. It was quite true that he hadn't been asked, though that was not of itself unusual. He was very little involved in the company's line management decisions. Nevertheless, the significance of calling a news conference at this particular time had been strangely overlooked – something compounded by the fact that too few of the Closter Drug working directors had been consulted over the matter either. 'We considered cancelling, but decided that would only make the thing worse,' he completed, without much conviction.

Chapter Two

'The bit in the *Standard* makes it much worse. Professor Garside was unhappy enough before,' protested the nearly bald man in the white laboratory coat.

His name was Stuart Bodlin. He was a Doctor of Science, unmarried, and dedicated to his work. He had been Research Director at Closter Drug for eight years. The hair loss was deceiving. He was only just forty, of slight build, and diminutive with it. His wide forehead and sunken cheeks gave him a skeletal look that was somehow emphasised by the over-large spectacles, as it usually was also by a pale complexion.

The paleness didn't apply now because the face was pink with anger.

'Well, by all means, let's address ourselves to restoring the happiness of the good Professor Garside at the earliest possible time,' said Dermot Hackle, the Marketing Director. He was a few years younger than Bodlin, tall, fair and athletic, with rugged good looks. His diffident air suggested effortless superiority while disguising an underlying arrogance.

'There's no call for . . . for sarcasm,' stammered Bodlin, getting angrier by the second. He was standing in the centre of the room, shoulders hunched, feet together, arms folded tightly in front of him. 'Garside is the best academic biochemist we could have got. He'd almost agreed to write his paper straight away. Just using the clinical data from the first trial results. He was so impressed with them. Like everyone else.' The speaker paused for grim emphasis. 'Well five minutes ago he rang Mary. He's decided now he'll wait for the results of the second trial.'

'I'm afraid someone had shown him the newspaper report. He didn't know there was to be a news conference, of course,' put in Dr Mary Ricini, the attractive twenty-nine year old Medical Director of the company. 'It'll mean another six months before he

16

does the paper.' She crossed her shapely legs under a short skirt: the eyes of two of the three men present registered the movement more than just perceptibly.

'Not necessarily six months, surely? Anyway, I'll talk to Garside myself. I suppose we should have warned him about the conference.' The speaker was Bob Larden, the Managing Director, a fleshy man of middle height, with dimpled cheeks but cold eyes. The gaze he now switched from Bodlin to Dermot Hackle showed impatience, though his tone had been irritated as well. Everyone in the room knew the news conference had been his own idea, like the decision not to tell Professor Garside and a few other key people that it was happening. 'One thing's certain, Stuart, we have to go ahead with it. The news conference, I mean. There's no alternative. Cancelling would only invite speculation. Dangerous speculation. I agree, the whole thing's unsatisfactory all the same.'

The four were in Larden's office at the company's Longbrook headquarters. This was off the Bath Road, twenty miles from London, between Heathrow Airport and the booming town of Slough. Albert Closter, the firm's founder, had built the place in the late twenties. It was a long, mostly single-storey building, rendered all over in dazzling white, and set on high ground beyond a rising grassed bank. In the middle, the flat-roofed, two-storey office block bellied forward in a wide curve, strapped by heavy metal windows at both levels. The windows were interrupted by an intimidating main door with a threatening, coffered entablature set behind a semicircular ripple of steps. Stunted round towers flanked this centre section and punctuated the start of the two long and low side wings, windowless on the front elevation – one housing the factory, the other the laboratories. There were more towers at the outer ends. The architect, Thomas Wallis, was said to have imagined the place as a desert fortress. Few people ever recognised his concept without prompting – and often not even then, the idea being a touch romantic for East Bucks. The place had recently been declared a protected building, some thought as a reminder to posterity never to do anything so boring again.

Larden's office was on the upper floor at the front. It was adequately furnished, but without ostentation or even much warmth. There was close carpeting, but blinds, not curtains, on the three windows – nor were there any pictures hanging above the fitted wooden bookcases. The leather upholstered chairs, the desk, the elaborate telephone and other desktop impedimenta were

17

all sternly functional. A long, rectangular table, in teak like the bookcases and the desk, was set at one side and used for meetings larger than the present one. The only uncompromisingly decorative feature in the room was a silver picture frame on the desk that held a colour photograph of a stunningly beautiful young woman with auburn hair.

'Look, we all agreed last night that the advantages of having the news conference outweighed the disadvantages,' said Hackle, this time seriously. He was seated, like Mary Ricini. Only Bodlin had elected to remain standing. He and the woman doctor had broken in on a meeting of the other two a minute before. It was shortly after two o'clock.

'I didn't agree,' the tight-lipped Bodlin protested quickly.

'Oh, come on, Stoo baby,' drawled Hackle in a breathy imitation of the late James Cagney. 'You wen along wid da rest of us guys in de ent, dincha?' he completed, in a high register. His mimicry was very professional, and could generally be relied on to bring down the temperature – except Bodlin's contemptuous reaction this time implied that Hackle had underestimated the heat.

'You did go along with us, you know, Stuart,' Larden insisted with a contrasting formal sharpness, but still making use of the point that Hackle had guyed.

'All right. Very reluctantly I did, and with a lot of reservations. I certainly said we'd regret having it. And we have. Already. Now the reason for it has been leaked by someone. Seromig has been . . . it's been cheapened. Cheapened and sensationalised before it's ever been presented professionally.'

Seromig was the provisional name given to the new migraine drug developed by Stuart Bodlin.

'Nobody's leaked anything. It'll all be in *Medical News* on Monday in any case. We're just making sure the significance of the first clinical trial isn't overlooked. And the *Standard* is hardly a sensational paper.' This was Hackle in a normal voice that was more matter-of-fact than reasoning.

'Well if that's so, why have they tried to pre-empt the story?'

'Better than tried. They seem to have succeeded,' Mary Ricini volunteered, also without emotion. Bodlin had brought her along for support, but her manner was a good deal less excited than his.

'And wasn't there supposed to be an embargo on any information till the news conference?' Bodlin now demanded. 'So there'd be

18

no mistakes in the reporting? Obviously someone's told the paper something.'

'Not according to Penny Cordwright. We've checked with her,' said Hackle.

Penny Cordwright's London public relations consultancy was handling all the arrangements for the news conference.

'And how would she know?' Bodlin demanded dismissively. His opinion of PR consultants was the same as Jumbo Crib-Cranton's, particularly when applied to Miss Cordwright.

Larden leaned forward, picking up the folded newspaper from the desk. 'She can't know for sure, of course, Stuart,' he said. 'But there's no hard fact in the *Standard* report. And they certainly got no extra information from us, or from Penny.'

'Did they try?'

'Yes they did. Like a lot of other papers. We've said consistently there'll be no comment till tomorrow,' said Hackle.

'The report simply says they expect we'll be announcing a development with one of our experimental projects. Probably the migraine drug. They must have been guessing, and got lucky.'

'Won't all the other papers want more information now?' asked Dr Ricini.

'Sure. So we'll keep 'em all guessing,' said Hackle with a grin. 'It's stirring stuff. Should help the flotation no end. As a major shareholder you ought to be delighted, Stuart.' It was a matter of record that his own shareholding was tiny when compared with the Research Director's – or, for that matter, the holding of any of the other working directors.

'There's more at stake than a penny or two on the new shares.' Still disconsolate, but his anger starting to abate, Bodlin dropped into an empty chair.

'Of course there's more than that at stake,' Larden said, quickly following through on an improving situation. 'But honestly, I don't think we've lost anything except a bit of Professor Garside's good-will. And he'll come round again. To be frank, I believe the paper he's doing will be a lot stronger if he uses the data from the second clinical trial, even if it means a delay. Don't you agree, Stuart?'

Bodlin frowned before replying. 'It's possible,' he acknowledged grudgingly, because the known facts confirmed it.

'Oh, better than that, surely?'

'All right. There are obvious advantages.'

'In other words, except for an irritating newspaper leak, we're in the same position as we were yesterday when we agreed, some of us with reservations,' Larden paused to nod at Bodlin, 'that a cautious, layman's update on Seromig to the media would be timely and helpful in a number of ways.' He leaned far back in his chair.

'The same position as yesterday except Professor Garside's going to take longer with a better documented paper,' put in Mary Ricini. 'And I have to say, Stuart, I'm going to be happier that he's using the second trial report. The data so far is fantastic. Much better than from the first one.'

The Research Director shifted in his chair. 'The data so far,' he repeated. 'OK, if the timing doesn't bother the rest of you, I'm sure it doesn't me.'

'Oh marvellous, Stuart. The patient sample in the second trial will be much bigger than the first too. And the weighting's much heavier on preventive treatment,' said Mary Ricini with enthusiasm.

The scientific paper they were referring to had been promised by Professor Garside of Middlesex University – but only when he was satisfied he had enough clinical as well as pharmacological data on Seromig to draw firm conclusions on its usefulness. Garside was the leader in his field, and universally respected. Bodlin was right in believing that he was the perfect author of a paper that would dramatically improve the chances of the new drug gaining official approval when the formal application was made.

'Mary's right,' Larden nodded. 'On the timing, of course we're working against the twenty-year calendar, as well as the competition. Remind me, someone, are we finishing the sixth or the seventh year since the company started on Seromig?'

'It's nearly seven years since we patented,' said Mary Ricini. 'We were a year ahead of the others then.'

All present were aware that two other much larger drug companies were working on a migraine treatment, and on lines chemically similar to their own.

'Seven years,' repeated Larden. 'Let's hope we're still a year ahead. The trial results coming through now are certainly exciting. Of course, we've known all along that when it came to clinical work we'd be governed by the nature of migraine.'

'That it's difficult to study,' agreed the woman.

'And how.' Larden pushed the newspaper to one side. 'It's a pity migraine clinics aren't like hospital wards.'

'Instead of a cross between out-patients and casualty.' This was

Dr Ricini again. 'With patients hardly ever available when they're actually suffering an attack. That's why treatment of acute attacks will always be hit or miss. Why Stuart's belief in preventive treatment has to be right in logic.' She leaned forward eagerly as she continued, her dark eyes alight as she pushed back a fold of jet black hair that had fallen becomingly across one cheek. 'It's why Stuart's been on a winner from the start, however long it takes.'

The Research Director shifted in his chair. 'My premise hasn't been justified yet, though. That'll take more time.'

In truth, the development of Seromig had been a good deal faster than that of most new drugs. After its pharmacological proving, it had been rigorously tested in animals for method and size of dosage, as well as for side-effects, and, to a degree, for effectiveness. Though you can't give a monkey migraine, you can induce changes in an animal's blood to match what happens in a human being during a migraine attack. You can then affect those changes with chemicals.

Because migraine is such a common ailment, the first human tests with Seromig had later been carried out on a group of migraine sufferers recruited from Closter's own staff, supervised by Mary Ricini. Afterwards, a series of outside clinical trials had been arranged through Dr Ricini with the medical chiefs of migraine treatment centres in different parts of the country. Even with the delay now expected over Professor Garside's paper, the new drug was still ahead of schedule.

'I have to get back to something in the lab,' said Bodlin. This palpably invented reason for his leaving put an end to the remaining tension in the room. It was clear that he had decided to accept the situation even if he wasn't totally condoning it.

'Of course, Stuart,' Larden responded, lifting an open palm as if in blessing. 'And listen. Nothing's lost. There's everything to win yet. Seromig is going to put us on top. Like the flotation. The news conference will help in both causes. Believe me.' He thrust himself forward in his chair with an expansive grin, his voice sounding a little too like a boxing manager's before a not very promising bout.

Bodlin gave a bleak smile, rose and made for the door, his hands stuffed deep in the pockets of the long white jacket.

'You don't need me for anything more?' This was Dr Ricini, getting up after Bodlin.

'No. Thank you, Mary. Thank you very much.' The repetition, together with Larden's meaningful expression and the woman's

21

unspoken acknowledgement, recorded the special thanks due to her for her well-phrased contributions. They both knew that Bodlin enjoyed compliments rather more than most people.

Less subtly, Hackle winked at Dr Ricini, and blew her a kiss. After the door had closed, he fell back in his chair with a sigh. 'Well thank God that's over without Bodlin actually chewing the carpet or climbing up the walls,' he said. 'You handled him beautifully.'

'So did Mary. I wish you'd done the same.'

'I thought I did my bit. Sorry. But you know I can't stand prima donnas, especially male ones.'

'Except that particular prima donna has the key to all our futures.'

'All right, Bob. But I backed you over the news conference, didn't I? Really, Bodlin's such a creep. A brilliant creep, of course, but with no commercial sense at all.' After his ten-year close working relationship with Larden, Hackle had earned the right – or thought he had – to be as open and critical about other colleagues as he chose. 'Are you going to call Mark Treasure at the bank?'

'I have. He isn't back from lunch.'

'Is the leak going to bother him?'

'Was it a leak? An inspired guess, you said.' His gaze held the other's as he went on: 'Yes, it'll bother him.'

'Not the medical aspect?'

'No. Only the City one. He's going to tell me again that the Stock Exchange gets very uptight over this sort of thing during the actual flotation period. He said that yesterday when he first heard about the news conference.'

'We should have asked him, not told him. Except he might not have agreed.'

Larden didn't respond to the last comment. 'About the actual conference,' he said. 'I've promised Mark we'll just present the bare data from the clinical trial. That we'll answer questions only with verifiable facts. No speculations.' He leaned back, hands clenched behind his neck. Like Hackle, he was jacketless, with shirt sleeves rolled up his forearms – in his case somewhat flabby forearms. His stomach was protruding more than it should have been, too. He eyed the other man, conscious of their contrasting physiques and the difference in their ages.

Larden's gaze then moved to the picture of Jane, his second wife. They had been married two years. He consoled himself that it took more than physical attraction for a man to earn an enduring

22

commitment from a woman like Jane. This was a sentiment that recurred frequently in his mind, and provided the reassurance he needed to combat a growing sense of sexual insecurity.

He watched the Marketing Director gather up the documents he had brought for their original meeting. Hackle remained good at his job, he thought, so long as Bob Larden was around to programme him. That hadn't applied so much in the past because it hadn't been quite so true in the past. Hackle was too frivolous by half – too privately irresponsible, and he seemed to be growing less not more mature. If his personal finances hadn't always been in such chaos, by now he might have been one of the major shareholders in the company, not one of the smallest. That point alone put a question mark over a lot of other things.

'Treasure knows Bodlin was against telling the media anything until after the journal article?' Hackle questioned.

'Yes, because Bodlin made sure he did. He knows Giles Closter-Bennet was against it too.'

Closter-Bennet was Finance Director of the company, the only remaining link with the founder, although that link was tenuous. He was not a direct descendant of Albert Closter. He had married Barbara, who was Albert's only surviving granddaughter, and added her surname to his.

'Closter-Bennet doesn't rate with Treasure,' Hackle offered dismissively. 'And of course, if the journal article had come out last Monday as scheduled, we wouldn't have needed a news conference.' He rubbed the big muscle of one arm. 'So, have you given any more thought to how soon you'll become Chairman?'

'Soon enough. I've told you we'll need a direct line to a merchant bank for some time yet.'

'You mean Treasure gives us extra advice and attention for a very small director's fee?'

Larden chuckled. 'You could say that. His mind's doubly concentrated, isn't it? As the head of our bankers he has a hell of a lot riding on us still. But as our Chairman he'll make sure the bank goes on indulging us if necessary.'

'I just think it'd be better if we went forward the way we planned now. With you as Chairman.'

'Plenty of time for that, Dermot.' The words were meant to encourage, but they also indicated that the subject was closed. When Larden moved up to be Chairman, Hackle expected to become the Managing Director. Both men knew this, but Larden

23

was the one who could make it happen. Larden lowered his gaze, pulled his chair up to the desk, and shuffled the papers on the blotter. 'And you'll be coping personally with the news media for the rest of today?' he queried, on an evidently concluding note.

'Any calls here from reporters are being redirected to the PR company,' said Hackle, rising from his chair. 'Penny Cordwright will keep the embargo till the conference tomorrow. Special queries she'll refer to me for clearance.'

Larden nodded, then frowned. 'I don't suppose we'll ever know if there really was a leak to the *Standard*.'

'I don't suppose so either,' Hackle replied.

But one of the two was lying.

Chapter Three

'I should make the effort and swim here every day,' said Molly Treasure, putting her lipstick and compact away, and closing her handbag with a decisive snap to match her words.

'I think you should too,' said her husband.

She glanced up sharply. 'Why? Do I look that much in need of jacking up?' she demanded.

Molly was one of the most celebrated high comedy actresses on the London Stage, and much in demand. Slim, vital, patrician, and with an appearance arguably more striking than that of many reputedly more beautiful women (which was just as well since she was not a perfect beauty: to begin with her nose was too pronounced) – with all of this, the lady was definitely not in decline.

'I meant you look terrific after a swim,' Treasure explained lightly. 'All of a glow, as they say in the Wrens.'

Molly considered the comment, then gave a tiny sniff of satisfaction. 'Thank you, darling. Swimming does give one a lift. Well, that's all right then.' She smoothed the top of the sleeveless, cotton shift dress with one hand, while picking up her glass of lemon juice with the other. Her one-week commitment to a lemon juice and salad diet was well into its twelfth hour.

The two were seated in the atrium bar of the Fitness Club in the basement of Augustus Court, a big new block of flats close to their home in Chelsea's Cheyne Walk. It was a relaxing place – stone flagged, fountained, furnished with pretty wrought iron chairs and tables, scented by exotic plants, and enlivened only by the muted chirpings of tropical birds: for the moment, they had the bar to themselves; there had been other members in the pool and the gym.

Coming here together for exercise before dinner was a treat the two seldom enjoyed on a week-night. Treasure was rarely home early enough. Molly was too often appearing in the theatre. She had just finished a successful revival of Bernard Shaw's *Captain Brassbound's Conversion*. Because the run had been extended, it had clashed with some filming, also now completed, but the days had been long ones. Her next professional engagement was not for three weeks, and a period without working after months of hyperactivity was inducing a niggling sense of indolence and, even more illogically, those suspicions of approaching decay.

'Did you read the script? The one that came this morning?' Treasure asked, picking up his whisky: they both made sacrifices in the cause of healthy living, but doing without a single serious drink before dinner was not yet one of his.

'The Ken Jago play? Yes, I read half of it this afternoon. Riveting first act. Then Jane Larden arrived. We spent ages debating over those fabrics. For the new covers in the big guest room. She'd been to so much trouble matching samples for me.'

'Do we need new covers for the big guest room?'

Molly smiled indulgently. 'Not if you think the old orange ones will go well with the new pink wallpaper. You liked the paper when I showed it you. The fabric I chose for the covers isn't made any more.'

Life was too short for him to want to know why. 'How was Jane?'

'Oh, gorgeous, as usual. She sent love. I've definitely decided her red hair is natural.' Molly gave the lemon juice a dubious look before taking a tentative sip. 'It's unfair to be quite that beautiful. Especially without taking pains.' She made a sour face over the juice, or, perhaps, the pains involved in staying slim.

'Beautiful if not all that bright.'

'That's not true. I think she's very intelligent. And she's really got a flair for interior design. Anyway she seems to make a fantastic living at it. Everyone's using her. Including Barbara Closter-Bennet, by the way.'

'Hmm. That must be a first for any designer.'

'Quite. The house in . . . ?'

'Later Burnlow,' he provided.

'Yes. Remember when we dined that time last year? It looked exactly as if it had been caught up in a 1939 time-warp.'

'Was it Jane who told you she was making a fantastic living in design?'

'Well, it's obvious.'

26

'I wonder. Her husband is certainly very successful.'

'So are you, but it doesn't stop me being the same. Some of the time,' she ended a touch disconsolately.

'That's different. I'd guess Jane Larden is an interior designer not for the money but because— '

'She'd otherwise lack fulfilment. You've said that before,' Molly interrupted. 'Maybe they'll have children. She's only twenty-eight. Bob Larden's not very old is he?'

'Old enough to have two grown-up daughters by his first marriage. He's fifty-four or -five. I don't think he wants children.'

'You may be right. About Jane not being happy. D'you think I should insist on paying her a fee for helping me with the guest room? It's a very small job. I mean she volunteered when I mentioned I'd been let down over the fabric. It was at their house-warming party.'

The Lardens had recently moved to a bigger house in Fulham, next door to Chelsea. This was a lot closer to central London than their previous place had been, and further away from the Closter factory twenty miles to the west, though the beginning of the M4 motorway was nearby.

'Offer a fee by all means,' said Treasure. 'She probably won't accept, but it might help with the fulfilment. I expect she'll get a discount on the stuff she buys for you.'

'I'd forgotten that.' She stroked her long throat and glanced up at the blue sky through the Gothic glass roof sections of the atrium. 'Did you see there was something in the paper today about Closter Drug?'

He nodded. 'There'll be more at the weekend. There's a news conference tomorrow.'

'About the new cure for migraine?'

'Yes. Ahead of an article in one of the medical journals on Monday. Bob Larden wants to be sure the news doesn't get overlooked by the national media.'

'Is it to help with the flotation?'

Treasure pulled a face. 'Indirectly it's bound to.'

'Touchy subject?'

'Fairly.'

'Is that because it's not covered by the thingy?' Molly wrinkled her nose. 'The prospectus? So why did you approve a news conference? You're Chairman of Closter aren't you?'

'I didn't approve it.'

'Oh. Another touchy subject?'

'Not any more. Anyway, I'm going to be there. At the conference. It'll be safer. If a bit like walking on eggs.'

'Was the new drug discovered by that sad little man? He was at the house-warming, but didn't stay. Doctor Bottle?'

'Bodlin. Yes. Brilliant chap.' It was how everyone described Bodlin.

'Bachelor. Looked as if he needed a good woman to smarten him up.'

'I don't believe Bodlin has much time for women.'

'Well a good man then.' She drank some more lemon juice as though she were enjoying it – or the self-deprivation involved in not having anything stronger. 'And Bob didn't find Doctor Bodlin? I mean he joined Closter Drug before Bob got there?'

'Several years before. He was hired by the previous owners. They hoped he'd produce some pharmacological miracles.'

'It seems he has. One at least. According to the *Standard*. So why did the previous owners take on Bob Larden? Bob and his macho lieutenant?'

'Dermot Hackle?'

'Yes. The one all the women fancy. But not as much as he fancies himself, I thought. Jane mentioned him today. Fair locks and lantern jawed. Would have made a wonderful matinée idol. Is he good at his job? He had us in fits with his imitations. At the party. D'you remember?'

'Vaguely. He and Bob are a team. Management and marketing. Yes, they're good. As a team.'

'I can't remember, does Dermot Hackle have a glamorous wife too?'

'A worthy but decidedly unglamorous one. You must have met her at the Lardens', too.'

'I do vaguely remember now. Mousy, nervous little thing is she? And they live in West Ealing? I hardly talked to her. I thought she was someone else's wife.'

'She's slightly older than Dermot.' Treasure shook his head. 'And yes, very nervous. She told me all about her two young children. Twice.'

'Will she be at the Savoy dinner next Thursday?'

'I should think so. When she'll probably tell me about them again. They'll all be there, I expect.'

'Not the children?'

28

'No, the other directors, and their wives, or husbands, or whatever.'

'Does Doctor Bodlin have a whatever?'

'Yes. He's an actor, I believe.'

'Oh? What's his name?'

'No idea. Never met him, and he doesn't show up at company events.' He picked up some nuts from the dish on the table. 'Bodlin usually escorts the lovely Doctor Ricini who doesn't seem to have a regular chap.'

'She's divorced isn't she?'

'Yes. I believe Ricini's her maiden name. Anyway, you're coming still? To the dinner? It's a chore, but they'll appreciate it. I'll appreciate it. You'll be lionised, I expect.'

'I'm looking forward to it. Not to being lionised,' she added modestly. 'To the excitement, I mean. Isn't it the day when you'll know if the flotation's been a success?'

'No, the day after. When trading starts in the new shares. When people who've bought them will know whether they've made a profit over the offer price of a hundred and ten pence.'

'Doesn't sound much.'

Treasure chuckled. 'The *Financial Times* thinks it's too much.'

'What do they know?'

'Rather more than you probably, darling. But thank you for the support.'

'Presumably it's all going to make Bob Larden very rich? What about handsome Dermot Hackle?'

'Not very rich in his case. He had no capital to invest at the right time. Five years ago. And none since then, either, or so it appears. Hughie McFee, the Production Director, has the biggest stake after Bob. You haven't met him yet. Nice Scotsman with a large, jolly wife. They weren't at the Larden party. They're very keen Scots. She's on the organising committee of an annual one-day Scottish Festival where they live. In Maidenhead.'

'Maidenhead?'

'Mmm. Sort of mini Highland Games in the afternoon. Scottish dancing in the evening. On a meadow next to the McFees' place.'

'How unlikely. But how splendid. How do you know about it?'

'Because some years ago she started sending us tickets at the office. Miss Gaunt used them, and she's been going every year since. She likes Scottish dancing. It's on a late Saturday in May. Quite soon, I suppose.'

'Isn't Maidenhead rather a long way for Miss Gaunt to go to a dance?'

Miss Gaunt, Treasure's middle-aged secretary, lived in Islington, on the edge of Central London.

'Oh, it's quite an event. Beside the river. She goes with an older male cousin. The Gaunts were originally Scottish.'

'Fancy,' Molly shook her head, and tried – without real success – to picture a tartan-sashed Emily Gaunt with a kilted, elderly kinsman dancing an abandoned Strip the Willow on the banks of the River Thames. 'Is Barbara Closter-Bennet involved in the reeling?'

'Not unless they do it on horseback.'

'But Later Burnlow is near Maidenhead.'

'Close by. Remember, we decided it was a village with more stables than bedrooms?'

'But the Closter-Bennets will be at the Savoy dinner on Thursday?'

'Sure to be.'

'Will the flotation have made them a lot of money?'

'Nearly as much as the McFees. She's fairly well off, although she complains to me at every opportunity about how little her family got for the company. That was thirteen years ago. When it was originally bought by Philer International.'

'Is Giles Closter-Bennet good at his job?'

Treasure pouted for a moment, then replied. 'He's an adequate accountant, but an unspectacular Finance Director.'

'Does that matter?'

'It would if ever the company had to operate entirely on its own.'

'Without advice from Grenwood, Phipps?'

'Without our involvement in financial management. As for Giles, I think he's run by his wife. I'm pretty sure she resents not heading up the company herself.'

'Could she have done?'

'She might. Her father controlled it, after all. She was originally against the flotation. She's come round now, but reluctantly. It wouldn't take much to alter her view again. Or rather her view as expressed through her husband.'

'Was anyone else against the flotation?'

'Yes. People who would have preferred it if we'd sold out to one of the big pharmaceutical manufacturers.'

'Isn't that rather unadventurous? And going backwards? Since Closter used to be owned by a big company?'

'Which wasn't in the drugs business. The situation's rather different now.'

'But won't everyone be better off when Closter goes public?'

'Not necessarily. Three or four of the international outfits have privately offered to buy Closter recently. At very fancy prices. Two directors besides Giles have been in favour of taking that route.'

'Who?'

'Doctor Bodlin and Doctor Ricini. They'd have been well enough paid for their stakes in the company. Like the Closter-Bennets, they don't really believe Closter's big enough on its own to handle an important new drug like Seromig. Not world-wide.'

Molly nodded slowly. 'So how does it handle things that have to be world-wide now?'

'Through agents, or through licensing agreements with overseas manufacturers. It's not as efficient as having Closter branches in other countries.'

'But less expensive?'

'For a one-product company certainly.'

'The one product being Seromig?'

'Will be. Provided nothing goes wrong with the remainder of the tests, and provided the Department of Health finally approves the product.'

'But Closter makes lots of other drugs, surely?'

'Yes, but nothing unique or exclusive. And nothing with serious international potential.'

'So are Doctor Bodlin and the other two right? Should Closter have been sold to a big company?'

'Not according to Bob Larden. He's convinced Seromig will make huge profits, which will pay for the development costs of the other new products in the pipeline, and eventually make Closter itself big and international.'

'That sounds more exciting. Is he right?'

Treasure gave an optimistic grunt. 'I hope so. It's a business gamble, but an acceptable one.'

'On Seromig being a success? Where does Dermot Hackle stand? You said he has no shares.'

'Very few,' Treasure corrected. 'He supports Bob, but possibly only because Bob is too determined to be persuaded otherwise. More to the point, the bank goes along with Bob.'

31

'Well I know Bob's the big noise in the company, but it's Doctor Bodlin who discovers the new drugs. If he doesn't believe Closter is big enough, why does he stay?'

'For several reasons. Seromig and the other new development formulas are patented in the company's name not his.'

'Is that fair?'

'Entirely. He discovered them in company time, and he's paid handsomely to do just that.'

'So why didn't he join a big company in the first place?'

'Because eight years ago, when he was thirty-two, Closter offered him his present job, with a totally free hand. He liked the title of Research Director and the terms. At that time he was an unknown academic and wouldn't have got either in a big company.'

'But he's changed his tune now?'

'For responsible reasons, and perhaps for the added personal one that in the interim he's acquired a successful track record. If he was in a big company now he'd no doubt be given a grand title and a free hand.'

'And that can't happen still?'

'It could.' He paused. 'Once Closter becomes a public company, any of the major drug manufacturers could make a takeover bid for it. A predator would find it costly, of course. At Grenwood, Phipps we're placing a substantial block of the shares with our main customers. After the flotation, they and the Closter directors will hold fifty-five per cent of the issued shares between them. They'll be looking for income and long-term growth, not a quick resale for profit. Except at a very sexy price indeed.'

'So anyone wanting to take over Closter would have to offer a lot more than a hundred and ten pence for the shares?'

'I'll say.'

'If it happened though, would it mean that Closter directors would have to be talked into selling their shares?'

'That's a possible scenario. But not the likeliest.' Treasure pulled a face. 'No, I really can't imagine a circumstance where all the directors would be ready to sell.'

'But if there were a takeover, the Closter directors with the larger holdings who make big fortunes next week could make even bigger ones? Could be why they've held out against selling so far.'

'Bob Larden, you mean? And Hughie McFee?' Treasure chuckled, shaking his head. 'I'm glad they can't overhear this conversation. Darling, your imagination is running away with us. Must be the lemon juice. I really don't believe anything dramatic is going to happen to Closter Drug. Other than a successful flotation, of course.'

But for once the banker was seriously wrong.

Chapter Four

'Doctor Ricini, it says in the handout that preventive treatment of migraine's been favoured in the past. That's because treatment after an attack's started is too late.' The speaker was male, old and paunchy, with a persistent cough. He was 'London Correspondent' for several small provincial newspaper groups, which meant the food and drink he consumed at news conferences was usually worth more than he was paid for his reports. He was in the front row, balancing a glass of amber fluid on a folder of information from Closter Drug. 'Is that the reason why Seromig is going to be a preventive treatment too?'

'Not quite.' Mary Ricini responded with a bright smile. She was in the left end chair, facing the audience, of the row of five behind the table. Next to her stood the wooden rostrum where she and a nervous Stuart Bodlin, now sitting beside her, had earlier made formal presentations. 'Seromig could have gone either way. Preventive or acute treatment. It still could, in the sense it's going to be a valuable therapy in both areas. As I said before,' she went on, wishing the questioner had been listening more carefully the first time, 'Seromig can provide quick relief at the start of an attack. Especially if injected, or given through a nasal inhaler. In one group of patients it arrested attacks in an average of twelve minutes. That's fast, but perhaps not fast enough.' She paused to gauge response to the premise, but there didn't appear to be one. 'In contrast, in two other groups of patients in the same trial series, Seromig in tablet form taken regularly over a two-year period eliminated migraine altogether in seventy-eight per cent of regular sufferers.'

'So why aren't you pushing it just as a long term treatment?' asked a barely audible, drab young woman in the second row. She was from *Tween* magazine (advertised as 'for girls in their teens who think over twenty').

'We're not pushing Seromig. It hasn't been marketed yet. When it is, it'll only be available on prescription. We'll detail it to doctors. Definitely no pushing,' corrected Dermot Hackle, leaning forward with the devastating smile that was almost guaranteed to captivate impressionable women of all ages. He was seated at the other end of the table from Mary Ricini, next to Bob Larden. Treasure was in the centre.

On the wall beyond the directors a banner announced CLOSTER DRUG in red letters two feet high on a solid yellow background, while on either side there were portable display stands exhibiting promotion material, and packs of the company's products.

'I meant, why bother researching it for acute attacks if it's so spot-on for the other,' the *Tween* woman responded, blinking several times, and reddening slightly: one hand moved subconsciously to improve the arrangement of a single lank curl hanging over one of her ears.

'Because although a regular daily dose of Seromig promises to eliminate migraine for most sufferers, we have to be certain that over the long term it won't inhibit natural chemical processes in the blood.' This was the woman Medical Director again. 'Really it's a matter of finding the right dosage.'

'So it's dangerous in the wrong dosage?' *Tween* returned suspiciously and more loudly.

'Not dangerous, except in massive overdose. But that applies to most drugs. Including aspirin.' Bob Larden had taken the question. 'As Doctor Bodlin explained earlier, Seromig is a synthesised variant of 5HT, a natural body substance. That's the transmitter we believe triggers the headache in migraine by expanding the blood vessels. Seromig, chemically known to us as $5HT_7$, neutralises this painful effect by constricting the blood vessels. That's the simplest explanation I can give you. But natural 5HT also has useful actions that we don't want to cancel out while we stop the migraine with an antagonist.'

'But the production of pain is a useful action too? A warning to the body, no?' The question had come in a husky voice and a German-American accent from a stylish young woman in a black beret, worn coquettishly over straight, sculpted dark hair. She had risen to speak from behind the others. The beret was setting off a crisp, red and white check shirt loosely clasped with a wide black belt over tailored black trousers. The wearer had come in after the presentation had started, and wasn't wearing one of the badge-stickers given out at the door: Treasure speculated that she probably worked for a fashion magazine.

'To say pain is a warning is a relative truth.' It was Larden who answered again. 'But you wouldn't get many migraine sufferers to accept it as just that.'

The reply brought a murmur of sympathetic approval, also a nasty coughing fit from the already florid 'London Correspondent'.

'And the clinical tests you haven't published yet. Are they going to confirm that you've found the safe dosage for acute and prophylactic treatments?' asked a donnish young man from *The Times*.

The *Tween* girl's eyes narrowed at the use of the word prophylactic.

'Naturally our aim is to find the safe and correct dosage,' said Dr Ricini carefully.

Most observers would have considered the attendance at the news conference to be disappointing – only a dozen reporters from the consumer press (the medical press hadn't been invited), no photographers, a man from the Press Association, no one from BBC radio, one from commercial radio who had left early, and none from television.

Penny Cordwright was worried about how long she could expect to keep the Closter PR business after failing to stimulate a better showing than this. She was a big bossy woman with a flowered blouse, a loud voice and a frenetic manner. She was hovering near the door at the back, still on the lookout for latecomers.

In contrast, Mark Treasure was relieved at the poor turn-out. It was clear from the numbers and quality of those who had come – and, more to the point, those who hadn't – that editors had not considered the occasion important. For reasons of his own, the banker supported their view.

The paucity of the attendance was also emphasised by the size of the room. It was on the first floor of the New Connaught Rooms in Great Queen Street – one of the biggest banqueting venues in London. By Connaught Rooms standards, the room was one of the smallest on offer, but would still have taken many times the number present for the advertised programme, which included drinks, a presentation followed by questions, then more drinks and a stand-up buffet lunch.

It was now after one o'clock. Treasure was hoping he could soon declare formal question time closed and the buffet open.

'And migraine is caused by something in the blood not something in the brain?' asked the earnest, middle-aged cookery correspondent from the *Daily Gazette* whose daughter suffered from migraine: she had come for that reason, and because the medical correspondent of the paper hadn't been interested.

Stuart Bodlin cleared his throat. The others at the table looked to him expectantly. 'Opinion is still divided on the root causes of migraine. Nobody knows the cause for sure,' he uttered in a more confident tone than he had used at the rostrum. 'But current thinking has veered to the idea that the aetiology is almost certainly vascular not neurological. Which applies equally to common migraine and to classic migraine with aura. That's why we've been searching for a very restrictive vasoconstrictor.'

All of this indicated that the Research Director communicated with a lay audience even less well without a prepared script than he did with one. The stony silence that greeted his accurate but, to most of the listeners, fairly meaningless pronouncement gave Treasure the opportunity he needed.

'If there are no more questions— ' he began.

'Will Closter Drug make a lot of money out of Seromig?' the *Tween* girl interrupted, spurred perhaps by the earlier question from the latecomer.

'If everything goes according to plan, and if Seromig is as successful as we expect, it could be one of the most important fifty drugs in the world,' Dermot Hackle supplied blandly.

'Can we have that in round cash terms?' asked 'London Correspondent', loosening his trousers with a violent tug at the crutch.

'Impossible at the moment. But it should be a very significant export earner for Britain,' said Larden.

'But you're not alone in the field. Aren't there two other manufacturers researching similar formulas?' asked the Press Association man who had been taking more notes than the others.

'Similar, but not the same. And we believe we're some way ahead of the competition.' This was the Managing Director again.

'And are you announcing Seromig now, before it's ready, to give a boost to your flotation next week?' demanded the black bereted girl.

'Certainly not.' Larden had spoken after a sideward nod from Treasure. 'The report of the first major clinical trials was scheduled to appear in the medical press last Monday. It's been delayed by a week, but the arrangement was made long before the date of the flotation was agreed. This news conference was called as a courtesy to you and your subscribers. The timing is coincidental. You must know too that the invitations were sent to medical correspondents not City editors.'

This failed to evoke better than: 'That's not a very convincing answer, but never mind,' from the questioner, who went on: 'Can Doctor Bodlin tell us whether in your expensive search for a treatment for migraine you ever considered the merits of the humble feverfew?'

'I wonder if we might know who you are and who you represent?' Treasure interjected firmly, and irritated by the insult to Larden.

'Sure. I'm Kirsty Welling. I suppose you could say I am representing the feverfew lobby. Actually I am working for *Natural World Tomorrow*.'

'Thank you, I'll make a point of getting a copy.' The banker smiled.

'For the benefit of anyone who doesn't know,' said Mary Ricini, 'feverfew is a white flowering, hedgerow plant. It's been used by herbalists for centuries.' She paused to let the information register. 'There are substances in feverfew which may well inhibit the release of natural 5HT in the body. But nobody's been able to isolate or evaluate them.'

'But you know those substances work?'

'We know they sometimes work in some people. The efficacy of feverfew in commercial form varies a lot. This has to do with the different methods of manufacture, and the varying shelf life of the products.'

'Have you ever experimented with feverfew on animals, Doctor Bodlin?' Kirsty Welling persisted after switching a wide-eyed, penetrating gaze from Dr Ricini to the Research Director.

'No. Why should I?'

'Would you have needed to if you'd seriously thought of it as the natural, obvious cure for migraine?'

'I might have done. The circumstance isn't likely.' Bodlin leaned forward, adjusting his spectacles on his nose so that they focused better on his attractive if discomforting questioner. 'We haven't been researching feverfew. So far as we're concerned, it has no future as a reliable treatment for migraine.'

Larden whispered an aside to Treasure who nodded before

saying: 'I think perhaps that's enough on feverfew. So unless— '

'Another question for Doctor Bodlin,' Miss Welling interrupted, her delivery quickening after a glance at the time. 'One of interest to humane readers in all countries. How many thousands of defenceless animals did you exterminate while experimenting to get so far with Seromig, Doctor?'

'That's . . . that's a grossly exaggerated figure.' There were signs of sweat breaking out on Bodlin's brow, and on the bald patch above it.

'You mean it was less than thousands?'

'Of course it was,' Mary Ricini interjected coolly. 'In answer to your loaded question, Miss Welling, we mostly used rodents. I don't have a note of the numbers involved, but relatively few were wasted. Those that died did so painlessly, and in the defensible cause of relieving human suffering.'

'At the expense of inducing animal suffering. How many animals other than rodents were involved, Doctor Bodlin?' the questioner returned. 'And please can he answer for himself?'

The Medical Director looked daggers at Miss Welling but remained silent.

'About a hundred and fifty, I think.' Bodlin mopped his forehead with a huge white handkerchief. 'Two hundred perhaps.'

'Or three or four hundred perhaps? So you can't be sure how many dogs, monkeys and other poor creatures perished in agony?'

This produced an instantly sympathetic stir from the audience.

'Oh come, Miss Welling. We all know better than that,' said Dermot Hackle in a patronising tone. 'Animal experiments are subject to strict procedures and inspection. Nothing perishes in agony.'

'We don't all know better, but a lot of us are learning something.' This was the *Tween* girl who had turned to nod approvingly at Kirsty Welling. 'So why do you have to murder dogs and monkeys, for God's sake?'

'It's necessary. Not to murder,' the confused Bodlin corrected hurriedly, while wishing again he hadn't been made to come: he disliked speaking to lay audiences at the best of times. 'It's necessary,' he repeated, in a voice so constricted that some listeners had to lean forward to hear him. 'In checking for toxicity for instance. You have to . . . to waste some subjects. So you can analyse all their organs. Every type of tissue. Without exception. Meticulously. You should understand, it's an essential step in the creation of safe drugs.'

'Thank you, Doctor, that was very illuminating and reassuring. Not that most of us needed reassuring.' This was Treasure, now quite determined to close the session. 'Time's pressing, I'm afraid. Thank you all for your attention. Let's get some lunch shall we?' he went on quickly. 'The buffet's ready on the left over there. Please help yourselves. And if anyone has more questions, feel free to ask them while we're eating.'

But few in the audience had been listening to the last words. Most heads had turned to learn the reason for the commotion at the back of the room.

The disaffected rumble from the door was first countered by stentorian protests from Penny Cordwright on high volume. Then even her stern admonitions were drowned by the chanting of the figures filing down the right-hand side of the room.

More than a dozen respectably dressed young men and women were making a determined advance in the direction of the official party. Penny Cordwright seemed to be bouncing herself at the leading members, like a large, out of control beach ball, but without at all impeding their progress.

'This is trespass. You've no right. Out! Out!' she cried, arms waving.

'Stop animal experiments! Stop animal experiments!' the intruders called back in penetrating unison. Since entering the room, each had donned a large round lapel badge bearing the words of the chant.

'Right, I'm getting the police,' Miss Cordwright now shrieked with decision, pushing empty chairs aside as she reversed her direction.

The directors at the table were dumbfounded.

The audience of newsgatherers waited expectantly on a bonus happening.

The insurgent group halted under the company banner fixed to the wall. Still chanting, the members quickly closed up in a straight line. Each one unfolded a large yellow oblong cloth, stencilled with a single red letter. The cloths were then held high in front of their bearers.

CLOSTER DRUG read the wall banner.

MURDERS ANIMALS was now appended immediately beneath it.

And standing on a chair with a serious-looking camera, Kirsty Welling was taking flash photographs at a furious pace, and in a thoroughly professional manner.

40

Chapter Five

'It all happened so quickly, you understand?' said the dinner-jacketed Bob Larden. He was answering Alison McFee, wife of the Production Director.

'But time enough for them to get those awful photographs.'

'Only just. Before we had their banners down. But they were well rehearsed.'

'Took you all a wee bit on the hop, I expect. Terrible.' The lengthened 'terrible' came out as a sort of brief Highland lament.

The jolly, short, and ample Mrs McFee, in an equally jolly and ample but long red taffeta gown, studied Larden intently over her champagne, the glass held two inches from her lips: there was a triangle of glazed smoked salmon on toast in her other hand, also poised in mid-air. She was blinking expectantly through spectacles with decorated frames so wide that Larden thought she looked ready for take-off. Abruptly her mouth darted to envelop the smoked salmon. She swallowed hard, then blinked again, but there was no intermediary sign that she had chewed anything.

'And Dermot punched one of the beggars?' said Hughie McFee, in a questioning way, as though the report might still need confirming. A lean, craggy Scot, with thinning, white wavy hair, he was standing beside his wife, feet well apart, knees a fraction bent, with both hands grasping a tumbler of undiluted malt whisky in the proximity of his navel.

'He hit him all right,' said Larden.

'Yes, Mark told me,' Molly Treasure offered, while wondering how Mrs McFee kept her glass up like that without her arm getting tired, also how the lady secured, let alone managed to consume, so many of the cocktail canapés that were being circulated but only fitfully. 'Very brave,' Molly continued. 'And here's the hero himself. Are you good at fisticuffs, Dermot?' she asked Hackle who had just joined them.

41

'He used to box,' said Rosemary Hackle, from beside her husband, but so quietly that only he heard. Nervously she pinched the top button of the white blouse she was wearing above a cheap but cheerful, cotton flowered skirt.

The Closter Drug directors, some with spouses, were met for a celebration dinner in a river-front suite at the Savoy Hotel. A long table was set for twelve on one side of the room, with a small bar in the charge of an attentive, tail-coated waiter near the door.

Mark Treasure and Jane Larden, who had been admiring the view of the Thames across the still busy embankment, had just turned to greet the Closter-Bennets, the last couple to arrive.

Bob Larden, the host, asked Molly and the others to excuse him. He moved across to speak to Stuart Bodlin who had been standing a little apart with Mary Ricini.

It was the first full day of stock exchange trading in the new Closter Drug shares, and six days since the ill-fated news conference.

'I have to say that punch wasn't intentional,' Hackle admitted, stroking the unusually square jaw. 'I was grabbing for one of the banners and happened to hit the face behind it.'

'Blacked his eye, didn't you?' asked Alison McFee, her head bobbing behind her glass.

'Dermot used to box,' said Mrs Hackle for the second time, but the words still went largely unheard. She was used to that. Shy and self-effacing, she had only made the effort to speak because she knew her husband would complain later if she stayed silent all evening. He called her a mouse. She consoled herself that she was a caring, faithful mouse. The others had been looking mostly towards Molly Treasure the celebrity: Rosemary Hackle had been looking solely towards her own husband.

'Mark said your victim left swearing he'd have the law on you,' said Molly. She looked cool in a simple, sleeveless black dress, her only jewellery a small diamond brooch and a pair of diamond earrings.

'When he was being helped out by two of his own lot, yes. The management hadn't quite arrived by then. They came soon after, of course, but the demonstrators disappeared damn quickly.'

'Is the man or the organisation, whatever it's called, likely to sue you for assault? To get extra publicity? Isn't that why they were there?' asked Alison McFee. As if by magic, a square of glazed caviare had materialised in her free hand.

'They're called Stop Animal Experiments. SAE for short.'

'Used to stand for stamped addressed envelope,' Molly interposed wanly. 'One supposes it's a ginger group. That concentrates on upsetting pharmaceutical companies.'

'That's what we think,' said Hackle. 'But we've never heard of them before. Anyway, no one's sued me yet. They may have been waiting to see if we're going to law against them. Or maybe they're planning a worse vengeance on me.'

'I hope not,' said Molly with feeling.

'You'll need to keep your wits about you for a wee while. Especially after dark,' advised Mrs McFee.

'Perhaps the SAE is pledged to non-violence?' said Molly.

'Not very likely. They're animal protectors not nuclear protestors.' McFee drained his glass.

'And the magazine, what was it called, *Natural World Tomorrow*? No one's ever heard of that either, have they?' asked his wife. She paused for enlightenment, but got none. 'Beats me how any of them got in at all.' Her lips closed over the stuffed olive she had just acquired.

'Oh, they were so utterly respectable,' Hackle said. 'I mean, hundreds of people go for lunch at the Connaught Rooms every day. If this lot had arrived waving placards and dressed for a demo, they wouldn't have got past the doormen. As it was, their banners were pocketed and they were better dressed than any of the journalists at the news conference. Of course, Penny Cordwright should have insisted on proper credentials from the Welling woman.'

'She didn't have an invitation?'

'Certainly not. But Penny was so disappointed by the turn-out, at that point she'd have let anyone in who owned a pencil let alone a notebook. She even provided La Welling with an identity sticker. Wrote her name on it. The woman never wore it.' Hackle pushed down the red silk handkerchief blossoming from his breast pocket, but not so deep as to spoil the insouciant effect. He swallowed some champagne. 'As for the other demonstrators, Penny Cordwright didn't react fast enough. Neither did the rest of us, I'm afraid.'

'Aye, it was a pity you let the lassie with the camera get away, Dermot,' said McFee, making it sound as if that had been entirely Hackle's fault.

'You talking about the Welling woman? That escape was well planned,' remarked Mary Ricini who had just moved to join them. 'She beat it to the door while two of the others tipped chairs over

43

behind her to stop pursuit. In any case she was working from behind a block of gormless reporters. I'm afraid we were just too slow.'

'Why did you let the animal rights photographer get away, darling?' Molly Treasure demanded lightly of her husband who happened now to be standing close by, but with his back to her.

'Because, at the time, I was doing my best to de-flag a nubile young woman,' he answered blandly, turning about. 'I succeeded too.'

'Sounds like a fertility rite,' rejoined Molly.

'She was the one holding up the N in animals,' said Mary Ricini. 'I was having a go at the man holding the A next to her.' Like Molly, the woman doctor was dressed in black, and just as fetchingly.

'The demo got minor headlines at the weekend, but Seromig was hardly mentioned,' said McFee. 'The earlier leak in the *Evening Standard* was almost fuller. All rather defeating the original Closter objective. That didn't displease our worthy Stuart Bodlin, but he'd paid for the privilege with some unpleasant haranguing from the audience.'

'Most of the national media stayed away from the conference. They picked up the Seromig story from the medical press report on Monday,' Dr Ricini offered quietly, with a glance at Treasure. 'There have been some quite full accounts since.'

'Which incidentally gave our competitors something to think about,' the banker commented.

'But did the demonstration do the flotation harm, Mark? In the City?' The questioner was Jane Larden, who was now on Treasure's right. She was a tall, bold beauty – her build a little more generous than slim – with high, pronounced cheekbones, almond-shaped brown eyes, and a shock of frizzed red hair. Despite the smile after her words, there was more of confidence than warmth in her general manner.

'The flotation might have been a marginally greater success without the demo,' said Treasure. 'The offer was over-subscribed, after all. Not by much, but even so, over-subscribed.'

'So the pictures in the two newspapers that chose to print them didn't damage us?' This was Mrs Larden again, with a shrug – an expressive movement of exquisite, bronzed bare shoulders. She was sheathed in a model gown made of a sparkling silver material. Alison McFee had already decided that the dress had cost more than both McFees spent on clothes for a whole year.

44

'I'm thinking they're neither of them papers that have a significant readership amongst the investing public,' said McFee.

'Is that why we're not suing anybody?' Mrs Larden demanded.

'The lawyers advised against any legal sword-rattling,' said Treasure. 'The less publicity the episode attracts the better. A law suit would have opened the thing up again. Your husband agreed. If we believed the rumpus or the following publicity seriously affected the flotation, that would have been different. Of course, to say that we murder animals is an outrageous lie and it should have been refuted. But I doubt any sane person believed it.'

'Doctor Ricini ought to sue the papers for publishing such a bad picture of her,' Molly protested. 'It was an insult, Mary.'

'I was too busy to say cheese when it was being taken. Anyway, the camera can't lie,' the attractive Medical Director replied modestly.

'Well it did in your case, Mary,' Hackle put in.

'How gallant you are,' said Jane Larden, touching his arm but without looking at Dr Ricini. 'Oh, I must check the table plan for dinner. And Dermot, get me some more champagne, would you?' She put her glass into his hand, then moved away in front of Mrs Hackle whom she had so far failed to acknowledge.

'We haven't said hello yet, Molly. I'm afraid we were adrift,' said Barbara Closter-Bennet a moment later, turning from Bob Larden, and not sounding overly apologetic. She and the actress embraced briefly. 'I've told the others already, Giles's car wouldn't start. Practically brand new too. BMW aren't stickin' the bits on as well as they used to. My father swore there'd never be anything to touch a Bentley for reliability. He was right too. In the end we came in the Range Rover.'

She was a spare, energetic figure in her late forties with a noticeably slender nose and mouth. Tallish and very upright, she wore her dark hair pulled back severely from a high forehead to a hollow chignon at the neck. Her long white dress had blue spots, and a ruffed V-neck that exposed an area of flat, freckled and very brown chest. The dress was gay but not gaudy, and while it wasn't exactly high fashion she wore it with easy, unconscious style.

Giles Closter-Bennet was following close behind his wife. Moon-faced and overweight, he was much the shorter of the two, and although of an age with her, he was wearing less well. His neck was too big for his collar, the ends of which were turning up around a badly knotted and somewhat soiled bow tie. His double-breasted dinner-jacket was too tight and would have looked a lot better unbuttoned.

'Shouldn't think the Savoy doormen get to park too many Range Rovers like yours, Giles,' said Molly with a smile as they shook hands.

'Up to the hocks in mud, you mean?' Barbara Closter-Bennet put in cheerfully. 'Giles did think to unhitch the horse-box before we left.'

'You both know Rosemary Hackle, of course.' Although there could be little doubt over the point, Molly wasn't clear whether the Closter-Bennets intended to greet the lady: most people seemed not to do so.

'I'm thinking you'll be pleased about the share price today, Barbara?' said McFee later, still chatting with the Closter-Bennets and Treasure. Molly and the others had drifted away, though Mrs Hackle was hovering indeterminately between groups.

'A hundred and twenty pence tonight.' It was Giles Closter-Bennet who replied to the question. 'Not bad, I suppose.'

'I think a premium of 10p is about right,' said Treasure with more assurance than the last speaker. 'It was higher during the day. Fell in the afternoon with some predictable profit-taking. But it steadied well before the close.'

'So Grenwood, Phipps got it right, Mr Chairman?' said McFee with a twinkle. He seemed more relaxed when he wasn't in the company of Dermot Hackle.

'Looks like it.' Treasure smiled.

'A bigger premium on the first day would have meant you'd set the offer price too low,' said Mrs Closter-Bennet with authority.

'Mmm. Last week the *FT* said we'd put it too high.'

'And it's worse for you bankers to do that,' the lady went on. 'You guarantee a flotation, so you have to buy in any unsold shares yourselves. As a shareholder I congratulate you on pleasing everybody, yourselves included.'

'Would you say the small private shareholder take-up was disappointing?' Closter-Bennet questioned, but tentatively. As Finance Director of Closter Drug, he had been closer to the mechanics of the flotation than most of the others.

'It came right in the end, didn't it?' said Treasure, 'The shareholder profile is going to be about average for a promising middle-weight public company. The accent's on institutional holdings, naturally. Insurance companies, unit trusts, and— '

46

'At least my shares now reflect the worth of the company,' Mrs Closter-Bennet interrupted. 'Not the shameful price my father was paid when he was made to sell out thirteen years ago.'

Her now dead father, an international horseman, and his playboy brother, had practically run the company into the ground through sheer neglect. They had been lucky to get any price at all for it, though naturally the buyer had not paid more than he'd had to. Treasure was aware of all this, but didn't comment. Barbara Closter-Bennet's pet grumble was well known – as was her conviction that her husband should be occupying an even more important position in the company.

'Barbara still feels we might have done better to sell out to one of the multi-nationals,' said Closter-Bennet. 'So do I sometimes.' He looked at his wife as if for support, or possibly commendation.

'I stayed ambivalent on that one,' McFee observed. 'That way, if the flotation had been a failure, I could have said I half told you so.' He chuckled. 'As it is, Giles, I think you and Barbara have to hand it to our Chairman for steering us in the right direction.'

'Oh, we're far from ungrateful. Or dissatisfied,' the other man replied almost too quickly. 'It was a democratic decision of shareholders after all.'

'Aye, but that's the very consideration that never fails to stir doubt and suspicion in my mind. Never fails,' McFee repeated, mischievously raising an eyebrow at Treasure.

Barbara Closter-Bennet frowned. She disliked flippancies on subjects that concerned her deeply – the three most notable being the disposition of her wealth, the well-being of her horses, and the acumen of her husband, in that order.

'I was just about to say that the multi-nationals aren't out of the picture yet,' said Treasure. 'On the contrary, you could argue they've just entered it in some force.'

'How's that?' asked McFee, now on his third very large whisky.

'National Pharmaceutical Industries have bought four per cent of the shares. Krontag of Zürich a bit over four and a half per cent, and the American ONR Drug Corporation nearly five per cent. All three pharmaceutical giants that may or may not be showing an intention to take a more substantial interest in us later.'

'Take us over, you mean?' demanded Mrs Closter-Bennet, intrigued but by no means aghast.

'Much too early to say,' Treasure replied.

'They'll wait to see what happens with Seromig,' said Closter-Bennet.

'There are also two quite large holdings registered in the name of Swiss bank nominees . . . ' Treasure paused in mid-sentence, looking over his shoulder with a frown.

It was Hackle's voice that was ringing across the room. 'That's a lie and you know it, Stuart,' he cried from where he and Bodlin were standing near the door. 'Why don't you bloody well grow up?'

'It's not me . . . not me who needs to . . . to . . . to grow up,' Bodlin returned in an uncontrolled, breathy hiss, too easily audible because of the sudden hush. He was stammering, which suggested he had already drunk too much: it was well known that he seldom drank at all. 'You can deny it as . . . as much as you like,' he went on. 'You . . . you could easily have compromised the company. And all because you were toadying to the Managing Director.'

Both men seemed oblivious to the embarrassment they were creating. Larden was now hurrying towards them.

'You'll take that back.' Hackle's hand went forward as though he might be about to take hold of Bodlin's lapels.

No one except Bodlin believed that a blow was intended, but the little scientist fell back defensively with a frightened whimper, away from the other's grasp. It was unlucky that he toppled over the chair behind him, and with arms flailing, crashed to the floor, tipping a fresh tray of canapés off the table.

Alison McFee gasped loudest in dismay.

Chapter Six

'So what exactly were they quarrelling over? Before dinner?'
asked Molly Treasure. She and her husband were being driven
home along the Embankment. Henry Pink, the chauffeur, was at
the wheel of the Rolls-Royce.

'Basically, just each other.'

'It wasn't to do with the wretched news conference?'

'Probably that, yes. But Stuart Bodlin loathes Dermot Hackle,
and Dermot scarcely ever acknowledges Stuart's existence. I don't
know which of them most irritates the other.'

'But Stuart's so important to the company.'

'So is Dermot.'

'Except Stuart discovers all the new products.'

'None of which has earned a penny yet, while Dermot directs
sales. It's thanks to him the company makes such good profits.'

Molly gave a doubting sniff, witness to the endurance of the
well-bred Briton's conviction that making things is virtuous whereas
selling them is vulgar. 'Anyway,' she said, 'it was the most exciting
moment of the evening.'

'Bob Larden stepped in very quickly. He smoothed the troubled
waters very effectively, I thought.'

'Like magic. One almost felt nothing had happened.'

'Nothing much had. Dermot has a very short fuse and knows
it. He was thoroughly ashamed of himself for the outburst, and
the bad manners. He was genuinely apologetic to Stuart and to
everyone else, the ladies especially.' He paused. 'Stuart won't have
forgiven him, of course. Or himself for drinking too much.'

'I don't think Stuart was hurt.'

'Just his pride.'

'I suppose it did put a damper on the evening for some.'

'Not really. Things picked up again quite quickly. They're not exactly a bumper fun group, of course. Was it a bore for you, darling?'

'Not at all. And your after-dinner speech was brilliant.'

'Not brilliant. Appropriate, perhaps. Not too long?'

'No, and very witty.' She squeezed his arm. 'Those two Swiss banks you kept mentioning, the ones who've bought shares for other people— '

'As nominees, yes?'

'Can you make them say whom they're acting for?'

'Officially no. Not unless either or both of them increase their shareholdings to a full five per cent.' Treasure was watching the traffic flow over Westminster Bridge as the car waited at the intersection in the shadow of Big Ben. 'There's a . . . a sort of legal stop light that comes on when anyone buys five per cent of the shares in a British public company. At that figure the buyer has to disclose exactly who he is, and if he's mounting a takeover.'

'But up to five per cent he can stay anonymous?'

'By having a bank buy for him. Which is fair enough. After all, investing money for customers is a pretty legitimate banking activity,' this banker added with pointed firmness.

'How d'you know these two banks aren't both buying for the same customer?' Molly persisted. 'So if each of them has just short of five per cent— '

'Which they have,' Treasure put in with a nod.

'So if it's really one buyer, he could now own nearly ten per cent of Closter Drug?'

'Except we don't know if it's one buyer. And if it were, and he eventually made a takeover bid, he'd already have broken the City Takeover Code by setting up what's called a Concert Party.'

'A Concert Party?' Molly repeated. 'Don't tell me. It can't just be something on the end of the pier. I know, it's a group of people acting in concert— '

'To buy shares on behalf of only one person or company.'

'And that's illegal?'

'If between them they have five per cent or more of the shares, and don't declare the fact.'

'And if they're found out?'

'They could be made to divest themselves of the shares.'

'To give them back?'

'Sell them back.'

'Well that's all right then.' Molly had tired of high finance. 'Hughie McFee was a very amusing dinner companion.'

'He's very pro Bodlin and anti Hackle. You probably noticed?'

'Yes, I did. Well, very pro Stuart Bodlin at least. Hughie didn't actually say anything against Dermot Hackle. Only that he hoped Stuart wasn't too upset after the row. Why do you ask? Is there a reason Hughie doesn't like Dermot? I felt there might be something.'

'I was just interested. There is a reason. It's supposed to be forgotten, but you can sense it affects Hughie's thinking whenever he has to make a judgement involving Dermot.'

'Are they rivals in the company?'

'No, it's nothing to do with the company. Well not directly. It's about Dermot and the McFees' youngest daughter. The unmarried one. They were . . . they were close friends for a while. Too close. Hughie strongly disapproved.'

'I don't suppose Mrs Hackle was wild about the idea either. Is the daughter pretty?'

'Very. Also very young and wilful. In the circumstances, Dermot was a fool to succumb to that sort of temptation.'

'You're suggesting it was the girl who did the tempting?' Molly challenged immediately.

'In this case, I think it could have been. They met at a Burns Night party at the McFees' house two years ago. Alison certainly blamed the girl in part. Hughie wasn't so obliging.'

'What happened?'

'Oh, it's all supposed to be over. The daughter's been packed off to an American university. Bob Larden told me the story some time back. I don't know why really.'

'Dermot's obviously a bit of a liability as well as an asset,' said Molly, wrinkling her brow. 'Not difficult to understand the reason, of course. He really is very attractive. Mary Ricini's obviously gone on him, and she's certainly not the only one.'

Treasure responded with a non-committal grunt. 'In Mary's case it could be she just admires the contribution he makes to the company.'

'That's too innocent,' Molly answered.

Treasure shrugged, then changed the subject. 'Alison McFee was trying to persuade me to bring you to that Scottish binge of theirs in Maidenhead.'

'Hughie had the same idea. Must have been a conspiracy. It's a week on Saturday. I said I wasn't sure if you'd be back from New York.'

'That was a sound blocking tactic.' The banker chuckled. 'I was just purposely vague. Incidentally, the American trip's no excuse. I'm only there two nights. Out this Sunday, back Tuesday.'

'I knew that. Well let's see how we feel about it on the day. It might be fun.'

'If it doesn't rain.'

'Oh, the main programme takes place under cover.'

'In a marquee?'

'A very superior marquee. A pavilion, Hughie said. With a pavilion you don't need poles to hold it up in the middle.'

'That should please any Poles attending.'

'Very droll. Anyway, Hughie made it all sound like the Braemar Gathering.'

'Well so long as I don't have to dance any reels.'

'Oh, come on, last time we did Scottish dancing you thoroughly enjoyed it.'

'That was at Gleneagles. The atmosphere was right. Maidenhead doesn't sound so convincing. Of course, I couldn't very well admit I'd already given our tickets to Miss Gaunt.'

'Oh, I did. Hughie's sending some more. In case. Are the tickets expensive?'

'Yes. Not that it'll break the McFees to give more away in future.'

'Are they rich from the flotation?'

'A lot richer than they were before it. At today's price, Hughie's shareholding would realise . . . let's see . . . nearly two and a half million pounds.'

'Making him the biggest director shareholder next to Bob?'

'About equal second with the Closter-Bennets.'

'Who you said were well off anyway. Before the flotation.'

Treasure smiled ruefully. 'Better off than Barbara pretends. She has quite large interests – horsy and landed – in South America. Her mother was Argentinian. I imagine a lot of her British resources went into the Closter management buy-out five years ago. It's certainly paid off this week.'

'You mean her husband put the capital in?'

'Yes, but it would have been Barbara's money. Giles was an unmonied and unspectacular accountant who married well.'

'His wife doesn't think he's unspectacular,' said Molly with feeling.

'I know. She thinks he should have been made Managing Director instead of Bob. He would have been apparently, if her family had gone on owning the company.'

'Would he have been any good at it?'

'A disaster I should think. I told you, he's not a bad accountant, but limited. Even so, the managing directorship was actually promised to him at one time, by Barbara's father. She and Giles are both still very aware of it. Barbara will be pushing for him to be promoted again if I bow out and Bob takes over the chairmanship.'

'Which is something that wouldn't please Stuart,' said Molly. 'He was on my other side at dinner. He hasn't much time for any of the others except Mary.'

'What did you talk about during dinner?'

'That was the problem. He had very little to say. Until I encouraged him to tell me about his work.'

'That must have been entrancing.'

'Well it was, in a way,' Molly offered slowly. 'What I understood of it. He explained all about Seromig, and the two other new drugs. A safer anti-depressant, he said, and a new er . . . '

'Antibiotic based on a derivative of quinolone,' Treasure completed.

'That's right. And much more complicated than the other one. Sounded as if it'd be ages before either of them would be ready.'

'Five years at least. And even that's optimistic.' He paused, watching the full moon's reflection in the river as the car sped by the Tate Gallery. 'But if Seromig's a success, the new drugs will fall into place very neatly as the next big profit earners. Especially after the Seromig patent runs out.'

'And if Seromig isn't a success?'

'It's bound to be a success if it cures migraine, which is what it's supposed to do. If it doesn't, a lot of money will have gone down the drain, and Closter Drug will just have to soldier on, doing what it's been doing for the last five years. It wouldn't be a disaster, but the company wouldn't be too exciting for investors.'

'Which would be a pity since it's just gone public?'

'Oh, it would have quite a few things going for it.'

'Even if the directors aren't exactly one big happy family.'

Treasure pouted for a moment. 'A degree of antagonism is often quite healthy in a management team. Bob Larden's a good catalyst.'

'I thought you were that. Stuart Bodlin says it's essential you stay as Chairman. That you give the company style.'

53

'How touching. I'm not sure a pharmaceutical manufacturer needs much style.'

'Well Stuart obviously respects you enormously.'

Treasure gave a cynical chuckle. 'That's not the reason for the loyalty. If Bob Larden became Chairman, someone else would have to be Managing Director. The likeliest contender would be Dermot.'

'Which wouldn't suit Stuart either.'

'Because he'd like the job himself.'

'You're not serious? I mean, I don't know much about running companies, but Stuart isn't at all the managing director type is he?'

'No he isn't, except you'd be surprised at the number of people who privately yearn for jobs that are way above their capacities. Not that if it came to it most of them would actually want to be promoted. Not to industrial stardom.'

'Why not?'

'Because it's the illusion they enjoy. While even deeper down in the sub-conscious they know perfectly well they lack the ability to match the aspiration.'

'So why the yearning?'

'Oh, sometimes envy of the chap already in the top job. More often, jealousy of whoever's really going to get it next.' He shook his head. 'It's a negative syndrome, but very common.'

'In the theatre too,' said Molly thoughtfully. 'And Giles Closter-Bennet is another yearner like Stuart?'

'Ah, there the negative syndrome has a related one attached to it.'

'You mean, related by marriage. Barbara?'

'That's right. The ambitious wife. Quite a common quantity in that sort of situation. I'm sure Giles wouldn't be ambitious on his own. It's only because Barbara expects him to be. Basically he's probably too lazy.'

'I suppose Hughie McFee doesn't have these hopeless ambitions?'

'Curiously enough, if it weren't for Dermot, Hughie would make a very competent managing director under Bob's chairmanship. He's very experienced, in the industry as well as the company. Very respected.'

'Not too old?'

'He's fifty-two. I agree he looks older.'

'Would he like the job?'

'Oh yes.'

'But Dermot's better qualified?'

Treasure hesitated. 'I didn't say that. It's simply that if anyone else were appointed, the mercurial Dermot would probably resign on the spot. He'd regret it afterwards, but he'd still resign.'

'And he's too valuable to lose?'

'Yes, he is. Immature in many ways, but exceedingly valuable.'

'It sounds as though Mary Ricini is the only director happy with her lot.'

'To an extent that's true. She's still learning the ropes of course.'

'Of medicine? But she's a qualified doc— '

'No, of management,' he interrupted. 'She's a high flyer. Already too good for the job she's doing. Give her a year or two, with broader experience, she could make a very good chief executive somewhere.'

'But not at Closter Drug?'

'Possibly. If she can be persuaded to stay long enough.'

Molly was leaning forward, screwing up her eyes to see something ahead of them.

Henry Pink was putting the car through a U-turn, just before Albert Bridge, and before swinging it into Cheyne Walk.

'Well here's your chance to start persuading, darling,' Molly said. 'That's Mary paying off a cab outside our house. I wonder what she wants at this time of night.'

Chapter Seven

Doris Tanner, secretary to the Managing Director of Closter Drug, counted the cups again. There were seven on the tray. Then she remembered there would only be six people at the meeting. Mr Treasure hardly ever came to the weekly directors' meetings, only to the formal monthly ones. And he definitely wouldn't be coming today because he was in America. She took one of the cups away and, focusing hard through her glasses, counted the pile of saucers. If her husband Bert hadn't made sexual demands of a very strenuous kind at five thirty on this same morning, Doris would not have been so dozy here at the office less than three hours later.

Bert was a caution all right. What with his thinking it was Sunday not Monday like that. She took away one of the saucers. Bert was an emergency fitter with British Gas, and worked odd shifts. That was why he sometimes got randy at inconvenient times: well, inconvenient for Doris – and that was apart from his getting the days mixed up. Still, it'd be time to complain if he stopped fancying her, which would be a long time off yet, judging by current interest. She smiled to herself as she put the extra cup and saucer back in the high cupboard behind her desk. The special crockery was stored there – where she could keep an eye on it.

The Tanners would both be thirty-seven in a month's time: they'd even been born on the same day. Bert liked to say that proved they were made for each other. They had put off having children for a long time, for money reasons, then discovered they had left it too late, or good as. After Doris's miscarriage two years before, they had been advised not to try for a baby again. Having to stay childless hadn't bothered them much. Doris had mentioned adopting once or twice, but Bert wasn't keen. They kept dogs instead – a pair of Alsatians. They had a neat, modern semi-detached house on a small estate a mile from the Closter factory. There was a handy-sized garden at the back.

'Morning, Doris. Lovely day. Got the coffee on, I see.' Bob Larden had come from the main corridor and into her office through the door in the small shared vestibule; the door to his own office was opposite. He was carrying his black leather document case, also the pile of professional journals he regularly took home on Fridays. He dropped the journals on Doris's desk. 'Present for you,' he said, smiling.

'Did you have a good weekend then, Mr Larden?' she enquired with a brightness that was still requiring effort. She usually addressed him as 'Mr', sometimes as 'sir': he wasn't the type of boss whom you called by his first name. 'It was ever such lovely weather,' she added in her smoothed-out, Lambeth accent. You didn't get Chelsea dolly birds doing the secretarial work around Longbrook, even in the top jobs like Doris's. And Longbrook bosses should be truly grateful for that great mercy, was what Doris always felt, and sometimes said. She moved the journals to her 'out' tray. 'Get out of London did you at all, Mr Larden?'

'Not really,' he said, his mind half on something else. Her question had reminded him that his wife had been working at a block of flats in Wapping for most of the previous afternoon and evening. The design job she was doing there had fallen behind schedule. He resented it when her work intruded on their time together. 'Played a bit of tennis Saturday morning.'

'Nice,' she said.

'And you?'

'Oh, we were very quiet. Enjoyed the weather.'

These were the standard Monday morning answers to the standard Monday morning questions. Doris was sure he didn't want to know about her weekend. He wouldn't half be surprised, she thought, if she'd told him what she and Bert had been up to at dawn. Talk about contortions – and all because Bert had bought a sex manual in a book sale. Mr Larden wouldn't have believed unglamorous Doris capable of such antics. Except he did look at her legs sometimes. She was no beauty – a thin rather than a slim brunette, with rather pronounced teeth – but she made the best of herself, and her legs were definitely her most attractive feature. She imagined his own sex life would be pretty boisterous with that young wife of his: she looked like a real raver from the photos – classy, but still a raver. Doris had never met Jane Larden.

Larden was still standing in front of her desk while he studied the meeting agenda he'd taken from his case. He stroked his chin

57

with his free hand. 'Doesn't look as if we'll need you in the meeting for anything this morning, Doris. Mr Closter-Bennet will take the minutes. Should be a short meeting too. I'll buzz if anything crops up.' He glanced at the electric percolator that was making erupting noises on her side table. 'Can we have the coffee before we start?'

'It'll be ready in two minutes.'

'Good.' He was glancing at his watch as he turned about to go across to his own office. It was 8.34. 'Everyone's cutting it fine this morning. Seen Mr Hackle?'

'I don't think he's in yet, Mr Larden.'

Regular informal directors' meetings took place in Larden's office every Monday morning at 8.45. They didn't last long, and were held so that progress could be reported on major company activities. Larden called them essential exercises in top level communication. On the first Monday of the month there was an official board meeting instead, at ten o'clock, usually with Treasure in the chair. Douglas Figg, the Company Secretary, normally attended all the meetings and took the minutes, but he had succumbed to shingles three weeks before. Closter-Bennet had been taking the minutes instead, without much enthusiasm. This was why Doris had sometimes been called in to take the occasional long note.

Hackle usually came to the Managing Director's office ahead of the others to discuss the agenda. Twenty minutes later, with the meeting well under way, he still hadn't appeared.

'If we're going to switch selling agents in Holland on the date we agreed, the Freight Department really has to know by the end of the month,' Hughie McFee was saying.

'We gave Dermot the credit clearance on that two weeks ago,' said Closter-Bennet sharply, shaking his head. 'We haven't had any contracts for signing.'

'Haven't we fired the existing agents?' asked Mary Ricini who wasn't directly involved, but interested.

'Yes, we have. So if we don't act fast we'll be left with no Dutch agent at all. Probably Dermot's got it in hand,' Larden scowled from his seat at the head of the oblong table, thinking there ought to be more people to accept delegated authority. Closter Drug had existed for long enough on this slim nucleus of working directors with little back-up, except in the Research Department, and with each member covering really unacceptably large areas of responsibility. The system had generated profit all right, but the strain was telling. He was about to say something on this subject when his secretary's head appeared around the door. 'Any news on Mr Hackle, Doris?' he asked.

'Yes, Mr Larden. I just spoke to Mrs Hackle. She says he had to go to Nottingham after lunch yesterday. On unexpected business. He rang from there to say he had to stay overnight. He was planning to drive straight here this morning.'

'Where was he staying?'

'I asked Mrs Hackle. He hadn't said.'

The likelihood of Hackle needing to go to Nottingham on unexpected business on a Sunday, and then having to stay the night without saying where, was silently but not very solemnly debated by all those present. At least one wondered at the naïvety of a wife who accepted such a flimsy story from a husband whose faithfulness wasn't exactly legendary.

'Thanks, Doris.' Larden shuffled the papers in front of him. 'We'll leave the Dutch situation till Dermot gets here. Traffic's bad on the M1 probably.' He cleared his throat.

'There's been a big accident near Luton,' Stuart Bodlin put in quietly. 'It was on the LBC news as I was arriving. There's a big tailback they said.'

'That's it then, I expect. And you can never get through on a carphone when there's a hold-up,' said Larden shaking his head. 'Let's move on to these draft budgets, shall we? I think we should— ' He stopped speaking, his eyes on the doorway. His secretary had appeared there again. 'Yes, Doris?' he said, a touch impatiently.

'I'm sorry, Mr Larden. There's someone on the phone who wants to talk to you about Mr Hackle. He says it's urgent. He won't give me his name. He sounds Irish.'

Larden glanced at the others, shrugged, then got up and moved over to his desk wearing a stony expression. 'Put him through.' He leaned across the desk for the telephone, and waited a moment while Doris switched the call. 'Hello, Larden here?'

'Would that be Mr *Robert* Larden?'

'Yes. Who's this?'

'Do you have the other directors with you, Mr Larden?'

'Yes I do. I understand you have an urgent message for me from Mr Hackle?' Doris was right, the accent was definitely Southern Irish. The voice was high-pitched but not excited.

'Well now, the message concerns all the directors. D'you think

59

you could turn on the amplifier I'm told you've got there? So everyone can hear?'

'Now look— '

'So everyone can hear what Mr Hackle has to say,' the caller interrupted, the voice sharpening. 'He's right beside me ready to speak. He's very anxious to tell you something.'

Puzzled, irritated, but beginning also to be alarmed, Larden pushed the conference button on the base of the instrument. 'The amplifier's on,' he snapped.

'Right you are then. Here's Mr Hackle.'

There was a pause, then came: 'Bob, it's me, Dermot.' The voice emitting from the loudspeaker was faint, strained but unmistakable. 'Can everyone hear me?'

Larden glanced round at the others catching their nods. 'We can hear you, Dermot. Only just though. Speak up, can you? Are you all right? Who's that with you?'

'Look, it's serious, I'm afraid. You see, I've been kidnapped.' The tone was a little louder now, the words well spaced. 'There's . . . they've got a knife at my throat, Bob. No kidding. They're going to kill me unless you do what they say. I think they mean it.'

It was an hour later when Dr Ricini rang the front doorbell of the twin gabled suburban villa in the West Ealing cul-de-sac. Then she stepped back a little, willing herself to exude calmness. She had rehearsed what she had to say several times in the car during the twelve-minute drive from the factory.

It was a pre-war house, quite large, but the grey, pebble dash walls were as sombre as the faded if spotlessly clean curtains in the bay windows on either side of the doorway. The white paintwork was badly in need of renewal, and some of the woodwork was plainly decayed. An estate agent would have described the place as desirable but in need of repair – which is exactly how Dermot Hackle had described it to his colleagues at Closter Drug when he'd bought it on a long mortgage five years before. It seemed nothing had altered since that time.

The small front garden was well enough tended. There was an area of recently mown grass, with a sundial on a stone pedestal in the middle. A flower border skirted the path up to the door and also the loose gravelled drive that ran from the gateway to the concrete garage on the right. Both halves of the dilapidated wooden street gate were propped open at drunken angles, looking as if they had been in that state for some time – possibly for years. There were red tulips in bloom in the border, some dead-headed daffodils folded back with elastic bands, and a row of pruned roses showing plenty of bud as well as leaf. Dr Ricini enjoyed gardening. She had a garden of her own in Windsor – and wished she was in it now, or anywhere but here.

She rang the bell again, debating what she should do if there was no one in. The door was opened almost immediately afterwards.

A breathless Rosemary Hackle stood behind the threshold in a dowdy blue dress. She used the back of the hand holding the yellow duster to push away a thick strand of unruly hair that was hanging over one eye. 'Mary, it's you. Sorry I kept you. Is it about the migraine test? I— ' she began, then stopped, with fright in her eyes. 'It isn't that is it? Oh God, something's happened to Dermot?' A hand had gone to her mouth, and she had paled.

'No, Dermot's all right. Honestly. There's nothing to worry about.' Mary stepped quickly into the hallway, closing the door herself, then she took Rosemary firmly by the arm. It was quite dark inside. 'Where shall we go? In the kitchen?' She'd never been to the house before. 'Along here is it? I think we'd better have some tea. Not now. In a minute. Let's sit down first. There's something I have to tell you. Are the children at school?'

'Yes. They both are. I was cleaning the bedrooms,' Rosemary followed Mary's example and took a seat opposite her at the plastic-topped table in the centre of the room. She still looked frightened. 'Tell me what's happened, Mary. Something has, hasn't it?'

Except for the newish paint on the walls and doors, it was a kitchen that hadn't been refurbished since before the time when built-in units became fashionable. But it was almost excessively tidy, and if the unmatched cupboards, the elderly Aga cooker, and the rest of the contents had seen better days, they were all as well burnished as the worn lino on the floor. There was an open, half-glazed door leading outside into the back garden. A large black cat was sitting on the step there, half asleep in the sunshine.

Mary leaned forward. 'Dermot's not hurt. But he's been abducted. Kidnapped. But don't worry, we're going to get him back safe.' She wanted to add how fervently she'd been praying for the past hour that that could be true.

Rosemary had let out a little whimper. 'Dermot kidnapped? Why? Who's kidnapped him?'

'We think it's the SAE. The Stop Animal Experiments lot, remember? But they haven't said so yet. They rang us, just after Bob Larden's secretary rang you. They let Dermot speak. We all heard his voice. He was very cheerful. He said he was being well treated.' She didn't mention the knife at his throat. It was bad enough that she had been made to suffer that and the other brutal disclosures herself without betraying her true devastated feelings to the men present at the time.

'The police? Mary, have you told the police yet?'

'Not yet. And we don't think we should. Not unless you say so.'

'Why not?'

'The kidnappers said we mustn't tell anyone. Not the police or Mark Treasure or Grenwood, Phipps. Not anyone, except you and the wives of other directors. If we do tell the police, the kidnappers say they'll know and . . . and then they'll hurt Dermot.'

'Kill him?' The whimper came again, only louder.

'Certainly not.' Her own stomach had jerked on the other woman's words. 'They're not going to kill him. He's much too valuable for their purpose.' She gave a reassuring smile – while forcing herself to believe her own words.

'But hurt him? Maim him? That's what kidnappers do isn't it? Oh God, help me!' Rosemary took a deep breath that was half a sob. 'Is it a ransom they want? We've got no money. Everyone knows we're— '

'They don't want anything from you. They want all the directors in the company to sell their shares in Closter Drug. Tomorrow. And not to try buying them back till next week.'

'I don't understand?'

'Neither do we really, but that's what they've said. If we obey, and don't tell anyone why, they'll let Dermot go.'

'That's all?' Her hands were cupped around her face.

'We're not to tell anyone at the Stock Exchange what we're doing. In other words, we mustn't admit we're being forced to sell shares. You see, if that were known, dealings in Closter shares could be stopped. The kidnappers know that.'

Rosemary seemed not to have comprehended the last point. 'When will they let Dermot go?'

'Quite soon.' Mary avoided giving a direct answer. 'As soon as they know we've done as they've ordered.'

'But how can we trust them? And how will they know what we've done?'

'They say they have informants everywhere. In the police, on the Stock Exchange, in the company, even at Grenwood, Phipps. They could be bluffing, of course. Except . . . Well if they're the SAE they're not criminals. I mean, not in the ordinary sense. Not in the sense they're in this for personal gain. Which added to something else— '

'There's no ransom?'

'Exactly. It could mean we're dealing with an organised group of cranks. A chain of animal nutters with committed members in all the places they say. They don't need to be high-ups. Just ordinary employees who have to see or pass on information.'

'Like secretaries?'

'Exactly. Secretaries, clerks, switchboard operators— '

'But why are they— '

'They're people simply out to make Closter directors give up their gains. The gains from last week's flotation.'

Rosemary was nodding furiously. 'But if it's the SAE— '

'It fits. The man who spoke to us on the phone had an Irish accent. The man who Dermot hit during the demo was Irish. I heard him. It could have been the same man. The problem is, there is no SAE. Nothing that we can trace.'

'But they broke up the meeting? There were photos?'

'Kirsty Welling and followers broke up the meeting. They called themselves the SAE. There were no faces on the photographs. Not of the demonstrators. They were all hidden by the banners. We now believe that was on purpose. So they couldn't be identified. They all melted into thin air after, too. Last week, when the lawyers were deciding what to do about the demo, they tried tracing the SAE and failed. They told Bob Larden on Friday the SAE didn't exist – just like the magazine, *Natural World Tomorrow*.'

'But the other animal protection groups— '

'Say they've never heard of the SAE either. And the journalist unions don't have a Kirsty Welling in membership.'

'So how could the SAE have kidnapped Dermot? I don't understand?'

'Bob thinks it's a small group temporarily recruited from the regular animal protection groups. It's not meant to survive. Its job is to harass Closter Drug. The demo was to spoil the flotation. The kidnap is to hurt the directors.'

'But why did they pick Dermot?'

'Maybe he was the easiest target for some reason.'

'Or because he hit the Irishman?'

'It's possible. It could also be because they know Dermot has fewer shares than the rest of us. He'd have been more difficult to pressure for that reason if someone else had been the victim.'

The other woman nodded slowly. 'But if they're not criminals, they're not going to harm him?' There was hope in the tone and in the eyes.

'Not if we do as they say.' She repressed the comment that fanatics could be a lot more dangerous than common criminals.

'So we must do as they say. Not tell the police or anyone. It'll be all right then. They'll let him go.'

'That's right, Rosemary. We've just got to sit it out.' And God, let it be true, she inwardly beseeched, for the man both these woman adored in their separate fashions.

Chapter Eight

'Stuart Bodlin voted to sell. From the very first. No hesitation at all,' said Giles Closter-Bennet, frowning into the gin and tonic he was holding.

'That man's too soft. His kind usually are,' his wife answered with feeling. 'Pour me another, will you?' She pushed her empty tumbler across the low, glass-topped, raffia-bound table. She took an olive from the dish there.

It was 7.30. Closter-Bennet had arrived home later than usual. The two were sitting outside on the well sheltered, stone-flagged terrace of their eighteenth-century farmhouse. The place belonged to Barbara Closter-Bennet who had inherited it from her father: it was on the edge of the Thames-side village of Later Burnlow.

Closter-Bennet picked up the gin bottle from the drinks trolley beside him. His weight and the movement made the wicker chair creak a little. The King Charles spaniel lying at Barbara's feet raised its head nervously at the sound.

The chair belonged to a set that Barbara's father had bought at Harrods more than forty years before: she was seated in another of them. If they creaked it detracted nothing from their resilience; they were sturdily built and good for many more years' wear. Naturally, the seats and the removable cushions had been renewed from time to time. The table had come with the chairs.

The garden furniture was indicative. There was nothing cheap or dilapidated about the Closter-Bennet home or chattels. Barbara had been brought up to invest in quality, proper maintenance, and to replace things only when the need was evident – not because something fancier had come out in plastic.

'Mind you, Bodlin doesn't like Hackle,' said Closter-Bennet, by way of emphasising the unexpectedness of his earlier report. He dropped two ice cubes into the gin, then added tonic.

'What's that got to do with it? Of course, the police should have been told immediately. And Mark Treasure.'

'He's in New York.'

'There are telephones.' She took the glass from him. As always, the action was a little awkward because her right wrist, damaged in a riding accident, had never mended properly.

'We couldn't telephone. We don't know who's to be trusted.'

'Oh come on! You don't seriously believe those criminals? What they told you about having spies everywhere? Naturally they were bluffing.'

'Mary Ricini doesn't think so.'

'Isn't she Italian?'

His face clouded. 'No, English.' He considered the evident incongruity of that claim when set against the lady's surname. 'I think her father was from Sicily. Before he came to this country. Her mother's from Leamington Spa.'

'So the girl's mind was filled with Mafia stories. They're always kidnapping each other there.'

He took it that she meant Sicily not Leamington Spa, but you never knew with Barbara whose prejudices were numerous, and not always predictable. 'We've taken no risks at all,' he went on. 'Not so far. The Irishman said if we told the police they'd castrate Hackle immediately. And then send us his . . . send us the evidence.' He had lowered his voice at the awesomeness of the threat.

Barbara gave a wince, but only a very small one. 'How disgusting,' she said, quite slowly.

'And they'll cut off his right hand if we warn the Stock Exchange about the plan.'

This time there was no visible reaction. 'It's probably all pretence. To frighten you.' She paused, her gaze straying to the secateurs in the flower basket near her chair. 'Hackle's right-handed, I suppose?'

'Yes, he is,' he answered, wondering if that particular enquiry had been seemly or essential in the circumstances. He hadn't yet told her about the final threat.

'And Bob Larden protested?'

'To the SAE, or whoever they are. Yes. He asked if they realised they were behaving like total barbarians. The chap just said that now we'd know how animals felt about vivisection. It was a good point in a way.'

'Nonsense.'

'Yes, dear.'

66

'But it's why you're pretty sure it's the SAE?' She dropped a hand to smooth the spaniel's head.

'The chap didn't deny it when Bob said so. Bodlin was convinced it was them from the start. He's very upset.'

'Not as upset as Dermot Hackle, I imagine,' Barbara offered drily.

'Of course not. It's just that despite what Bodlin says, he's never really felt easy about the animal experiments we do. Especially the terminal ones on mammals.'

'He has an affinity with monkeys? Quite understandable, I suppose. He looks like one. Like an undernourished baboon that's lost some hair.'

'He was the only one at all affected by the protest the other day.' Closter-Bennet scratched his stomach under his trouser top. 'It's hard to explain. He's become a vegetarian, for instance. Quite recently. Perhaps you'd feel the same way as him if you had to destroy a perfectly sound horse, say. Even in a good cause.'

'But I could never find myself in such a position. If his work bothers him so much, the man should switch to something else.'

'We couldn't do without him.' He knew it pleased her to be gratuitously perverse.

'Nonsense. No one's indispensable. Daddy always said that.' Her eyes became thoughtful, but she wasn't ruminating on her dead father whose pronouncements hadn't warranted much of her attention in his lifetime. 'What if Hackle didn't survive? When Bob becomes Chairman, they'd have to make you Managing Director, of course.' Her still narrowed eyes delayed immediate comment from her husband. 'Yes, I must remember to confirm that date with Jane,' she added.

'About the new decorations here?'

'To talk about them.' Even a sound ulterior motive would not be allowed to precipitate commitment in so unresolved a matter. 'There's no hurry. But I ought to be in touch with Jane. It'll be appropriate, in the circumstances. We might have them both to dinner here again, too.'

'We don't know that Bob's going to be Chairman.'

'He will be. Quite soon. Mark Treasure never intended to stay on after the flotation.'

'In any case they wouldn't make me Managing Director.'

'Who else is there?'

'Bodlin?' he offered tentatively.

67

'You can't be serious?'

'Hughie McFee then?'

'Not the breadth to be a managing director.'

'Someone from outside then?'

She made a tutting sound. 'For God's sake, Giles, if you don't value your capacities, how can you expect anyone else to?'

He shrugged, then emptied his glass. 'What we're talking about is academic. If the managing directorship becomes vacant, it's bound to go to Dermot. He won't come to any harm. We're going to protect him. Do what the SAE order.'

Barbara seemed to be occupied with other things as she answered: 'We'll have to see about that.'

He assumed she was referring still to the managing directorship. 'Pretty well everyone was committed to selling their shares,' he said, gloomily.

Her jaw stiffened. 'I thought you said some of them were undecided?'

'That was about whether we should go to the police.' He shifted in his chair. 'Well . . . Bob hasn't actually committed himself on the shares. But I think he'll decide to sell in the end.'

'I assume you haven't committed my shares?' Her words were almost menacing. Then without waiting for a reply she asked: 'You realise it's my decision, not yours?'

He shifted in his chair, making it creak again. 'The shares are in my name.'

'But bought with my money, five years ago. Out of what was left of Daddy's fortune. Your kidnappers have no right to regard those shares as belonging to a director. They belong to me. I'm not a director.' Angrily she lit a cigarette.

'I don't think the SAE would understand the distinction. I think we'll all have to sell. If we don't they say they'll . . . they'll put down Dermot Hackle tomorrow night.'

'Put down?' Her hand dropped instinctively to the dog again.

'That's what they said. Like an animal. And that won't be the end of it either.'

'More shamming, of course. So what would be left for them to do if they put down Dermot Hackle, for heaven's sake?' She pronounced 'put down' in a manner that gave the possibility no credence.

'They say after that they'd go on hurting us all in the slow way. Because we'd have rejected the fast one.' He paused. 'They'll

68

abduct the wife or the child of a director. Both, in time. That's unless we relent and sell. And they'll do the same if we ever admit there was a kidnapping.'

This time it wasn't only Barbara's jaw that stiffened. Her whole body had gone tight at the mention of the word wife. Because of her movement, the startled spaniel sat up too. With their astonished, aggrieved expressions, lifted noses, and popping dark eyes, at that moment outraged mistress and pet looked uncannily alike.

'This telephone call you got must have gone on a rare long time,' said Alison McFee. She stuck the long cooking fork into one of the potatoes in the saucepan on the cooker.

'Four or five minutes, I suppose. It was pretty one-sided,' her husband answered. He was in shirt sleeves, taking apart the defective plug on the lead to the electric kettle. There was a glass of neat whisky beside him. Like Closter-Bennet, he had arrived home later than usual. 'I don't think anyone was timing it.'

'But someone could have been alerting the switchboard to try tracing the number.' She stood back from the cooker and glanced around to where he was standing at the draining board. 'Except, of course, you wouldn't have dared. In case the kidnappers found out. I'd forgotten that. How terrible.' She shook her head and used the fork to push about the lamb chops on the grill.

He had given her a similar account to the one Closter-Bennet had given to his wife – except Hughie McFee had early on explained that they had no choice but to part with their shares to save Dermot Hackle's life. Again like Closter-Bennet, he had stressed why it was essential that the wives told no one about the kidnap either now or possibly ever.

They were in their big, square kitchen, an invariably untidy area but well equipped and practical. The McFees' home was a substantial, red-brick, Victorian villa, with later additions, and grounds of several acres running down to the towpath on the outskirts of Maidenhead.

After all three children had left home, the couple had taken to spending most of their time either in the kitchen or in the adjoining conservatory – an iron-framed, stone-floored, Gothic appendage, shaped like a glass marquee, and promoted from its earlier status as a playroom. The conservatory was warm, except in the very depths of winter, and adaptable for eating, sitting, reading, napping and watching television or boats on the river. It was haphazardly but effectively furnished to cover all those activities, making for a comfortable muddle: Alison McFee was anything but house-proud. For a good deal of the year, the room was also pleasantly scented by the exotic plants that McFee nurtured along the ledges, or brought in from his greenhouse.

It was to the conservatory that Alison now drove her husband. Although the electrical repair job wasn't completed, her cooking was.

'When they phone again tomorrow, can you have the call traced in some way then?' she asked, while unloading the tray of food on to the big round white-painted table in the centre of the room. Less than half the table surface had been cleared for the meal; the remainder was occupied by, amongst other things, a collection of seed catalogues, a broken clock, some travel brochures, a length of green netting in need of unravelling, an office stapler, a stack of unissued tickets for the Maidenhead Scottish Festival, and the previous day's copy of *The Times*, folded to the cookery page.

He drew up a chair, a collapsible, high-backed tubular steel affair with arms and loose cushions, quite different from the wooden, upholstered one his wife was using. 'The man told us they were using Dermot's own portable phone. From his car,' he said. 'You can't trace a call from one of those.' He seemed to be considering the overfull table, his gaze pausing quizzically on the green netting. Then he withdrew his napkin from its holder, before adding broccoli from the nearest serving dish to the grilled meat his wife had put before him. 'You see, there's no way of pinpointing the location of a portable phone,' he completed.

'You don't say?' She shook her head in surprise, took the serving dish from him, helped herself to vegetable, then leaned over to deposit the dish in a neutral area of the table, but one already occupied by the *Radio Times*. 'You'd have thought it'd be a mite easier than with an ordinary phone.'

'The system operators would like it to be. Too many portables are stolen. Thieves use them with impunity till they're reported, like the SAE are doing now, with no chance of their being tracked down. The system operators are working on a solution to that one. But it won't be in time to help Dermot Hackle.' He poured her some water as he spoke. She drank nothing else with dinner at home. He preferred to sip Scotch. As usual, he had brought his glass and the bottle to the table with him.

'But what if you were to ring them? Is it the same? If you know Dermot's number surely— '

'We've tried already. This afternoon,' he interrupted. 'For another reason. We got the standard message when a subscriber is choosing not to answer. They were obviously not in the business of accepting calls. In any case, the locating problem's the same. Or nearly the same.'

'His poor wife, Rosemary. She's such a frail creature.' Alison spooned some potatoes on to her plate from the other serving dish, recharged the spoon, considered, then put the second helping back in the dish. 'What's happening about her? She's been told?'

'Aye, and Mary Ricini's moved into the house. It seemed the best solution. It's hit Rosemary very hard apparently.'

'What else would you expect, Hughie?'

'I meant about it being the best solution. Because she might need sedation, and maybe medical counselling over the next few days. We couldn't risk her taking herself off to her own doctor. Having to explain things. She understands that. And she gets on with Mary.' He cut into his lamb chop.

'And what about the Hackle children? Let's see, the girl must be a teenager now. The boy about nine.'

'They're not to be told what's happening. Not unless it's absolutely unavoidable.'

'Of course. But they must be told something.'

'Only that their mother's unwell, and that Mary's staying because their father's been caught up with meetings in the Midlands. That should hold them till Friday, if necessary.'

'Is that when he's to be released?' Alison shook her head and gave a ruminative smile. 'Rosemary wanted to bring the family here to the Festival on Saturday.'

'I doubt they'll be in the mood for dancing. But then, he could be freed earlier. If the kidnappers are satisfied, and Bob can persuade them.'

Alison looked up from her plate. 'And if they're not satisfied? Are they really going to harm him, or is it all threats?'

'Threats, I hope. But we must still do as they order.' He chewed for a moment while considering the prospect. 'They don't have the risks ordinary kidnappers run. For instance, they don't have to pick up a ransom.'

'Isn't that when kidnappers are usually caught?'

'I should think so. I'm no authority, but it stands to reason.'

71

'It's when they're always caught on the TV. D'you suppose this SAE group is really not interested in money?'

'We don't know it's them for certain, of course. They haven't admitted it.'

'But who else could it be?'

'You're right. Bob's assumed it's them, like the rest of us. But he won't accept they're not on the make. Not in some way.'

'But they don't have to be out for money. Not if they're people committed to a cause.'

McFee dabbed his mouth with his napkin. 'Bob's not the sort to get committed to a cause beyond self-interest, so he's not really in the market for people of the other kind,' he observed cynically.

'But what can the SAE stand to gain, except better treatment for animals?'

'It's difficult to say exactly.' His eye roved from his now empty plate to the dish of apple crumble Alison had brought in earlier.

'We're going to lose a great deal?'

'Aye. Not the lot, but a great deal.'

'I suppose it's only money. And money canna buy happiness,' she added. It had been a favourite phrase of theirs in the early days of their marriage.

'And we're paying to save a life.' McFee looked solemn. 'I just wish it was a life worthier of the sacrifice.'

'Every life is worthy of saving, Hughie.'

'But this one less so than most. You're very forgiving.'

'So are you or you wouldn't be ready to help.'

He didn't respond directly. 'The SAE have told us we have to sell twelve million, eight hundred and fifty thousand shares. Beginning at ten in the morning. A million shares every fifteen minutes. On the open market. Till they're all gone.'

'That's a very exact figure?'

'And they knew it exactly. Of course it was in the prospectus for anyone who could add up. It's the total number of shares held by all the directors. It's just short of sixteen per cent of the whole company. It's going to be a terrible jolt.'

'You mean the price of the shares will drop?'

'Like a stone. And when it's known it's the directors who are selling, the stone could turn into a bomb.'

'So the two-and-a-half million pounds our shares were worth on Friday— '

'Could fetch less than half that, I'm afraid.'

72

'A million and a quarter's still a lot of money.' Her tone allowed that they they were not about to be reduced to penury. 'Have some apple crumble.' She removed his dinner plate, stacked it with her own, on top of the seed catalogues, before passing him a dessert dish. 'I still say you're a good man, Hughie McFee. To give up so much for someone you don't care for at all.'

He poured some Scotch into his glass. 'If anything happens to stop Dermot Hackle becoming Managing Director when the time comes, I wouldn't want the cause to have been my doing. Not in any way.'

'Because you'd be made Managing Director instead?'

His eyebrows lifted. 'That doesn't follow.'

'But you always wanted that. You know, I hadn't thought . . . ' She hesitated, absently helping herself to an overgenerous portion of the pudding. 'That couldn't be why Dermot's been kidnapped? Dermot as opposed to Bob for instance? Or any of the other directors?'

'I don't know what you mean.' The sharpness of his comment surprised her.

'Neither do I really.' But his response made her want to try again. 'Because Dermot has more enemies in the company than anyone else? More rivals, maybe? Could that have anything to do with what's happened? Or what will happen next?'

'Certainly not,' he said, again with untypical fierceness.

Alison absently added more cream to her crumble.

73

Chapter Nine

'Is Mummy very ill, Emma?'

'Just an upset tummy.'

Tim Hackle, who was only just nine, lined up his mouth over his plate before disgorging another cherry stone on to it. 'Will she stay in bed for the rest of tonight?'

'Probably. Doctor Ricini's giving her something,' said his sister. The two were finishing supper in the kitchen.

'So why have we got a doctor living with us?'

'She isn't living with us. Just a couple of nights while Daddy's away. D'you want some more cherries?'

'Oo, yes please, Emma. Did the doctor bring the cherries?'

'I think so.'

Out-of-season fresh fruit was not a regular feature of the Hackle family diet. Emma put a handful of cherries on to Tim's plate. Resisting a desire to take some more for herself, she then rose from the table, picked up the dish of fruit and put it in the refrigerator.

'Are the cherries a present for letting her stay?'

'Perhaps.' Emma returned to her seat and poured herself another cup of tea.

'Like the chocolates we took to Auntie Susan? When we went to Bedford?'

'That's right.'

Thirteen year old Emma was very like her mother – quiet, self-denying and self-effacing – but quite capable of supervising the household when her mother was indisposed. Mary Ricini had already said as much, approvingly, a few minutes earlier, before she had gone up to sit with Rosemary.

Tim pulled away the stalk from a cherry between his teeth. 'Why didn't Daddy say he wasn't coming home?'

'He didn't know till it was too late.'

'But if he was going to Nottingham, why did we see him at Heathrow in the afternoon? He doesn't fly to Nottingham. Not usually, does he?'

Since almost every one of Tim's utterances ended in a question, it was surprising that over the course of time he hadn't become at least marginally better informed.

'We didn't see him. Not for sure,' said Emma.

'Twenty-three.' Tim had been counting his cherry stones. He was a good-looking child. Mary Ricini had remarked that he'd inherited his father's captivating smile, while silently judging that a match for his father's bedroom eyes was coming along nicely too. 'I saw him,' the boy offered, in a contrary half-whisper.

'You only thought you did.' Emma looked troubled. 'You haven't told Mummy?'

''Course not. You gave me 10p not to.' The hurt look would have done justice to a bishop wrongly accused of misquoting the Lord's Prayer. 'It was him though. With that lady.'

The two had taken a bus the few miles to the airport after lunch on the previous afternoon so that Tim could see the new Aeroflot airliner take off. He was an avid plane spotter. They had been waiting for a return bus at the terminus in the centre of Heathrow when Tim had spotted a familiar-looking car. It had certainly seemed like the one their father drove, and it had been heading for Terminal Two.

'We never saw the faces,' said Emma.

'I saw Daddy's. I'm certain. Nearly certain anyway. And I saw the number plate,' he ended with a rush.

'No you didn't.'

'Some of it.' He rubbed his nose. 'Most of it. Why can't I tell Mummy?'

'Because, I don't want you to. And you promised not to.' She knew that the promises he made for money were the ones he honoured: in so doing, he kept the way clear for negotiating similar contracts in the future.

'Is it because she's got a tummy upset? She didn't have that yesterday. Not when you said not to tell her.'

Emma was a sensitive creature, as well as an observant one. She had grown up a good deal in the previous year. There were many things she knew about that depressed her mother. She sensed that her father's being with a pretty young woman at Heathrow, an hour after he'd left the house to drive directly to Nottingham,

75

would qualify as another of those things. 'Mummy doesn't like Daddy flying. She worries. In case there's an accident.' It was a good try.

'We'd know by now if there'd been an accident, wouldn't we?'

'If he hasn't got the car he'll be flying back. She'd worry about that too. And it probably wasn't him we saw anyway.' She looked at the time pointedly, got up, and began to clear the table.

Tim brushed the hair from his eyes and gave his sister a bright-eyed smile. 'Can I watch telly till half past then?' he pleaded.

Emma nodded, relaxing inside herself. Reason had triumphed where bribery hadn't totally – with his favourite programme providing the coup de grâce.

She knew it had been her father's car all right, with her father driving it. She had seen him quite clearly, also the woman in the passenger seat, before Tim had even noticed the car.

There was no way Emma could know that by declaring what she and Tim had seen, she might have reduced the danger for her father. No one had told her he was in any danger. That being so, you could understand why she deemed it important not to report something she was instinctively certain would make her mother miserable.

Something similar had happened before. A friend had told her mother she'd seen her father with a woman going into a London night-club. Unknown to the others, Emma had overheard the conversation. Her mother had dismissed the report saying the woman had been a customer of Closter Drug, that it had been a business date, that she'd known about it. But her mother had been sad for days afterwards, and Emma believed she knew why.

So Emma's reticence now was not only innocent but also maintained with the best of intentions.

In contrast, there was someone else closely connected with Closter Drug who, unlike Emma, knew about the kidnap and who had been with Dermot Hackle after the children had seen him. That person had no justification for remaining silent – but plenty of reason.

'Thank God that's over,' Jane Larden sighed and fell back into the front passenger seat of the Mercedes. 'I don't know how you managed to be so cool all evening.'

'With some effort.' Larden started the engine, then moved the car towards the exit in the nearly empty underground carpark of the National Theatre on London's South Bank. Their guests of the evening had driven out just ahead of them.

'I wasn't any help, was I? I'm sorry, darling, I'm just numb still.' She leaned across and kissed him on the cheek, her hand moving to caress the inside of his thigh.

'You were fine,' he replied, only half meaning it, but as always affected by her touch. The news about Dermot Hackle had moved her deeply – much more than he had expected. He had realised too late that it would have been better to have delayed telling her anything until the evening was over.

'It's just as well it was theatre and dinner after, not just dinner. I don't believe I could have coped with Roger and Sybil through a long meal tonight.'

'They're not an easy pair. But he's an important customer. I thought of cancelling, but it seemed the wrong thing to do. For a lot of reasons. They enjoyed themselves, at least. It was a good play.'

'Was it? I couldn't concentrate.'

The two had met earlier as arranged at one of the theatre bars. She had arrived by cab. He had driven directly from the factory. There had been a few minutes to talk before their guests had appeared. He had given Jane the bare bones of the kidnap story then. They had not been alone since. Their meal at Ovations, the theatre restaurant, had ended a few minutes before this.

'So when exactly did they take Dermot?' Jane asked as he was swinging the car into York Road.

'We don't know. Some time last night probably. He'd rung Rosemary. From Nottingham we assume. He said he'd have to stay over. Hughie McFee did a discreet check on all the places where he might have stayed. He wasn't registered at any of them, and there was no reservation.'

'What about the person he went to see? You said it was a business trip?'

'There was no appointment in his diary. Nothing his secretary knew about.'

'Was it someone who rang him at the weekend?'

'Could have been. His wife doesn't remember any particular call. We've a number of major customers in the area. But we don't know which one it was, and we could hardly ring them all asking if they'd seen him.'

'Because they'd know he'd gone missing?'

'That, and because we simply don't know whom we can trust.'

She gave a little shiver. 'So it's possible Dermot didn't go to Nottingham at all? I mean it could have been a ruse to get him away from home?'

'Possibly.'

'In which case no one there's going to know anything about him anyway.' She paused. 'If the SAE are using his car telephone, I suppose it means they're using his car too?'

'Not necessarily. It's a portable phone like this one.' He nodded at the instrument below the dashboard. 'They're more likely to have abandoned the car.'

'So can't you report it as stolen? If the police find it, you'd have an idea where to start looking.'

He shook his head. 'So far we've avoided any contact with the police. The Irishman was adamant about that.'

She nodded understandingly. 'When Dermot spoke, did he sound normal?'

'Normal, but his voice was faint. He could have been some distance from the phone. Maybe tied up with someone holding it for him. That's just guessing.' He had caught a new look of distress on her face.

'But they haven't hurt him?'

'He said not.'

'But they'll kill him if you don't do what they say?'

'That was the threat. I don't believe they would.'

'But you can't be sure. And there were other threats, you said?'

'If we tell the police.' His tone was purposely dismissive. 'Since we haven't, there shouldn't be any danger.'

'And you'll sell the shares?'

'You realise what that'll mean?'

'The price will drop afterwards?'

'Not just afterwards. As soon as we start selling. In those sorts of quantities. The exercise could cost me five million.' He looked grimly at the road ahead.

'Over half the value of your holding?'

'That's my estimate, yes. But only an estimate.' His knuckles were white as his grip tightened on the wheel. 'It could be worse than that. The reward for five years' grinding effort more than halved in one day.'

'But you can buy back the shares?'

'No one's to buy back this week. Or to let anyone else buy for

78

them. That includes bank nominees. Otherwise the deal's off.'

'But how can these people know who's doing the buying?'

'They say they can. Because they have moles everywhere. So far we've accepted that much as fact.'

'Because of the risk to Dermot otherwise?'

'Yes. They won't release him till after the stock market closes on Friday. To make sure we're held to our word.'

'So you can buy back on Monday? Won't the share price be low then?'

'It may be. It depends on what game they're playing.'

'But isn't their game what you said? To hurt Closter directors? Like the demonstration last week was to spoil the flotation?'

'I keep telling you, we just don't know what they're planning next. Can't you understand that?' he added hotly, and on the verge of losing his temper.

There was a heavy silence in the car for a while.

'I'm sorry, darling,' he said eventually, reaching for her hand.

'Don't be. It was my fault. You must be under a terrible strain.'

'Let me try to explain. It could be these people are aiming to destroy confidence in Closter management permanently. Because if we agree never to admit there was a kidnap, not ever, because of what they might do to directors' wives and children, no one can ever know we sold the shares under duress. And we'll never be able to convince the Stock Exchange otherwise.'

'But if you could convince them?'

'We could almost certainly get them to rescind tomorrow's forced sales. As soon as Dermot's released.'

'To cancel the sales? So that everything goes back to square one?'

'Yes. But if we don't admit the kidnap, people will just believe we've lost faith in the company ourselves. And the products. That we took the capital gains on our shares while the going was good. Even the puny gains on offer by mid-morning tomorrow.' He hit the steering wheel twice with a clenched fist. 'And dammit, they've only been able to pick on us because we're small.' He hit the wheel again. 'Our management group's still far too small. We're vulnerable, you see? There's no flexibility. There can't be. Not yet. Especially not in a crisis.'

It seemed to his wife that he was now more concerned in remonstrating with himself than in explaining anything to her. 'Is Closter really so much smaller than all the other drug companies?' she asked.

'Much smaller than any with a real breakthrough product on the stocks. Anything negative that happens to us now can shatter our credibility. At the most critical time.'

'The credibility of Seromig?'

'Absolutely. So it'll take us that much longer to convince the Department of Health that the drug is ready. Safe. It'll be the same with the Food and Drugs Administration in the States. It'll become a matter of . . . of atmospherics not facts. D'you understand? And it could set us back years. Make Seromig totally unprofitable.'

Jane's eyes narrowed. 'You're not suggesting the SAE is in league with a competitor? Someone who wants to hold back the launch of Seromig?'

He thought for a moment. 'No. Not any of the ones working on a migraine cure. Not any of the ones we know about at least. It'd be too obvious. In any case, why should an animal protection group be teamed up with a drug manufacturer? Any drug manufacturer. The whole industry uses animals in development work.' He paused again. 'Unless the animal protection bit really is a front. A front for a drug company that wants to knock down our value before buying us out.'

'To get control of Seromig?'

'And our other development products.' His forehead stayed creased. 'It would need to be a company big enough to get Seromig approved afterwards, despite any setback. To make up for any time we could lose on the programme now. But that would make it an even less likely ally for a piddling outfit like the SAE.'

'You mean the drug company would need to be big? And with a sound reputation of its own?'

'And one that indulges in kidnapping to gain its ends.' He shook his head. 'Doesn't fit, does it?'

'Nor do the firms that wanted to buy Closter while you were still a private company.'

'Right. For one of them to be involved would be even more incredible. But we could still be talking about a takeover.'

'That's a bizarre idea, surely?'

Larden took a deep breath through his nose. 'Possibly. But I've been having a lot of those all day.' He shifted in the driving seat as he turned right off Fulham Palace Road. 'It's still tempting to say to hell with them, whoever they are. Better still, to convince ourselves we're being harassed by a bunch of cranks with no backing and no connections. That way we don't need to accept they've an intelligence system following our every move. Nor a bunch of hit men ready to abduct wives and children. If I believed all that, I'd be free to do as I like. To tell the SAE to drop dead.'

'But you have to sell your shares tomorrow. You said everyone would.'

'Not if I tell them not to. If I say we call the bluff of those bastards.' He drew the car up outside the three-storey house where they lived. It was in the centre of a terrace built at the turn of the century. The street had been gentrified recently.

Jane made no move to get out. 'Look, Bob, you can do what you like once we get Dermot back. I mean tell the police, the Stock Exchange, everyone. I'll take my chances about being abducted. I don't know about the other wives. Their children too.' She brought her hands together under her chin. Her gaze was straight ahead. 'But the police would have to give us protection. And with Dermot to help, they'd possibly find the kidnappers anyway.'

'That's a brave— '

'Let me finish,' she interrupted, turning to him suddenly. 'All that's after we've got Dermot back. As things stand, you have to do as they say.'

'But if we're half certain they're bluffing?'

'Only half though. They could murder him. You can't risk that.'

'But you've just said you'd take your chances— '

'After Dermot's free. That's different,' she broke in again. 'We'd know then what we'd be in for. In advance. Dermot's their prisoner now. He had no option. No chance to protect himself. You've got to get him back.'

'In every case of kidnap I've heard of the police have been told,' he hedged. 'The police or a security agent.'

'Not in every case. There've been some where the victim's family has paid up without telling anyone till after. And in any case, that's it normally. A cash payment's made. So a pick-up has to be arranged, meaning there's a chance the kidnappers can be caught. In Dermot's case the swine are running no risk of any kind.'

He nodded, partially agreeing. 'At first, I couldn't believe that was it.'

'But you do now? That they're safe so it's even more vital you do as they say.'

'By selling our shares? Losing half their value? Perhaps more?'

'Yes, and making the other directors do the same.'

'I can't make them.'

'You said just now you could stop them.'

He was examining the car key in his hand, avoiding her gaze. 'I still believe we should call their bluff. Dermot would support me, I'm sure.'

'That's nonsense, and you know it. If it were the other way round, if you were the prisoner, Dermot would be moving heaven and earth to get you free.'

'Perhaps because he'd have nothing to lose if the shares were sold. He hasn't any. Not to speak of.' He still hadn't appreciated his wife's determination.

'That's a bloody callous thing to say.'

'I just don't believe— '

'Look at me, Bob.' Her tone was icy. 'I'm deadly serious. Please do exactly as the kidnappers say tomorrow. If you don't, I'll leave you. For ever. I'm sorry, but I mean it.'

Chapter Ten

'But Mr Larden, if every director's unloading shares, there has to be a reason.' The man on the other end of the telephone was called Poundown. It was a singularly appropriate name for the Financial Editor of the *Daily Gazette*.

'And I've told you, the reason is personal.'

'And I'm sorry, but our readers will want a better one than that. D'you know it's less than a week since this paper was recommending the shares? At the flotation price? With no reservations? We were the only paper to do that.'

'I know that very well. It's why I agreed to talk to you, Mr Poundown,' Larden responded, wishing now he hadn't felt obliged to do any such thing. He wiped his brow with his handkerchief, then his neck, under his already loosened collar. 'The advice you gave last week was perfectly sound.'

'How can you say that, Mr Larden?' The speaker sounded genuinely shocked – unusually so for a journalist. The *Gazette* readership was a shade below middling – rated by numbers, class, income and brow. Its City news staff was, in turn, a shade below middle-weight, and being constantly depleted. The paper was usually cautious about the financial advice given to readers, more often than not taking its lead from the early editions of better informed journals. Recently it had been aiming to sound more independent and strident, with apparently bolder market tips – but still only affecting if not total certainties, then at least investments that were proof against abject failure. Except Closter Drug wasn't proving to be anything of the kind.

'You gave sound advice because the price of our shares yesterday was more than justified. Measured against current trading and future prospects,' said Larden, aware his words were hollow as well as pompous.

'That was yesterday. What about the price at midday today?'

It was now twelve thirty. The price of the shares had been in free fall for nearly two hours.

'It's showing a temporary drop for technical reasons. I'm confident the price will recover.'

'That's what your PR outfit says. It's hard to credit, Mr Larden. Why should the price recover if the directors are selling out? You have sixteen per cent of the company shares between you. The word is you're offloading the lot. Is that true?'

'The directors of Closter Drug have been through a lean time for five years. Between us we probably had too many shares. It can happen after a management buy-out. So we're taking the chance to go liquid. We know the company's strong enough to stand it.' He had both elbows on the desk, one hand supporting his drooping head, the other holding the telephone. His posture was as collapsed as the logic he had just propounded.

At an early morning meeting the Closter directors had all agreed, as a final resort, to do as the kidnappers demanded.

At nine o'clock, the Irish spokesman had telephoned for their decision. Larden had fought hard for a delay. The Irishman had dismissed his plea, angrily this time, and put Hackle on the line to beg for his life, and to repeat that his captors would show no mercy. Bodlin had gone a deathly white at this. Mary Ricini had been close to tears.

So Larden had agreed to the kidnappers' terms.

The call had been taped, like the one the day before, except for the opening moments. Only a year earlier the company had installed sophisticated tape machines in the offices and homes of all directors. These were to record not only messages but also, when required, ordinary calls as well. It had all been to do with security in the broad sense. The machines were intended to provide records of conversations involving technical or contractual data. After the first call from the kidnappers, it was Mary Ricini who had suggested that all machines should be set to tape everything, in case the SAE chose to phone a director other than Larden. The others had agreed, though some would forget to do anything about it.

Hackle's captors had accepted one concession in response to Larden's reasoned argument. Mark Treasure was to be told about the kidnapping – but not until he returned from the USA later in the day. Significantly, the kidnappers had known which flight he was taking. Despite the concession, Treasure had to be made to pledge that he would tell no one except his wife about the kidnap.

84

If he reneged on this, the Irishman had said, it would very soon go hard for some director's wife or child.

Later, Larden himself warned Penny Cordwright at the PR company that there might be enquiries from the media during the day about the sale of shares, and that such calls would be routed to her. He told her broadly how she should respond, but he implied the matter didn't have much importance. This had been bad judgement on his part, sparked by wishful thinking.

The instructions had mildly surprised Miss Cordwright, but she hadn't believed she would have to act on them. She had assumed the sale of directors' shares Larden mentioned would be a minor affair, involving a relatively small number of shares, and unlikely to cause much, if any, media comment. She hadn't even questioned the wisdom of the action. There was presumably justification for the directors taking a profit on part of their holdings now if they chose. She was quite unprepared for what came next.

At eleven thirty, when the 'minor affair' had already acquired the makings of a major financial news event, Miss Cordwright had got back to the Managing Director for fresh instructions. She had been told her response shouldn't alter. With a second call though, she had succeeded in getting Larden to talk to the *Daily Gazette*, because it had been the only paper unreservedly to commend the flotation in the previous week. It seemed a Judas act not to give it special treatment now. Larden had also calculated it would be the paper most likely to find some kind of justification for what was occurring, if only to support its own previous judgement on Closter Drug.

'And you are one of the directors selling out, Mr Larden?' Poundown persisted.

'I'm a seller, yes. For pressing personal reasons. Like the others, I've been overstretched financially for some time. There's a chance to relieve the pressure now, and I'm taking it. Naturally I expect to be a buyer of the shares again before long.'

'How long, Mr Larden?'

His gaze lifted to the photograph of his wife on his desk. 'That's difficult to say.'

'Is all this the result of a bad report on Seromig? A setback there?'

'No it isn't. Quite the opposite. Seromig is likely to be a major advance in the treatment of migraine.'

'So isn't this a crazy time to stop being a major shareholder in the company?'

'Not if you have an overdraft the size of mine, Mr Poundown.' He did his best to sound light-hearted. 'I'm sorry, you'll have to excuse me now. I'm late for a meeting.' This was half true: Closter-Bennet had just come through the door. 'Look, why don't we talk again soon? Early next week, perhaps? Things will be in better perspective then.'

'One last question, Mr Larden. Are you and the other directors selling *all* your shares in Closter Drug?'

He hesitated for a moment before he said: 'Yes.'

'Thank you, Mr Larden.'

It had been the question he had most wanted to avoid answering, but to have lied would have given the SAE grounds for maiming Dermot Hackle. He couldn't risk Dermot being hurt, not after what Jane had said last night.

He put the phone down and fell back in his chair, mopping his brow, his eyes still fixed on the picture of his wife.

'The share price is down to seventy-two pence, and it's still dropping,' said Closter-Bennet after firmly closing the door behind him. 'People in my department have found out it's the directors who are selling. A lot of them have shares themselves you know?'

Larden shrugged. 'So do people in every other department. So what d'you suggest we do, Giles?' he questioned acidly.

The Finance Director looked more discomforted than before. He wasn't given to making snap executive decisions. His agreement to sell his shares had been made at his wife's instigation, and not merely because they had been paid for with her money in the first place.

Barbara Closter-Bennet's normal sangfroid had evaporated in the face of the kidnappers' threat about directors' wives.

'It's just worse than I expected,' her husband continued now. 'My broker keeps calling, advising me to stop selling. He'd sold half my holding by noon, as instructed. He doesn't understand, and I can't explain. It'll be much worse this afternoon when he unloads the second half.' Closter-Bennet spoke as though his problem was unique. He dropped into a chair, and began literally to wring his hands.

The directors had agreed about the shares being sold in timed stages, the last at three o'clock. They hoped that this would reduce the impact on the market as much as possible and spread the losses fairly between the reluctant sellers.

'If I call a meeting of employee shareholders now, there's

86

nothing I can say that'll mean anything. Not till the rot stops this afternoon when trading closes,' said Larden, quietly but firmly. It was an astonishing admission by someone who normally lectured others on the importance of prompt staff communications. 'Today I can only repeat what we're saying to the newspapers, and nobody's believing that,' he went on. 'We just have to sit it out. We'll make a staff announcement tomorrow.'

'To encourage people to hold on to their shares?'

'Those that still have any. More to emphasise Seromig hasn't turned into a failure.'

'And it hasn't. And the shares are a perfectly sound investment,' Closter-Bennet protested limply. 'Perfectly sound,' he repeated, with even less conviction than before. 'They are, aren't they, Bob? God, the bastards have got me believing we're washed up now. When does Mark Treasure get in?'

'On the Concorde. At six. I'm meeting him. Bringing him straight here.'

But it was after ten that evening when Larden had eventually ushered Treasure into his office. The flight had been delayed before leaving New York.

The other directors had been waiting for them, all except Mary Ricini who was at home with Rosemary Hackle.

'The price dropped to thirty-nine pence at the end of the day,' McFee was saying, some minutes after Treasure arrived.

The Scotsman and Closter-Bennet were seated on one side of the table, with Larden and Bodlin opposite: There were glasses and coffee cups strewn about the surface.

'There was real panic selling after three o'clock,' McFee went on. 'My broker rang later, just before the market closed. He said it was as well I got out when I did. Though he wasn't exactly offering congratulations. He was sore that I'd fobbed him off with a spurious reason for selling in the first place.' He shook his head. 'He's convinced the company's in deep trouble.'

'I imagine the whole Stock Exchange thinks the same,' said Treasure. He was seated at the top of the table, his usual place at their board meetings. There was a glass of Perrier water and a portable tape recorder in front of him. They had earlier played over the two recordings of the calls from the kidnappers. 'When did anyone last talk to Grenwood, Phipps?'

'Laurence Stricton rang me several times. The last time around six.' This was Closter-Bennet.

Stricton was the executive in the bank's Corporate Finance Department who had been in charge of the Closter Drug flotation. He was young and very bright. Treasure wondered what he had made of the situation since he evidently hadn't been given the true reason for what had happened.

'My chauffeur gave me a message to ring Laurence,' he said, glancing at the time. 'I'll do it in a minute. Just tell me, all the directors' shares had been sold by three o'clock?'

'That was the arrangement, Mark.'

The others nodded agreement with Closter-Bennet.

'And the lowest price up to that point?'

'Around sixty pence. It went lower still immediately after. When the evening paper came out advising people to sell. Because the Closter directors weren't giving adequate reason for offloading their own shares. That's what the paper said.'

'And because of an unattributed report that Seromig had gone wrong. I wonder who fed that in?' said McFee. 'The SAE probably.'

'Almost certainly,' Treasure responded.

'Anyway, the newspaper advice was reported on all the television share services. That really got small private shareholders selling with the rest.' The Finance Director had pushed his chair away from the table and had his head bowed as he spoke, eyes focussed on the floor between his feet. 'Laurence Stricton said the institutional selling was heavy from noon, except for some very large holders, customers of the bank, who accepted the bank's view.'

'Which was that the whole thing was caused through ill-considered action by the directors?' Treasure put in.

'Yes. And that there was definitely no setback with Seromig,' Closter-Bennet completed, glancing up at Treasure. 'I felt very badly about keeping Laurence in the dark.'

'Mark knows we couldn't let anyone into our confidence. Not anyone,' said Larden abruptly.

'The bank's customers who accepted its advice shouldn't regret it,' said Treasure.

'Did we do the right thing, Mark?' It was Stuart Bodlin who had asked the question. This was the first time he had spoken since the banker's arrival.

Treasure shrugged. 'You took a quite reasonable course.' The words created an almost tangible sense of relief amongst the others. 'It's no ordinary kidnap. There's no ransom to be collected. Until we get Dermot back, I don't see how anyone can find out where he's being held or who's holding him.' He leaned back in his chair. 'You tried delaying things. If you'd hired security specialists they'd probably have advised that. They usually do.'

'You think we should have hired specialists, Mark? But . . . but the SAE said— '

'They said if we contacted anyone like that they'd find out,' Larden interrupted Bodlin's halting words.

'Aye, and that the consequences for Dermot would be the same as if we'd told the police. You heard that on the tapes.' This was McFee, who had got up and was replenishing his whisky glass from the tray of bottles on one of the bookcases. 'We decided it would have been too great a risk to take. They sound like murdering zealots, and we took them to be just that. We made our decision and stood by it. No heel tapping.'

Treasure admired the resolution in McFee's tone. The determined voice at Closter directors' meetings was usually Larden's, but tonight it was the Scotsman who had taken over from the desperately demoralised Managing Director.

The banker inwardly wished the group had handled the emergency in a different way, but there was no purpose in saying so now. The damage was done, but, in his view, it was possibly still repairable. Meantime Hackle appeared to be safe, and the threat to others was at least in abeyance. 'It'd be useful if we knew the SAE's ultimate intention,' he said.

'Haven't they achieved it already? What else is there for them?' asked Closter-Bennet.

'If it really is them at the back of everything,' the banker answered.

'Who else could it be?' questioned Larden.

'I've no idea, but if it's the SAE there's a big flaw in their strategy. From what you've told me they've got no publicity and they're not looking for any. There's no suggestion that Closter has been brought down because it experiments on animals, and you've been forbidden ever to disclose there was a kidnap. It doesn't fit. Crusaders, zealots as Hughie describes them, aren't normally so reticent. It defeats their purposes.'

'Perhaps they'll start crowing tomorrow,' said McFee, returning to the table.

Treasure shook his head. 'But they can never do that without repairing all the damage they've done so far. Because they'd be disclosing the truth about what's happened. That you've been criminally pressured into starting a run on the shares. That there's nothing basically wrong with the company.'

'They'll still have crippled us all financially,' Larden said, but leaning forward with rekindled interest.

'Not necessarily. For instance, if you can buy back the shares while the price is still low.'

'The SAE will still have rubbished Seromig,' said Bodlin, with all the feeling commensurate with being the drug's discoverer.

'No. They'll have set it back. No more than that, surely?'

'Long enough possibly to make it unprofitable.' This was Larden.

'Not even that if they admit to what they've done,' Treasure insisted.

'So you're saying what they've achieved is only short term?' said Bodlin thoughtfully. 'Too short term? And that can't be enough for them?'

'It might have been enough if a ransom had been paid. Providing funds for the cause of stopping animal experiments. But there hasn't been. Even though large sums of money have been involved.'

'Lost, you mean? By us?' said Larden.

'And by other shareholders, of course,' Closter-Bennet added in a sanctimonious aside, as though his concern might be primarily for the others.

'But our loss could still be someone else's gain?' said McFee slowly.

'Precisely,' the banker replied. 'Otherwise, it might have made more sense for the SAE to do something much more dramatic and admit it.'

'Like burning down this factory, you mean?'

'That might not have done the company more long term harm, but at least it would have advertised the cause of the SAE. It's much more the sort of thing fanatics do if they're simply pushing a crusade.' Treasure glanced around the faces at the table. 'No, I think the whole thing makes more sense if the SAE, or someone behind them, have an end result in mind we don't know about yet.'

'One that can't have been achieved so far?' asked McFee.

'Certainly.' Treasure got up and went over to the document case he had left open on Larden's desk. 'By the way, there can't be any doubt that's Dermot's voice on the tape?' he asked, while removing a black leather notebook from the case.

'None at all,' said Larden. 'It's a bit muffled. Strained. But it's Dermot all right.'

'If there is any doubt, it's easily resolved,' McFee put in. 'His voice is recognised by the voice locks in the high security wing.'

In answer to Treasure's puzzled expression, Bodlin explained: 'I don't believe you've been in the research labs recently, Mark. The main door is now opened by voice, in combination with a card-key.'

'You mean you have to say a codeword?'

The scientist shook his head. 'You just need to speak. Into a receiver.'

'High-tech cloak and dagger,' said McFee with a wry smile. 'Except one of Stuart's boffins proved last week a tape recording works just as well as the real thing.'

'The makers are trying to find out why,' offered Bodlin, in an apologetic voice, as though he were responsible for the shortcoming. 'Of course, you still need to use the card-key as well. But Hughie's quite right. If that's Dermot's voice on the tape the sensor will recognise it.'

'Well that's something I can settle on the way back from having a leak. Something I've been needing to do for some time. So if you'll all excuse me,' said McFee. 'Shan't be a jiffy.' He picked up the tape recorder from the table and, with a nod to Treasure, left the room with it.

The banker punched out a number on Larden's telephone that he had read from the notebook. 'I'm calling Laurence Stricton at his home,' he said. 'There's one outside possibility we haven't checked on yet. He will have. At least I hope so.' He looked down at the voice-piece. 'Hello Laurence, Mark Treasure here. Sorry it's so late.' He paused briefly. 'Yes, I got your message, but I'm afraid the plane was delayed. I just got in. I'm at Closter Drug. With the directors. Anything new on their— ' He stopped speaking to listen to Stricton. He was frowning a moment later when he put in: 'Damn. It's what one guessed could be happening, of course.'

The telephone conversation lasted another two minutes and was very one-sided, Treasure making mostly monosyllabic contributions until he concluded with: 'Look, I think we'd better meet. My house? In half an hour? I expect Bob Larden will be with me.' He looked across at Larden who nodded. 'And you'll bring Fritzoller's letter with you? Good. See you shortly then. Goodbye.'

He put down the phone just as McFee re-entered the room with the words: 'It's Dermot's voice on the tape all right. Sprung the lock like butter. But I'll tell you something else that's very odd, he's— ' The Scotsman stopped in mid-sentence when he saw Treasure's expression. 'Sorry. Something's happened?' he asked, looking round at the others.

'Yes. We've found that elusive end purpose. With a vengeance,' said the banker. 'A takeover bid for this company has been formally in progress for roughly an hour. The bidder is Krontag Pharmaceuticals of Zürich. Earlier, between eight and nine o'clock, they bought a substantial number of Closter shares, at pretty knockdown prices. We don't know the precise number of shares yet.'

'And that was the outside possibility you meant, Mark?' asked Bodlin.

'Afraid so. Alters the scenario a lot, of course.'

'But . . . but the stock market's been closed for hours,' protested Closter-Bennet.

'Not in Tokyo it hasn't,' said Treasure. 'All the orders were put through the Japanese offices of London security houses there. The deals can't be confirmed till morning, but they'll be honoured first thing.' He snapped his case shut. 'The eight London security firms who've been making markets in Closter shares were only too pleased to unload them after hours this evening. At first, at almost any price. They were all expecting the price to go down again tomorrow.'

'But it'll have gone up again by now?' said McFee.

'Naturally. But the Krontag brokers made most of the killing before anyone twigged what was happening. They arranged to have the orders spread between the market makers, all of whom were operating with a caretaker staff at that time of night. Laurence is sure Krontag will have picked up more than thirty per cent of the company, and quite a bit of it at below fifty pence a share.'

'But with thirty per cent they *had* to make a formal takeover bid for the rest. That's the regulation.' This was Closter-Bennet in a tone now combining both bewilderment and outrage.

'They have. Mark just said so,' said Larden brusquely, bringing the knuckles of his clenched fists together.

Treasure nodded. 'A letter to me from Doctor Willy Fritzoller, the Chairman of Krontag, was handed in at Grenwood, Phipps at

92

nine. Much earlier, Miss Gaunt, my secretary, got what was made to sound like a routine call from a secretary at another merchant bank, saying a letter was on the way to me this evening from one of their customers. She wasn't told the subject or the name of the customer. Miss Gaunt smelled a rat and sensibly told Laurence Stricton. They both stayed on to accept the letter. The other bank was probably hoping it wouldn't be opened till the morning. Ethically, though, they'd covered themselves with the advance message.'

'Which bank is it?' asked Larden.

'Schenlau. They were playing a tactical game, of course. Under the regulations, Krontag had to admit they held more than five per cent of the shares once that was the case, but they weren't obliged to announce a formal takeover bid for the whole company till they owned thirty per cent. That happened probably around nine o'clock.'

'But through deals that still can't be confirmed till morning?' This was Closter-Bennet.

'That's true. In the circumstances that's a technicality, but one no doubt they'll quote later to emphasise the apparent rectitude of their actions. You see they stopped buying on the open market at nine, and announced their bid and the price they were offering in the letter to me. Any shares they acquired after that would need to have been bought at the Krontag formal bid price.'

'Which is?' asked Larden and Closter-Bennet, almost in unison.

'One pound twenty-five pence a share. That's the minimum price they could offer to comply with the Takeover Code.'

'Being the highest price paid for our shares in the last six months,' said Closter-Bennet dolefully.

'Or more precisely in the last seven days, since Closter only went public last week,' Treasure continued. 'I believe— '

'It's inconceivable!' Larden thundered suddenly, this time banging the table with his fists.

'That a company of the eminence of Krontag should be mixed up in a kidnap?' said Treasure. 'I agree.'

'But what's the alternative?'

The banker sniffed. 'Coincidence?' He picked up his case. 'We'll have to see. You ready to leave, Bob?'

Chapter Eleven

Dr Willy Fritzoller, in his middle sixties, was a courteous, stooping bear of a man. His immense head was strangely square, an impression heightened by the cut of the close-cropped, wiry grey hair which seemed to flatten the top of his skull. 'You are alone, Mr Treasure? This is not what I had expected,' he said, as the two shook hands.

'There's a reason.'

'So. And you must have started very early this morning?' The voice was low and powerful, the consonants distinct.

'By New York time, yes. I was there yesterday. Flew into London last night. But perhaps you knew that?'

The other shook his head. 'Only that it's unfair for you to have travelled again so soon.'

'I'm used to it. I'm only glad you were free this morning.'

The Swiss-German bowed gravely in an overly mannered way. 'If you'd come in the middle of the night, I'd have been available, Mr Treasure. For so distinguished a visitor.' The lids over the dark eyes opened wider and lowered again in a fluid, character-istic movement before the speaker went on. 'And how is Lord Grenwood?'

'Berty's very well, thank you.'

'We meet sometimes at Ascot races. Royal Ascot, yes. Also, once, I remember, at Christie's. During a sale. That was a few years ago. He's retired now, I believe?'

'He's still titular Chairman of Grenwood, Phipps.'

'But not active. Not since you became Chief Executive. Also I see the bank has become even more successful under your leader-ship. And you have time for important outside directorships.' The eyelids made their double, punctuating movement again. 'Like the chairmanship of Closter Drug.'

'The bank has an enduring interest in the company.'

'Of course.' Fritzoller considered for a moment. 'You understand the present situation is a little embarrassing for me?' He spoke slowly and with feeling. 'More than a little.' He gave an enquiring smile, eyes searching for a reaction.

'I can imagine it might be.'

'Business affairs used to be more civilised.' The big hands unclasped then stayed in an abject pose. 'Letters are now delivered at dead of night. Shares are bought through stock exchanges that never sleep. Tch! Who wants such things?' The shoulders heaved a dismissal. 'But that's the way it is.' Both hands were now thrust deep into the side pockets of the dark, generously cut jacket. 'But I'm forgetting my duties as a host. Some coffee perhaps? It's ready over there. Come and sit down?'

They were in Fritzoller's office on the top floor of the Krontag Tower in the industrial suburb of Glattbrugg, eight kilometres north of Zürich, but only four kilometres south of the airport.

The sixteen-storey tower was on high ground in the middle of the Krontag factory complex – something even more substantial than Treasure had expected. Though the company had remained private, it was one of the world's ten largest pharmaceutical manufacturers.

The low-ceilinged corner room, with two curtained glass walls, had been designed as a private study. External sound was excluded. The cooled air came without any suspicion of draught. Internal sounds were muted by deep carpeting and heavy wood panelling. There was a collection of well-lit paintings displayed along the two inside walls. Amongst the pictures, Treasure had identified a Pissarro, a small Corot, and what was unmistakably one of the Picasso 'blue period' oils of circus clowns.

Willy Fritzoller was a renowned collector of fine art, an indulgence that in terms of cost, at least, fitted with his being the largest shareholder in Krontag, as well as its Chairman. The banker felt that the paintings by themselves had justified the several identity checks he had gone through from the main gates of the factory onwards. He mused also that tape recordings would certainly not be acceptable door-openers in any of the top security zones at Krontag.

The part of the room to which the two men now took themselves was away from the ornate, antique partner's desk where Fritzoller had been seated on the visitor's arrival. Here there were winged armchairs, in soft leather, grouped in a semicircle to offer panoramic

95

outside views. To the east was the Zürichberg range of mountains, shrouded now in a green-blue haze. To the south, beyond the city skyline in the middle distance, there were glimpses of the Lake of Zürich, sparkling in the mid-morning sunlight.

A silver coffee service was arranged on a circular marble table, together with an inviting selection of Swiss pâtisserie.

'Please help yourself, Mr Treasure,' said Fritzoller as they settled in adjacent chairs. 'It would be appropriate, I think, to invite Mr Grubber, our International President, to join us, yes?' He reached for the telephone on the table.

'Better not, if you don't mind. What I came to talk about concerns only the two of us.' Treasure was pouring coffee as he spoke.

The older man was surprised and showed it. 'This is really so, Mr Treasure?' he said, taking his hand off the phone. 'As Chairman of the Krontag holding company, you understand I'm not so familiar with the details of our foreign . . . er . . . merger intentions. Not so that I'd wish to conduct negotiations without the presence of the executives involved. We have many such projects.'

'Naturally. But your takeover bid for Closter Drug isn't the purpose of my being here.'

'It's not?' There was even more surprise than before.

'Not in any sense I believe you'd expect. You wrote to me yesterday, in my rôle as Chairman of Closter. You gave notice that Krontag was making a formal bid for the company. A formal acknowledgement of that notice, with my initial reaction, will be sent to you shortly.'

'But not given to me verbally today? Informally perhaps?'

'Oh, informally I can tell you the bid will be fiercely opposed because it's inadequate. Woefully inadequate, as you must be aware. But I repeat, I haven't come to discuss that.'

'You haven't come to ask us to withdraw the bid?' asked Fritzoller carefully.

'Not today certainly.'

'Good. It's not likely we could do that, Mr Treasure. We're very familiar with Closter. We wanted to buy the company before it went public. A year ago Mr Grubber had informal discussions with your Mr Larden, Doctor Bodlin and Mr . . . er . . . '

'Closter-Bennet. Yes, the discussions were reported to the whole board.'

'But our approach came to nothing. The present offer is a much bigger one than anything contemplated then. It reflects the progress made since that time by Closter. We hope it will be more attractive to the now many more shareholders in Closter. Who knows?' The eyelids provided emphasis.

'Indeed. Meantime, I'm here to tell you in confidence about a related but different subject.'

Fritzoller scowled. 'In confidence? Not to be shared with anyone else? That's correct behaviour? In the circumstances?'

'Yes it is. A man's life may depend on it.'

'A man's life?' The other leaned forward in his seat. 'You're serious, Mr Treasure?'

'Perfectly serious. Let me explain. Yesterday the working directors of Closter sold all their shares in the company. This amounted to a very substantial holding. As a result, the price of the shares dropped by more than half. In the course of last evening Krontag, or Krontag nominees, started buying. By nine o'clock your letter was delivered to my office. It said that you owned just short of thirty per cent of Closter. That meant you had to make a formal bid immediately, of course, which you did in the letter. I assume you signed the letter much earlier and sent it to your London bankers some time in advance. So it was ready when needed. In other words you signed it some time before you actually owned the shares?'

The big man shifted slightly in his chair. 'It was a formality only. It was to be delivered when we had the maximum number of shares permitted. Not before. Because it wasn't necessary before.' He gave a quick and slightly mischievous smile. 'But immediately after, of course. So as to satisfy your Takeover Code.'

'It's been suggested to me that you may have controlled over fourteen per cent of Closter shares before yesterday – in fact since the flotation last week – and not just below five per cent as you'd already reported. The extra shares are said to have been those we knew were held in the names of two Swiss banks, but which we now understand were for turning over to you at the appropriate time. With the twenty-five per cent of Closter shares you acquired last night, that would make up your holding in the company to just over thirty-nine per cent. Only twelve per cent short of control.'

'Who has made these suggestions?'

'They've been made to the team at Grenwood, Phipps who handled the flotation. If they're right, that you arranged a Concert Party in Closter shares, you could be in deep trouble with the

97

Securities and Investments Board in London. You already have a problem explaining to them why you've broken your earlier assurance. That your original holding was no more than a prudent investment, not the down payment on a takeover bid.'

'I know nothing of the arrangement with your SIB. Such detail would be in the hands of our Finance and Legal Divisions. They are very efficient. Very proper.'

'I see.' It was Treasure's turn to smile. 'Such matters are sometimes too complicated to sort out quickly, of course. In any case they're not my concern at the moment.' He drank some coffee before continuing. 'The sale of shares by Closter directors yesterday could have produced a very attractive situation for buyers who knew what was happening.'

'Except there were no such buyers around, Mr Treasure. I believe the price went on falling all day.'

'On the assumption that something was wrong with the company. That the development drug Seromig was a failure.'

'Something had to account for your directors' action.'

'But Krontag knew better?'

'We were advised that the directors were selling their shares because they needed money. That it was nothing more than that.'

'All the directors?'

Fritzoller shrugged. 'That was our information.'

'But you didn't start to buy until eight o'clock? After other substantial shareholders had panicked. They had also unloaded a huge volume of shares, so the price was at rock bottom.'

'Our advisers watched the market carefully. We bought when it seemed prudent.' For someone who had affected earlier not to be familiar with the detail of Krontag's acquisition activities, the doctor was doing remarkably well.

'You were aware there was nothing wrong with Seromig?'

'We've followed the development of the drug.'

'You mean you've been conducting your own trials with our patented formula and come up with the same results as we have? Very wise. To understand what you're aiming to buy.'

'Such practices are common and quite legal.'

'Agreed. Krontag have certainly made a coup. We estimate that you bought approximately twenty million Closter shares yesterday at an average price of sixty pence. That's a saving of twelve million pounds on the market price of the previous day.'

'We are offering to pay one pound twenty-five each for the rest of the shares.'

'You'd have had to offer a damned sight more than that for them, and for the ones you bought yesterday, if the Closter directors hadn't sold and started a run.'

'All that is obvious perhaps, Mr Treasure?'

'So obvious that you signed that letter to me possibly on Monday, post-dated for yesterday? That was not so much recognising the obvious as being incredibly prescient.'

'I didn't say I signed the letter on Monday.'

'If there's an enquiry, you may need to be able to prove exactly when you did sign it, Doctor. Also when it was delivered to Schenlau, your London bankers, and by whom.'

'But how could the letter matter that much? And how could we have known beforehand that the Closter directors would be selling?'

'That's certainly the question you're going to be asked, Doctor. They received instructions from someone about selling on Monday. They actually did sell yesterday. Under duress.'

'Under duress? How is this possible?'

'Because one of them was kidnapped. His name is Dermot Hackle.'

'Kidnapped?' The doctor shook his head in what seemed evident bewilderment. 'I don't understand. You mean he is held a prisoner?'

'Since some time last Sunday. The other directors have sold their shares to save his life. The single beneficiary of that action has been Krontag.'

Fritzoller looked suddenly much older. For a moment he said nothing, only clasped and unclasped the big hands in front of him. 'How can Krontag be the beneficiary?'

'Isn't that obvious?'

'But it is something quite separate. A coincidence?' The eyes narrowed. 'Also the kidnappers will receive some ransom, no?'

'The nearest thing to a ransom has been the twelve million pound saving made by Krontag on the purchase of Closter shares yesterday.'

'And the police know of the kidnapping?'

'Not yet.'

The eyes and the face muscles evinced some relief. 'But you've told your security advisers?'

'We've told no one for fear of reprisals. The kidnappers are animal rights fanatics. They call themselves the Stop Animal Experiments group. SAE for short. Have you heard of them?'

'Never.'

'Neither had anyone else until very recently. They're an undercover action group, unknown to regular organisations in the same field. But they claim to have informers everywhere. They could even have them inside Krontag.'

'You believe this?'

'So far we haven't dared not to. Hackle has a wife and two young children.'

'It's not possible that they have informers here.' The voice held solid conviction.

'On the contrary, whoever's been advising you over Closter must be in the confidence of the SAE. There's no other logical explanation for what's been happening. When everything's disclosed to the police it's inevitable their enquiries will start right here, at Krontag. They'll have no better lead to work on.'

'But that would be unthinkable, Mr Treasure. Unjust. My company is not involved in criminal activities. Not possibly. The accusation you speak about . . . the scandal that would follow, it would be unfair and an outrage.' But it was the word scandal that had been given the most emphasis. The agitation Fritzoller was showing was a natural enough reaction from the head of a major entity in a sensitive industry.

Treasure built on his advantage. 'I'm afraid a scandal looks unavoidable,' he said.

'So when are you telling the police?'

'I'd say as soon as Hackle is released. That's supposed to be on Friday evening.' He paused. 'I ought to tell you that the SAE intend the kidnap should never be disclosed. If it is, they threaten to hurt the families of Closter directors. For that reason, we may just hold back on telling anyone for a short while. Until we've completed protection arrangements.'

'But can you protect people against what you call fanatics?'

'I believe we have to give the authorities the chance to catch those fanatics. Before they try the same trick again. Most of the Closter directors agree with me. If we didn't tell the police it would let Krontag off the hook, of course. But only temporarily. A crime as big as this one can never be hushed up for ever. Too many people know about it already. Including you now, Doctor.'

100

Fritzoller took a deep breath. 'Krontag is involved in no crime, Mr Treasure. Not possibly. We have been advised throughout in the Closter Drug matter by outside consultants. They are completely independent of this company.'

Fritzoller was running for cover, and both men knew it.

'I believe you,' said Treasure quietly. 'That's why I'm here. I need the name of the consultants.'

'That may not be possible.

'The name of the consultants,' Treasure repeated, 'in exchange for my word that I will never disclose to anyone how I got it, without your permission. You must in turn promise me to tell no one about the kidnap. No one. Not until we are ready to inform the police.' He paused, holding Fritzoller with a purposeful stare. 'Our common intention to co-operate ought to be on record from this moment, don't you think, Doctor?'

Chapter Twelve

To avoid giving notice of his arrival, Treasure paid off the taxi in Hirschengraben, just before the corner with Hendrickstrasse.

Number Two, Hendrickstrasse was clearly identified some yards down the other street, on the far side. The Gothic number was inscribed on oval white enamel plaques on both the gateless gateposts. It was a substantial house, in grey rendering, with grey painted shutters to all the windows. The building was set back behind a low wall in the once residential road of overall grey edifices designed in the heavily gabled, old Swiss-German manner. Few of the windows in the houses were curtained, which suggested that most of the properties had been turned over to offices: Hendrickstrasse was close to the centre of Zürich. There were few garages, but cars were squeezed into the paved forecourts of the houses, as well as parked along both sides of the street.

The substantial front door of Number Two was painted the same drab grey as the rest of the house, but it was enlivened with polished brass fitments. It stood at the top of four stone steps and was sheltered by a heavy protruding lintel with bold scroll supports. A telephone entry system offered the names of four tenants in a glass-framed, neatly lettered directory. The names were all business titles, but Lybred and Greet AG, the one supplied by Willy Fritzoller, was not amongst them. Discouraged, Treasure turned about and descended to the basement, down steep, mean steps.

The shutters to the two basement windows were tightly closed. They faced on to a narrow area with barely two feet of space between them and the retaining wall of the forecourt above. The windows behind the shutters could not have provided much light to the interior. Even so, if there was anyone inside, the shutters would surely have been opened.

The sudden loud clatter from behind him startled the visitor. He swung about involuntarily as something fast-moving brushed

102

past his legs. It was a black and white cat that had leaped sideways off the lid of a dustbin where it had probably been sleeping. The lid had shifted and toppled to reveal a clean but significantly empty bin. The cat stopped at the top of the steps and settled there, observing the intruder with a reproachful, unblinking stare.

The basement door was directly under the steps to the main door above, its menial appearance in this way shrouded from the street. It had no fittings, brass or otherwise, except for a small and palpably inadequate vertical letterbox. A fat envelope, decorated with coloured advertising material, lay on the doorstep evidently because it had been too bulky to go through the letterbox. Just as clearly, the package had been lying where it was now for some time.

The prospect that Lybred or Greet were either of them inside was beginning to seem more than just remote.

There was a bell push to one side of the door, set under a metal frame of the size to hold a visiting card. But the frame was empty. Treasure pressed the bell. A strangled but still encouraging ring sounded from inside. The caller waited, going over in his mind the encounter that had brought him to Hendrickstrasse.

Once Dr Fritzoller had been persuaded to do what Treasure asked, the older man had acted with speed and, it had seemed at the time, with efficiency. He had been outraged at the prospect of his company being involved as an accomplice to a kidnap – or as an apparent beneficiary at the end of one. If Treasure's story was true, and, in view of the source, the doctor accepted it had to be, the chances of eliminating such possibilities seemed slim. But Fritzoller calculated that the size of any scandal could be measurably reduced if he co-operated. Further, the banker had made promises that were definitely dependent on the two men acting together now. That both saw good reason for not bringing in the police at this point had improved the sense of interdependence.

So Fritzoller had parted with information that the predator company in a hostile takeover bid would not normally have divulged. And he did it without reference to anyone. This was as much because Fritzoller was at heart an autocrat as because Treasure had insisted that Hackle's life could depend on their exchanges remaining confidential. The only other person involved had been Fritzoller's private secretary, a comely, middle-aged lady of conservative appearance who had quickly come in with a single thickish file in response to her employer's telephoned order.

'Lybred and Greet is the name of the merger and acquisition consultants we have used to handle the takeover of Closter,' Fritzoller had announced.

'Retained on fee or commission?'

'Fee only.'

'In two parts?'

'Yes. A substantial advance, and . . . ' He had hesitated.

'And an even more substantial final payment. But only after the successful completion of the takeover?'

'Precisely, Mr Treasure. Please don't press me on the actual numbers involved. Without legal advice I don't believe I should give you those.'

'Understood and accepted. Can you tell me who approached whom in the first place?'

'Yes. Lybred and Greet approached us. They were a new firm, with experienced principals, specialising in the merger of pharmaceutical companies. Their headquarters are in New Jersey. There's a small subsidiary European company registered here in Zürich.'

The Krontag Chairman had not personally met either Hans Lybred or Helga Greet, the principals. He had emphasised this by repeating the disclaimer several times. Lybred and Greet had never been used by Krontag before, nor had they come through recommendation – nor, Treasure ruminated as he stared at the basement door, was it likely that anyone from Krontag had ever visited their Zürich office. Simply, Hans Lybred had impressed Dieter Grubber, the Krontag International President, with his inside knowledge of Closter Drug and with the assurance that he had access to much more of the same.

Certainly the file that Fritzoller had referred to constantly, through the rest of the encounter with Treasure, had subsequently yielded a great deal more information on Closter Drug than it had on Lybred and Greet.

Of course, the Krontag directors had been well aware that Closter had a potentially important new drug in Seromig. The information had been common knowledge for years. But Lybred and Greet had produced copies of confidential clinical reports they claimed had not yet been shown to anyone else outside Closter. The reports in the file were authentic copies all right: Treasure was well aware that they confirmed the astonishing efficacy of Seromig.

Krontag had thus been more than ever spurred to renew its

previous attempt to acquire Closter. And Lybred and Greet had added yet more enticement to the prospect.

'They said a crisis was about to break at Closter,' Fritzoller recounted. 'When it happened, there would be a dramatic fall in the price of the shares. The position would be short-lived but to the advantage of a buyer ready to step in at the critical time. We had only to leave the timing of everything to Lybred and Greet. That way it was certain that a substantial part of the Closter equity could be snapped up at bargain prices.' Then the doctor had insisted: 'Herr Grubber had no reason to believe the crisis would be precipitated by a dishonest act.'

In Treasure's view, Grubber had been unbelievably naïve in not demanding to know the cause of the 'crisis' – either that, or the man had been sufficiently suspicious of that cause to want to stay ignorant of it. That Grubber and others hadn't asked the obvious questions could only be inferred, of course. Fritzoller was unable to confirm the point either way.

The doctor did go so far as to say that Grubber might have been 'too anxious to buy Closter, so that natural prudence gave way to the acquisitive instinct'. Treasure had made no comment on this remark which he felt, grimly, might be destined to feature as the most famous understatement of the year.

Fritzoller had later reluctantly agreed that the Lybred and Greet package seemed to have been based on not just one dubious act but a series of them – although the evidence for this was so far only circumstantial. Treasure had insisted that a criminal conspiracy must have existed between Lybred and Greet and the SAE kidnappers. Proving that Krontag was never a party to this conspiracy could reasonably excuse the Swiss company from blame. Helping to outwit the criminals now would be a step in that direction. It had been on a reiteration of this sombre but – for Fritzoller – compensating note that the two men had parted.

The banker rang the basement bell again. There was still no response. He pushed open the flap of the letterbox and listened. There was no sound of any kind from within. This did nothing to still the gnawing concern that Dermot Hackle could be a prisoner within feet of where the caller was standing. It was a bizarre thought, but several kidnap victims had been transported over national boundaries recently.

'Hello,' Treasure called through the letterbox. 'Is anyone there? *Ist jemand zu Hause?*'

Silence followed: Treasure let the boxflap spring closed. He moved beyond the door, intending to circle the house. There was only one window down the left side, shuttered like the ones at the front. He passed along the narrow basement defile to the rear of the building. Here the basement area was wider, but grated over at the top and blocked vertically halfway along. There were no windows at all on this side, and no door either, only a nearly horizontal trap-door arrangement at ground-floor level, next to the back door up there. This probably gave access to a basement fuel store via the permanent concrete shoot that was blocking Treasure's further progress. He returned the way he had come, and climbed the steps to the forecourt. This time the still suspicious cat stayed where it was.

A few minutes later the banker had walked right around the building. The doors to the fuel store had been locked and, like the shutters elsewhere, gave every indication that they had not been disturbed for a very long time. There were no unshuttered basement windows anywhere.

Treasure's progress had not gone unobserved, though none of the office workers – one man and a pair of giggling young women – who had watched him from separate windows in the house had paid any enduring attention. The man, on the second floor, had made a vaguely helpful expression but then disappeared from view. The young women, on the floor above, had seemed only to be appraising the good-looking Treasure, not questioning the reason for his circling their place of work.

The banker decided to return to the front door and to call up the ground-floor occupants on the entryphone. Enquiry from them might produce information at least about the most recent activity by the basement tenants. It was as he rounded the front of the building that he heard a car door slam close by. A moment later, he became vaguely aware of a taxi driving away on the road outside, beyond the parked cars there, and on the forecourt.

He had reached the steps to the front door when he turned about at the sound of footsteps approaching from the street. The figure coming into view took him totally by surprise.

'Kirsty Welling,' he uttered in astonishment, then quickly wished he hadn't.

The young woman had been hurrying through the gateway, a parked Audi car separating the two still. She was clasping a tall, overfull, brown-paper grocery bag. Her gaze had been down while

106

she rummaged in an open shoulder-strap bag with her free hand. But there was no mistaking the assured, coquettish face and shapely figure. Even the beret was the same. Only the sharply sculpted hair was different: instead of black it was auburn.

Her head was up now, the expression on her face turned from blankness to fright as she saw Treasure.

'*Nein—*' She had begun the pointless denial as he moved around the car towards her. She looked about in panic. Then, with no warning, determinedly she heaved the brown bag straight at him, turned, and fled into the street.

Treasure jumped backwards and sideways as the bag, and what was left of its contents, burst at his feet. Oranges, tomatoes and potatoes, plus a carton of milk had already found their target by then, and more fruit and vegetables continued to bounce in his direction off the bonnet of the Audi. There was a piercing squawk as he slipped and fell. His left foot had landed on the now totally outraged cat, all its suspicions proved, that shot from under him for the second time that morning.

Miss Welling was rounding the corner into Hirschengraben by the time Treasure gained the street. She was frantically hailing a taxi but it hadn't stopped, so she ran on, glancing behind her. Treasure hurried after her, moving as fast as he could, though not as fast as Miss Welling. The sharp pain in his left ankle was excruciating.

The girl was on the far side of the street now and sprinting into the paved precinct of the Kunsthaus art museum, an islanded, concrete building that Treasure had noticed on his arrival earlier. Here there were many more people to dodge, and to confuse pursuit. There was also a choice of routes around the gallery or even into it. Sure that his quarry had purposely chosen familiar ground, the banker blundered after her, fearful of losing sight of the green-shirted figure, but aware that she was gaining ground.

On the other side of the museum he lost sight of her. He was about to double back, thinking she had done the same. Then on impulse he went to the railings at the end of the precinct and spotted her again, well ahead of him. She was struggling through the lunchtime crowds on the long stone stairway leading down to the shop-lined Heimstrasse, the street that ends its own long descent there and disgorges into the even more bustling Heimplatz.

And on the far side of the Platz, to the right of where he had briefly paused above the steps, Treasure could see what he

107

took to be Kirsty Welling's objective – a line of empty taxis on the rank.

Dodging, jumping, twisting down the steps after her, enduring the ankle pain, mouthing apologies, and creating protest in his wake, Treasure reached the Heimstrasse not so far behind the girl. He had seen her try to cross here, but a crowd of others had been waiting to do the same at a crossing light and under the forbidding gaze of two policemen.

Miss Welling was now running on down into the Platz, to the next crossing, and still fifty yards ahead of her pursuer. The lights ahead of her were changing, and the traffic in the widened thoroughfare was stopping already before the crossing. As soon as a gap opened, Kirsty Welling moved off fast. In a moment she was alone in the central reservation between the sets of tramlines, and she scarcely hesitated there.

She was already halfway to the far pavement when the accelerating motor-bike hit her.

The rider had come from behind a slowing tram on the right. Like the girl, he had been trying to beat the lights. There was a deafening screech of brakes, and a shower of sparks as the machine slewed across the metalled surface.

The bike swung full circle and over on to its side. The upset rider was pinned underneath. Then man and machine were threateningly impelled towards the crowd on the pavement. Women screamed. Everyone fell backward. People were toppled in the press, the ones at the back pinned against shop windows.

The running girl had been knocked high in the air by the impact, her arms and legs splayed. She seemed to hover before coming down limply, like a rag doll, falling head first with a sickening, audible thump just short of the gutter. The beret, the shoulder-bag, and one shoe flew away from her in different directions while she was still in the air. The contents of the bag spilled out as it hit the road. It was Treasure who was to gather them up.

'She's badly injured. Fractured skull. Her pelvis and the right leg also fractured. We operate straight away.'

'Will she survive, Doctor?'

'She has so far.' The young houseman in the white coat smiled and continued to practise his English. 'So she has a chance, yes. She's young. She seems healthy.' He paused. 'Also very pretty. Her face is not marked, that's lucky. Not so lucky, she's in a coma still.'

'How long will that last?'

The doctor shrugged. 'That's always impossible to say. Hours? Days? Weeks sometimes. We must hope not too long. You said you're not a relative?' The gaze had become curious.

'No. A business acquaintance. Her parents live in Schaffhausen.' The wallet had revealed as much. 'The police are contacting them.'

The two were in a corridor at the hospital in the Ramistrasse. Treasure had followed the ambulance the short distance in a cab. He had been waiting here nearly an hour.

'But you saw the accident?'

'Quite by chance, yes,' he lied. 'I gave all the information I could to the police. There were other, closer witnesses.' This was true. The police hadn't detained him or troubled to question him at length.

'That's just as well. If you live in London, you won't want to come back later. To the court. Not for a . . . for a business acquaintance.'

Was there a touch of sarcasm in the voice?

'Quite. I'd come if necessary, of course.'

'Of course.'

'The motor-cyclist. He's all right?'

'Cuts and bruises only. The police will prosecute the guilty party, I expect.'

'It wasn't the lady's fault. All the witnesses agreed. The lights had changed to green.'

'As you said. You'll excuse me now?'

'Of course. Thank you for telling me all you have, Doctor.'

'Not at all.' The young man looked at Treasure speculatively again. He seemed to be about to ask a question, then thought better of it. He was wondering if the witness knew the patient a lot better than he was admitting. Was she his girlfriend – something the proper and probably married Englishman couldn't afford to acknowledge? Except he was deeply concerned about her condition. Awkward, the doctor acknowledged to himself, but not his business.

'I'll be in touch with the hospital about her progress.'

'Yes. Do that, sir. It's a service. Goodbye, then.' The doctor turned on his heel.

Treasure also turned about, his hand going involuntarily to the pocket holding the diary and the ring with the latchkeys on it. He'd picked up both articles from between the tramlines, along with the other contents that had spilled from the handbag. He wasn't stealing – only borrowing the two items he hadn't replaced, and in his view for a wholly defensible reason.

There was an empty taxi standing outside the hospital. Treasure got into it. '*Zwei Hendrickstrasse, bitte,*' he ordered.

He was sure the keys would open the basement door. He'd had plenty of time to scour the diary during his wait at the hospital. He had already called his secretary, Miss Gaunt, from a payphone there, and without offering an explanation for the instruction he had given her. If he was right that the kidnappers' ubiquitous moles could not possibly be listening in on such a call, then his cautious phraseology had certainly been overdone. It was simply that he was still avoiding unnecessary risk. Miss Gaunt had understood what he wanted her to do about the telephone number – the significant one in the diary.

For the first time in the fourteen or so hours since he had learned about the kidnapping of Dermot Hackle the banker felt he was making positive progress. He had thought as much from the moment he had caught sight of the credit cards in the handbag.

The real identity of the young woman in the accident wasn't Kirsty Welling. Treasure was sorry about her injuries, but pleased that she was effectively in custody for the next day or two at least.

The name on the credit cards was Helga Greet: it was on the passport, too.

Chapter Thirteen

As Treasure was leaving the hospital in Zürich, Bob Larden and Stuart Bodlin were drawing up in Bodlin's car outside the Larden house in Fulham. They had been to a meeting with Professor Garside, at the Royal Society of Medicine.

'Well we've achieved one positive thing today,' said Larden edgily, when, shortly afterwards, he was ushering the other man into his study on the middle floor.

The room was as gracious as the owner's factory office was stark. It was small, square, and bookcase-lined to ceiling height, with a glazed case for sporting guns in one corner. The curtains were heavy velvet. There was a leather-topped, antique desk, with two chairs in sympathy, and several simulated oil lamps offering electric illumination in three strengths. More sophisticated electronic gadgetry was hidden inside two matching, early nineteenth-century chest-commodes set behind the desk on either side. It was all a demonstration of Jane Larden's design capability in the 'practical classical mode' – a term that went some way to justifying the fake lamps and the vandalising of the commodes.

'I can't get over how indifferent Garside was to the takeover.' Bodlin shook his head. He had made the same point earlier, during the drive from Harley Street.

'Or the crash in our shares yesterday,' Larden agreed. 'Of course, he knew that was nothing to do with Seromig. And it doesn't matter to him who owns the company. What's important is his attitude to Seromig.'

'Which hasn't altered. Even after the cheapening news conference.'

'The conference didn't bother him. These protected academics aren't nearly as touchy as people assume,' said Larden unfeelingly, since it was Bodlin who had made the dour predictions about Garside's attitude – and had continued the lament up to the time of today's encounter. 'You were right to be sensitive about him, I suppose,' he added, in mitigation. 'I'm glad we didn't postpone the meeting. Though we had plenty of cause.'

'Garside's still postponing his paper.'

'No disadvantage in that. It'll be a more definitive effort now. Mary Ricini said that, remember?' Larden waved a hand in the direction of a leather armchair. 'Sit down, Stuart. I'm sorry Jane's out. I'll make us some tea. Unless you'd prefer something else? Something stronger?'

'Tea's fine, thanks,' the other answered abruptly. The last time he had accepted alcohol had been at the Savoy dinner, and what had happened afterwards still made him uncomfortable, especially with someone who had been there.

'Then I'd like to go over those notes Garside gave you,' said Larden. 'Just the headings. You're still going back to the office?'

'I need to, yes.'

'There's no point in my attempting it. Not with Laurence Stricton from the bank meeting me here. He's coming at six. To update me on what's happened since lunch.' Larden had been at Grenwood, Phipps up to the time of the Garside meeting. He breathed out heavily. 'God, I'll be glad when this week's over.'

The unguarded comment still only hinted at the turmoil Larden was enduring over his future with his company and his wife: he was reluctant to admit, even to himself, that he might have lost control of both. Counting his assets gave a short-lived buoyancy to his spirits.

His Closter shares had fetched 4.4 million pounds yesterday, even from the forced sale. He had a four-year, watertight contract as Managing Director of the company whoever owned it. Above all, he had paid a crippling price – half the real value of his shares – to keep his wife.

Only the final fact had a hollow ring. Jane's ultimatum in the car two nights before had rocked Larden to the core. He hadn't chosen, or dared, to press her since then about its true meaning – whether she had been insisting he had to save Hackle's life for reasons of humanity, or whether it was because Hackle meant more to her than her husband did.

'I'm sorry? . . . Yes, Laurence Stricton's very good,' he said now, in answer to a comment from Bodlin that had hardly registered.

'And Mark Treasure wants us to oppose the bid? Even if it has nothing to do with the kidnap?'

Larden moved towards the doorway. 'You still believe the two aren't related?'

'Krontag are very respectable,' Bodlin answered defiantly.

'And they're involved in a very unbelievable coincidence.' Larden rubbed the side of his cheek. 'Treasure has strong feelings about that. But he doesn't want any public comment till we've got Dermot back in one piece.'

'Treasure's gone to Zürich?'

'Not officially.'

'What's that mean?'

'Good question,' Larden commented with a frown. 'He's making an off-the-record call on Willy Fritzoller. The bank set it up early this morning, but they're not acknowledging it's happening. Not to outsiders. Treasure wants to give Fritzoller a private chance to extricate Krontag if he wants. If he doesn't want, we'll know where we stand. Also where Krontag stands.'

'Treasure's going to tell Fritzoller about the kidnap?'

'Yes. Assuming – hoping he doesn't know about it already. Not that he could admit it if he did know.'

'I'm positive he doesn't know.' Bodlin looked down at his bunched fists.

'Even if someone else in Krontag does?'

'Grubber, possibly. He's an odd man.' Both Bodlin and Larden knew the Krontag International President from their abortive meetings with him during the previous year.

'It wouldn't have to be him, surely?' Larden questioned, then paused, considering Bodlin and his words more carefully. 'Perhaps you're right. Difficult to credit though.'

The other glanced up. 'Treasure's risking the SAE will find out what he's doing?'

'Could find out, not will. It's a calculated risk. As our Chairman it's reasonable he should make a personal response to the takeover bid. Chairman to Chairman. He's determined no one else will be involved, and he's going to make Fritzoller swear to keep the confidence. Till Dermot's free. If Fritzoller won't agree— '

'He will,' Bodlin interrupted fiercely.

'Or agrees and then still gives us away to the SAE?'

'Not possible,' the other insisted, even more fiercely.

'Again, it wouldn't have to be him, of course. What if Fritzoller's private secretary, say, is an SAE mole? What if she can listen in to what's said in his office? Who knows?' Larden shrugged. 'Well

I hope you're right. I'll get that tea. Make yourself comfortable.'

'I'd like to make a phone call.'

'Help yourself. Sit at the desk if you want. It's probably easier.'

As Larden descended the stairs into the hall, the street door flew open. His wife came in, flushed and ebullient, wearing a crisp yellow dress, carrying a slim folio case and looking as if she hadn't a care in the world. She started when she saw him, recovered, then moved forward quickly to embrace him. 'Darling, I didn't think you'd be back till tonight.'

'The Garside meeting went on longer than we expected. There was no point in my going to the office.' He continued to hold her close to him – not caressingly, but tentatively, his hands around her waist. In a way his action seemed to increase the tension existing between them. 'Stuart Bodlin's in the study. He's making a phone call. I was going to make us some tea.'

She pouted, drawing away from him a touch awkwardly. 'I'll do that, darling. But could you have it down here in the sitting room? I have to fax a drawing to a client urgently, do some photoprinting, and make phone calls at the same time. I can do all that up there. Then I have to go out again. Incidentally, my bloody carphone's on the blink again.' She moved around him, heading for the kitchen at the back of the house.

Although she shared an office in Victoria with two other designers, it seemed to him she used it less than she did the house for business. 'We'll come down,' he called after her.

'Thanks.' She looked back over her shoulder. 'Anything new? About the takeover?'

'Not really. Nor about Dermot,' he added, his gaze holding hers until she looked away. 'The SAE aren't phoning again till tomorrow. That reminds me, I haven't checked for messages yet.'

It was then that Larden saw Bodlin standing on the landing at the top of the stairs.

Bodlin's face was even more ashen than usual as he emerged from the study, clutching his briefcase to his chest. He looked and behaved as if he had just received shocking news.

'I'm sorry, I . . . I have to leave. I'll explain later. All right?' His speech was faltering, like his steps on the stairs as he clung grimly to the banister.

'Something happened? You all right?'

'I'm OK, yes.' He shook his head. 'Garside's notes. They're on the desk.'

'Hello, Stuart. How are you?' This was Jane who was returning from the kitchen.

Bodlin, who had now reached the hallway, looked back at her with a sort of horror. He made as if to speak, then, instead, stumbled to the street door, wrestled with the lock to get it open, and fled.

Doris Tanner looked down at her less than prominent bare breasts, frowned, and pulled the sheet over herself. 'Scrawny I'm getting, and that's a fact,' she said, then sighed and wriggled a little further down into the bed.

'Go on. I've seen a lot worse,' her husband answered with feeling. He looked at the bedside clock. It was nearly four fifteen in the afternoon.

'Thanks very much. Seen a lot worse lately have you? Topless customers, is it? Courtesy of British Gas? Oh Mr Engineer come quick, I think the leak's in the bedroom.' She giggled and dug her right elbow into his side.

'Leave off, love. And I didn't mean nothing like that. I meant on the beach.'

'That was last year.'

'That's right. You was the best-looking bird there. Will be again this year as well. Far as I'm concerned, anyway. Pass the cigarettes then. Any tea left in the pot?' Bert Tanner took his arm from around her shoulders. He was short and muscular, with a gravel voice, crew-cut hair, a boxer's nose, and a mild countenance that could prove deceptive.

There was a faded tattoo on his left forearm showing a heart pierced by an arrow. The word Mother came underneath this in a flowery script. Doris had been on at him for years to have that tattoo removed. It was a relic of six youthful years in the regular army. He'd promised to have something done about it when his mother died. His mother was barely sixty and in robust health.

Like his wife, Bert Tanner was a Cockney from south of the river, but without her acquired polish. If asked, he would have said you didn't need phony polish in his job – just knowledge and experience, and he had plenty of those.

Bert had been awake for half an hour. He was due on duty at the gas maintenance depot at six thirty. He didn't like the shift he was on this month. It paid good overtime, but he didn't see much of Doris. This was the first time they had been in bed together all week – and they were only there now through a chance variation in her routine.

Doris normally reached home shortly after five thirty. Today, Bob Larden, her boss, hadn't been to the office at all. He had told her she could leave early to make up for working long hours on the previous two hectic days. She had come in just as Bert had been waking up.

He inhaled deeply on his cigarette. He never smoked at work, and not much anywhere else nowadays, except here. 'There's nothing beats a cuppa and a smoke in bed,' he said. 'Well only one thing, and we've just had that.'

'You are coarse,' she said. 'Sit up properly then.' She passed him the tea she had poured. The tray was on the bedside table beside her.

He pushed his back up the pillow till his neck was resting on the top of the newly upholstered bedhead. 'Ta.' He sipped noisily from the mug, then balanced it on the undue expanse of stomach below what until recently had been a recognisably barrel-shaped chest. 'Nice drop of tannin in that.' He turned his head to look at Doris. 'What's for my breakfast, then?'

'You want to lose some weight before we go to Minorca,' she said, fingering the mane of black hair below his navel.

'Thought you liked me the way I am?'

'The way you used to be. Not gross.' She pinched his flesh.

'All right then. Two rashers instead of four from now on. Is Mr Larden still on a diet?'

'Shouldn't think so. Poor sod's got too much to worry about to think of diets.'

She lay back on the pillow, eyes roaming the room contentedly through a slight but flattering mist since she didn't have her glasses on. The place was much prettier since their last redecoration. They were always decorating, the two of them; improving their home. This room faced south with a bay window that got the sun all afternoon. Sunbeams were streaking in as strong as stage lighting. She had enjoyed making love under what she'd imagined as spotlights. Not that anyone could see through the net curtains. The sun was also lighting up the new dressing table: she'd draped that with the same yellow and green fabric as the curtains. She'd made the curtains herself too.

Lazily she slid her left foot back, bending her knee upwards so that the sheet fell away from her bare leg in a mildly erotic sequence. Then she straightened the leg, twisting it about in the air while pointing the foot. 'I've still got nice legs, haven't I?'

116

'Very nice, yes.'

He put his hand on her other thigh, then patted it under the sheet. She sensed this was more an involuntary gesture of approval than a sign of rekindling passion, and she didn't mind.

'My legs'll be nicer still with a Mediterranean tan. Can't wait for the holiday.'

'Will the shares pay for it? Like you said last week?'

'If we want to sell them. Easily. Now the price is back to a pound twenty-five.'

Bert shook his head. He didn't understand high finance: the building society was good enough for him – and more reliable than shares going on recent experience. All he knew about their Closter Drug shares was that they'd bought them at a special price with two hundred pounds from their savings; against his better judgement. That was five years ago when the management had taken over the company. The value of the shares had gone up to two thousand, four hundred pounds last Thursday. He'd said it was too good to be true – and it looked as if he was right when the figure dropped to eight hundred pounds yesterday afternoon. Today Doris said it was back to two thousand, five hundred because there was a bid for the company.

'Can we get the money out now?' he asked.

'We'd have to sell the shares for that. I asked Mr Closter-Bennet. He said not to. Not yet.'

'You think he's right?'

'Well he's the Finance Director. He ought to be right. I'm sure Mr Larden'll say the same. He did yesterday, even when the price was right down. He said I wasn't to tell anyone else though. What he'd told me. About not selling. Funny that.'

Bert gave an uncertain sniff. 'Any news of that Hackle?'

They always referred to Larden as Mister. Hackle was just Hackle – and there was a reason.

'If you ask me, he's done a bunk.'

'Go on? With a woman?'

'I wouldn't think so. Money more like.'

'Sticky fingers in the till?'

'It's hard to say, and I don't see how it can be that. Not really. But something very fishy's going on, all the same.'

'He went off last Sunday?'

'Sunday afternoon. From home. He's supposed to be seeing Midlands customers. Well Lorna, that's his secretary, she knew nothing about it, and he hasn't rung into the office once. Any calls for him have to go to Mr Larden or one of the other directors. That's if Mr Larden's not there. And they're automatically recorded. Anyway, with all this takeover business, he wouldn't stay away from the office. Stands to reason.'

'What about the call to Mr Larden from the Irish bloke? The one on Monday?'

'That was about Hackle. That's all I know.' She turned on her side towards him. 'Doctor Ricini is staying with Mrs Hackle.'

'Looking after her?'

'Seems like it.'

'And you don't think Hackle's with another woman? Right bugger he is. He hasn't tried it on with you since?'

'Hasn't needed to.'

'Better not neither.'

'It was only that once.'

He hoped that was true. If ever he found it wasn't he'd kill the bastard. 'Bloody animal,' he said.

Late one evening, in the previous autumn, Hackle had returned to the office, found Doris Tanner alone, and made a pass at her. It was obvious he had been drinking. She had made him leave her alone by threatening to tell her husband – which she had done, weeks later, after making Bert promise not to do anything about it. Despite her protests, Doris had been secretly flattered by the attentions of the Marketing Director: it was the reason why she had told Bert, without mentioning Hackle's condition. She'd have been more complimented, of course, if Hackle had been sober when he'd groped her – and probably have allowed him to go further than she had. She sometimes fantasised about that.

'He's had Doctor Ricini panting for him for the last six months,' she said.

'Is that a fact? Sleep with him, does she?'

'Lorna thinks so. Only he seems to have gone off our lovely young Medical Director just recently. Most likely taken up with someone else, Lorna said. She doesn't know who though. I know she wishes it was her. She's potty about him.'

'Blimey, does he have every bird in the company begging for it?'

''Course not. He doesn't have me for a start. He is dishy though, and . . . and sort of sophisticated, I suppose.' Her words tailed away.

'And he's a married man with two kids, like you said.' Bert was strong on fidelity. 'What about his wife then? What's she saying to Doctor Ricini who's looking after her? "Finished with my hubbie, have you? Who's he in bed with now, d'you know?" Cor! I'd give him sop .isticated. If he ever lays a hand on you again— '

'So what about laying a hand on me yourself?' She snuggled closer.

'That's different.' As he put the empty mug on the table he noticed the time again. 'I have to leave at quarter past six.'

'Well it's not going to take you that long is it? Please yourself of course.' She feigned hurt feelings, half turning from him.

'I'll do just that then.' He pushed away the sheet and ran a firm hand down her body.

She swung back to him, twining her arms around his neck.

He had been working out that he'd have time to shave and dress, take the dogs for a run, eat the 'breakfast' Doris would cook for him, and make love to her once more now. Bert was a methodical man. 'This is the life,' he growled.

'So why . . . d'you have to leave . . . so early?' she asked, between the lovebites she was making down his chest and abdomen.

'Didn't I say? I'm working out of Chiswick tonight. We're short-handed at Chiswick. Further to go than Hounslow.' There was a pause. 'Oo, it's bloody marvellous there.'

But she knew he didn't mean Hounslow.

Chapter Fourteen

'Are you leaving in the morning, Auntie Mary?' called Tim Hackle, missing the rubber quoit again. He and Mary Ricini were playing in the back garden of the Hackle house. Tim wasn't good at games that required too much physical co-ordination.

'Perhaps. More likely I'll stay for tomorrow night.' As always with Tim she did her best to make everything sound as casual as possible.

'That's good.' He gave her his endearing, slightly wicked smile. He retrieved the quoit from a flower bed and threw it back towards her across the lawn – but too high, and not far enough, despite his nearly propelling his whole self with it. 'Sorry.' He pushed up a dangling blue shirt sleeve, but the other one dropped down while he was doing it.

'Shall I roll them up for you?'

'No thanks, I can do it.' He did so, but not very neatly. 'Does that mean Daddy won't be home again?'

Mary, in stockinged feet, picked up the rubber ring, hopped backwards lightly for several steps, then aimed it accurately towards the small boy – who missed it again. 'I expect that depends on how busy Daddy is.'

It was becoming a touch more difficult to satisfy Tim's curiosity about his father's whereabouts. His sister Emma was no problem. Whatever her view on what was happening, she pressed no one for explanations, and kept her own counsel.

'Can we play the football game on TV now, Auntie Mary?'

'Because you always win? You're a terror. All right.' She pushed the hair from her eyes.

He skipped to her side, then pulled up a sock to his knee below the short trousers. She leaned on him while she slipped on her discarded high heels. He took her hand and squeezed it affectionately as they made for the open kitchen door. 'Why are you staying now Mummy's better?'

120

'You want me to go away?'

''Course not.'

'Well don't push your luck then. I like being here.' She had found that the best way to cope with his ceaseless questions was to neutralise them with counter questions.

'Mummy is better isn't she?'

'She's fine. Don't you think so?' The woman doctor was glad to have him relate her presence more to his mother's needs than to his father's absence.

'She looks all right.'

'But you see it's not only a matter of her being better. She's helping me with the research I'm doing on migraine. On those bad headaches she gets.'

'That's with the new medicine?'

'Right. If she gets another attack I have to be here to check on what happens.'

'Can I have a drink, Auntie Mary?' he asked, when they were in the kitchen.

'There's some orange juice in the fridge. I'll have some too.' It was juice she had brought herself, along with more fruit, fresh fish, and the extra groceries she had been providing on the pretext of contributing her share to the household costs. She had also given the children presents. There had been TV games for Tim, and a pretty blouse for Emma. It was a home where luxuries were rare but appreciated. Rosemary Hackle was clearly short on housekeeping money. She was certainly grateful for Mary's help, and unaware that the giver went to some trouble to disguise the extent of her benevolence – or else Rosemary was too preoccupied with other things to notice.

For her part, the pretty young doctor was compensating these three people in every way she knew for something she felt she had deprived them of in the recent past. Of course, it was a tortuous sort of formula that balanced wholesome foods against the stolen affections of Dermot Hackle. She was not even sure she had ever truly possessed those affections, but whatever the cause of her unease she was taking the opportunity to make up for it.

The emergency plan had worked well so far. Neither of the children was ever left alone out of school hours.

Rosemary was with her daughter now, meeting her out of school and taking her to a dental appointment arranged the week before. Accompanying her daughter to the dentist was something Rosemary would have done in the normal way.

Mary Ricini had left Closter Drug that afternoon in time to pick up Tim at his school at three thirty – something his mother usually did. Routines hadn't been noticeably changed, nor arrangements cancelled. The children weren't aware that they were being protected from special danger.

The alternative of Emma and Tim being sent away to safety somewhere, in the middle of the school term, would have created too many questions – in their own minds as well as other people's. It had been Mary herself who had devised the lower-keyed solution. Its credibility depended on the children accepting that the woman doctor needed Rosemary as much as Rosemary needed the woman doctor. The migraine research had met the situation admirably – particularly at night when normal medical supervision wouldn't be available outside a hospital. It explained to the children why Mary was sleeping at their house, and also satisfied the concern of Bob Larden and the other directors that there should be two adults there after dark.

Mary hadn't been alone with Tim before, or not for any length of time. She preferred his company to that of his sister. He had all his father's pleasing traits. She hoped he would never develop the unpleasing ones. She watched him now guzzling the orange juice, eyes sparkling at her beguilingly over the top of the glass, blond eyelashes flashing.

'Daddy's been away a long time,' he said, standing on tiptoe as he washed the empty glass under the tap.

'Not that long, surely? Only from Sunday lunchtime.'

Tim wrinkled his nose. 'Emma and I saw him after that,' he offered in a conspiritorial voice. 'We haven't told Mummy. Emma says we mustn't. She gave me 10p not to,' he added, as if proud of this less than objective reason for his reticence.

'Have you told anyone else?'

'Only you.'

'Where did you see him?' She was doing her best to keep her interest at a low sounding level.

'At Heathrow. Emma took me to see the new Aeroflot plane take off.'

'What a coincidence. Did Daddy see you?'

'Don't think so.'

'About tea-time was it?'

122

'Three o'clock. That was the take-off time.'

'Was Daddy watching the take-off too?'

'No. He was in his car. With a lady.'

'That would be his secretary, I expect. Short girl with dark hair?'

Tim shook his head. 'She's called Lorna Smith. It wasn't her. This one was ginger.'

They both heard the front door slam, together with voices in the hall. Mary quickly moved across to Tim, her mind racing. She knelt beside the boy and whispered. 'Emma was right. Better not tell Mummy. Not at the moment. Nor anyone else. All right?'

'Yes, Auntie Mary.' He looked over her shoulder. 'Hello, Mummy.'

'Teeth all right, Emma?' Mary enquired brightly, getting up as the girl came into the kitchen behind her mother. The black family cat was also in train.

'Fine, thanks. Just a scaling.'

'Tell you what, Tim and I were just going to play a TV game. Could you play instead of me?' She turned to Rosemary. 'I've just remembered something I should have done at the office. I'll have to go back. Shouldn't take long. Let's see, it's four twenty. Back in an hour, I expect.'

But it was after seven o'clock when she returned.

At a quarter to five, Alison McFee was locking the door of her Austin Metro in the basement carpark of the supermarket. She had already done her shopping – just enough to get the money back on the parking token. Food prices were higher in Chiswick than they were in Maidenhead where she normally shopped, and parking was free in the supermarket there. She was careful with her money, not mean, but careful. It was why she still felt these trips to Chiswick were an extravagance, despite the improvement in her figure. The feeling was worse this time, too.

Up to last Monday she had been confident that she and Hughie were going to be rich because of the Closter flotation, that a few modest extra expenses could be justified. Now the shares were gone, her prudent Calvinistic upbringing had reasserted itself. Even though the shares had fetched a million pounds, she had almost decided to cancel the rest of her treatments – almost, but not quite.

She left the carpark by the street exit wearing her dark glasses.

She hadn't told Hughie anything about the slenderising course.

This was partly because she hadn't been certain till the last but one visit to Ivan Popinov that his treatment was working on her. Now she was pretty sure that it was. The results weren't startling yet, but even Hughie had remarked on how svelte she was looking all of a sudden. That was an exaggeration probably, but she thought she was definitely on the way to a better shape. She had told Hughie it was due to dieting and exercises, but it was scarcely that. Alison found it impossible to keep to a serious diet.

After crossing Chiswick High Street, she hurried down the narrow lane beside the furniture store.

What Mr Popinov did was to dissolve or redistribute the excess flesh. It was what his advertisement in *The Lady* had promised. The diet part wasn't rigorous and she'd got used to the foul-tasting vitamin drink. As for the process of 'dissolving and redistributing', that was the most abandoned experience Alison McFee had enjoyed in her whole life, though she tried not to admit it to herself quite as baldly as that – to stem a much more insidious sense of culpability than the one caused by the cost.

The road into which she now emerged was residential. The new block of flats where Mr Popinov lived was some distance to the right. The basement carpark there was strictly for residents only, with apartment numbers painted on the bays. That was why she had taken to leaving her Metro at the supermarket. On the first visit to Mr Popinov she had looked for space in the basement of the flats without success, and eventually parked outside in the street. She hadn't noticed until she came away that the street parking was also restricted to residents. If the car had been clamped or towed away, she wouldn't have known how to cope. She relied on Hughie to handle all brushes with authority, but she would have had to explain to him why she was parked in a Chiswick sidestreet, twenty miles from home.

Mr Popinov used some electric ray equipment for part of the treatment, but Alison was sure it was his massaging that was working the miracle. He had fingers like steel when they needed to be, but a velvet touch for the rest of the time, so soothing and gentle – and other things too that she didn't care to admit to herself. He was quite young and very good-looking, or more distinguished than just good-looking perhaps, with his high forehead and pointed black beard – he reminded Alison a little of pictures of the last Tsar. The white medical jacket he wore, buttoned at one shoulder, was cut like the summer uniforms officers wore in those days. He was

Russian of course, but from one of those Baltic states. He had told her about his background on the first visit, but Alison had been nervous at the time and forgotten the details. She hadn't liked to ask again. She did recall he had aristocratic connections.

She crossed to the other side of the road to be out of the sun.

Of course Mr Popinov's conduct was absolutely proper. There was a receptionist, a pleasant young woman, and quite pretty. She came into the consulting room, when called, to help with the equipment, but went back to her desk in the waiting room at the massage stage. But she was there all the time, on the premises as it were, so there couldn't be any suggestion of impropriety.

Alison McFee's still stout little body experienced a tremble of pleasure at the thought of impropriety with Ivan Popinov, though she quickly suppressed it.

She was especially glad the assistant wasn't present during the manipulative part of the treatment. It was then that the patient had first felt a spiritual as well as physical rapport with Mr Popinov. She had never experienced faith healing, but she could imagine now what it must be like.

Mr Popinov had a healer's touch all right. It was why the treatment worked so well. Faith was better than dieting: he was spiriting away her excess pounds – she was convinced of it. But it involved a very delicate relationship (she hesitated to use the word intimate), and one that could easily be shattered by the presence of a third person. Alison was much too modest to give herself over to such a spiritual experience if there had been anyone other than Mr Popinov in the room – especially when he took away the towels. That was prior to his moving his magic, searching hands slowly down her body, from her brow to her feet, while he exhorted her in an urgent whisper to relax and allow the unwanted tissue to dissolve and drain away through the very ends of her tiny toes.

These body sweeps, as Mr Popinov called them, were the key to the treatment. Alison could quite see that now. The sweating they induced was incredible. They made her feel utterly exhausted. It was prudish of her to have been so obviously embarrassed over her nakedness the first time. She blushed at her past inhibition. What a goose Mr Popinov must have thought her. That was if he noticed, and he probably hadn't. The concentration and effort he put into the sweep sequence would obliterate trivia from his mind.

She quickened her step, then restrained it again after a sobering glance at her watch.

Since the second visit she had tried always to be just on time. On that occasion she had been nearly forty minutes early. She had found it embarrassing to be sitting waiting with the patient who had the appointment ahead of hers. Treatments lasted half an hour. Then the patient before the other one had come out of the consulting room, joking with Mr Popinov in a show of familiarity that Alison found very nearly irreverent. This patient had then turned out to be the first one's friend. The two had come together and were returning together, so Alison had had to wait the next thirty minutes in the company of the second.

Both the other patients had been glamorous, younger than Alison, and hardly at all overweight: they had also had a great deal more in common with the pretty receptionist than with her. They had treated Alison with what seemed at worst cynical disdain and at best the kind of humouring she sometimes applied to her aged mother. It had made her very uncomfortable, as though she was somewhere where she shouldn't have been, up to something unworthy or even immoral. That this had been her guilt complex asserting itself and not because of any intended slight by the others was neither here nor there. She came to Chiswick partly because she didn't care to attend for similar treatment any nearer her home where she might run into people she knew. Now she found the presence of sophisticated strangers equally irksome.

She was nearly at the entrance to the flats now.

She hesitated before crossing a side road because of the white VW Golf. It was approaching from the other side of the flats, but slowing, and with its flashing indicator suggesting that it was going to turn into the road she was about to cross. But the car turned earlier than that – into the entrance to the basement carpark of the flats.

Alison's heart gave a leap as she identified the single occupant of the Golf. It was Jane Larden.

It was a substantial block of flats, but Alison had a horrifying premonition that Jane was heading for the same destination as herself. Oh the mortification of it! – for lumpy, fifty year old Alison to find herself in that waiting room with the gorgeous Jane of the perfect body profile. Jane would be coming for treatment to keep her natural shape. Alison was just hoping to alter the ravages of time and overindulgence – and if she was totally honest with herself, it was a pretty forlorn hope at that.

Despite the cheek kissing and the affected greetings when they met, Alison was sure Jane would be inwardly laughing at her. It would be the same as with the two pretty young patients on the second visit – only worse. And Jane was bound to tell her husband.

Alison stood at the kerb edge desperately wondering what to do. Thank God she had been wearing the dark glasses. She was sure Jane hadn't seen her – not yet. Seconds later a plan formed in her mind. She would allow just time enough for Jane to park her car and take the lift, then follow her into the basement. There were indicators above the lift doors in the building, and if Alison was quick enough, and if no one else had used the lift meantime, it should be possible to tell which floor Jane had gone to. If it was Mr Popinov's floor then Alison would find a telephone and cancel her appointment.

Surprised at her own ingenuity, Alison scampered across to the basement ramp, then down into the building. She soon found the empty white Golf because of its colour. It was parked in a bay on the left. Alison looked around feverishly for the lift. It was some distance to the right. Before she reached the door she could read the indicator above it. The light was steady on the figure 3. Mr Popinov's flat was on the fourth floor.

Alison was breathless but satisfied. Whatever reason Jane Larden had for being here, it was now almost certain that it wasn't to see Mr Popinov. It was the end of the afternoon. Jane had driven in less than a minute before. No one else had entered or left the building. There was no one else in the basement. If the lift had gone to the fourth floor it would almost certainly still be there, because if anyone had used it since Jane, it surely wouldn't have been just to go down one floor? It had taken a moment for Alison to work out the last conclusion.

She felt she could stop worrying. Then, for the first time, she wondered what authority if any Jane had for parking down here. It was probably the usual thing – that people like Jane always got away with breaking rules that people like Alison never dared to challenge. The notice at the entrance said RESIDENTS PARKING ONLY – TRESPASSERS REPORTED TO THE POLICE. Jane certainly wasn't a resident. Perhaps she had a resident's permission?

Out of curiosity, Alison walked back over to the white car. It was parked in a bay marked $3/14$. That had to mean the bay belonged to flat 14 on the third floor. Thankfully it fitted the hypothesis that Jane was visiting someone on that floor. The next bay had exactly the same marking. So flats were allocated two bays. The second bay

127

was also occupied – by a car larger than Jane's, but enveloped by a lightweight car cover. It was the same kind of cover that Hughie had for his company Mercedes and never used – well, there was never any reason with their big garage at home.

On her way back to the lift, Alison did a small detour looking for the bays marked $\frac{4}{23}$. That was the floor and number of Mr Popinov's flat. She found the bays. They were both occupied – one by an expensive red Porsche, the other by a dilapidated Mini. She wondered who the smaller car belonged to – Mr Popinov's receptionist, or his wife (if he had a wife), or a favoured patient perhaps? Alison thought the first idea the most likely: Mr Popinov's patients were expensive, like his prices – no doubt a wife would be the same.

While she was on her way up in the lift, Alison came to a decision. When Hughie got home this evening she would tell him about the treatment. Then they could decide together whether she should go on with it – whether it was worth it, worth the price. She was tired of deceiving him. 'Deceiving' was too strong a word, of course, but she had always hated to do anything or to be anywhere that she couldn't tell him about, and that would diminish her if someone else told him. Nearly running into Jane Larden had been a stern reminder.

By the time Alison rang the bell to Mr Popinov's flat, she was feeling a whole lot easier. Already she couldn't wait to get home ready to tell Hughie what had been happening. It was then that the other thought struck her, the one that prompted her to return to the basement after her treatment – just to make sure of something.

Of course, it was just one of those silly compulsions, probably. But she needed to be certain in her mind that it was just the cover that was similar.

Chapter Fifteen

'Exactly what have you been doing?' asked Molly Treasure as her husband got into the back of the Rolls again beside her.

The car was parked in front of the ponderous main door to the Closter Drug factory. Molly had been waiting in it with Henry Pink, the chauffeur, while Treasure and Giles Closter-Bennet had gone inside the deserted building. That had been a quarter of an hour earlier, at just before 8 p.m., which accounted for the impatience in Molly's voice. The two men had promised they would be only a minute or two.

'We've been testing a theory of Mark's. He was right, as usual,' said the perspiring Closter-Bennet, getting into the front passenger seat.

'We'll go to that address in Chiswick now please, Henry,' Treasure instructed. 'You know where it is?'

'Yes, sir. Miss Gaunt explained.'

'What theory?' demanded Molly.

'It's a bit complicated to explain, darling,' said her husband leaning back in the seat.

'You mean I'll have to listen extra carefully?'

'Sorry, I meant tortuous. The door into the research laboratories works on a voice lock. There's a recording of Dermot Hackle's voice that we knew worked the lock. Giles got the tape out so we could demonstrate it.'

'Trouble is, there's another voice on the tape that also sprang the lock. It shouldn't have,' Closter-Bennet put in, turning round, with a bit of a strain, to look at them both. 'Mark knew it would.'

'No. Only guessed it might,' Treasure corrected.

'We couldn't be sure after that that anyone's voice wouldn't do the same thing,' said Closter-Bennet.

'Yours or Mark's for instance?'

Closter-Bennet shook his head. 'Mine would because it's in the . . . the authorised voice bank.'

'That sounds very grand,' Molly said.

'Not really.' Closter-Bennet wasn't sure whether she was being serious. 'All the directors' voices are on it.' He faced front again because twisting his neck around was making him dizzy.

'But not Mark's voice?'

'Only the full-time directors,' said Treasure. 'Anyway, my live voice didn't do the trick. Then we figured that maybe all recorded voices might.'

'So you had to make a tape?'

'Yes. Which is why it all took so long.'

'And a lot of dashing about,' added Closter-Bennet breathily, and still warm from the exertion.

'What are we going to do in Chiswick? More conjuring tricks?' asked Molly.

'We're looking up an address Miss Gaunt got for me from directory enquiries,' her husband answered.

'They don't give addresses.'

'They do if you're Miss Gaunt,' Treasure said flatly. His secretary had a cousin who was married to a manager in the right part of British Telecom. 'Giles, you really don't have to come with us, you know. It's out of your way.'

'I'd like to come. I can easily pick up my car at Heathrow later.'

Molly frowned. It was out of her way too – well, metaphorically if not directionally. She had gone to the airport with Pink on impulse, and in the hope that her husband would take her to dinner on the way back. She hadn't known then that Treasure had telephoned Closter-Bennet from Zürich airport asking him to meet the flight.

'Who lives at this Chiswick address?'

'Nobody. Not permanently. But it's a possible link with the SAE,' answered the banker. 'Miss Gaunt's found out it's a furnished flat. One of six in the same ownership, in a new block. Available for short or medium lets. She got on to the letting agents through the owners of the building.' Miss Gaunt was nothing if not thorough. 'The telephone number was in Helga Greet's diary under last Sunday's date.'

'Helga Greet, or Kirsty Welling that was?'

'Mmm. Incidentally, we called Zürich from Giles's office. The operation was successful, but she's still in a coma.'

'But at least she's alive?'

130

'Yes.'

'You started to tell us about the basement flat in Zürich.'

'Nothing more to tell really. I went there. Opened the door with Miss Greet's keys. It was a very ordinary furnished flat. No sign of recent occupation.'

'Tidy, you mean?'

'Yes. Beds made. No dirty dishes. No garbage. A lot of junk mail in the letterbox, and a month-old magazine in the living room. Nothing really personal anywhere. No clothes. No papers.'

'You made a very thorough search,' said Closter-Bennet earnestly from in front.

'With good reason and to no purpose. Probably Helga Greet and her partner just use the place as a pied-à-terre. And a business address to impress. It'd do that all right, for customers who didn't actually go there.'

'Darling, what would you have done if you'd been taken for a burglar?'

'Referred the taker to Doctor Fritzoller. Indirectly, Krontag is probably paying the rent for the flat. In their fee to Lybred and Greet. Anyway, if it came to it, Fritzoller would have bailed me out. He's co-operating totally.'

'And Miss Greet was on her way into the flat when you saw her?' asked Molly.

'Unfortunately, yes.'

'What happened wasn't your fault.'

'Certainly not,' Closter-Bennet added firmly, supporting Molly. 'Case of a guilty conscience. I wouldn't be surprised if the kid . . . '

He left the last word uncompleted and broke into a heavy and palpably phony fit of coughing. He had remembered in time about Henry Pink not being privy to the kidnapping.

'You don't think Krontag is involved in anything but the take-over?' asked Molly, her words more circumspect than Closter-Bennet's.

'I'm pretty certain they're not,' said Treasure thoughtfully. 'I'm not even sure that Miss Greet or her company is responsible for the nastiest aspect of what's been happening.'

'I don't follow you?'

'I'm not following myself at the moment.'

They reached Chiswick in ten minutes' fast driving along the M4 motorway. The block of flats was called Mereworth Court: it was

131

where Mr Popinov lived and practised. There were two police cars and an ambulance parked outside.

Treasure frowned at the vehicles. 'Hope they're not ominous. I think you'd better stay in the car, darling,' he said to his wife, as Pink brought the Rolls to a halt.

'Not this time,' Molly responded firmly. She had the door half open already.

Treasure shrugged. 'Wait for us here then, Henry, will you? What's the number again?'

'Flat fourteen on the third floor, sir.'

Entry to the building was through unlocked double doors into a large six-sided, tiled hallway. There were two lifts in the wall opposite the entrance, with front doors to individual flats in the other ones.

'No porter. No entryphone,' remarked Molly as the three got into one of the lifts.

'But every flat has a very wonderful burglar alarm system. That was the sales pitch the letting agents gave Miss Gaunt,' said her husband.

'Entryphones are often a snare and a delusion,' said Closter-Bennet, but he didn't elaborate. He was pawing at his neck. The too-tight collar button of his shirt had come off, as a result of all that turning about in the car.

The door to flat fourteen was to the right of the lift, and wide open when they got there.

Standing just inside the hallway to the flat was Hughie McFee. He was in earnest conversation with a short, sandy-haired man.

'Good God! Mark!' exclaimed McFee, looking up in surprise. 'And Giles and Molly? You've got the news already?'

'What news?' asked Treasure. 'Is Dermot Hackle here?'

'He's here, yes. And very dead, I'm afraid. His body's in the living room, through there.' He made a despairing gesture with his arms. 'Sorry, Molly. It's going to be a terrible shock for everybody. I found him. The police doctor's here. It seems he died of cardiac arrest. Some time during the last two hours.' He turned to the man beside him. 'This is Detective Inspector Furlong.' He introduced the others to the policeman, then went on. 'I had to explain about the kidnap. No need for secrecy now, of course.' This was no doubt what had accounted for the presence of someone of Furlong's rank.

Treasure still felt uncertain about the disclosure.

'Does Rosemary Hackle know what's happened?' asked Molly.

'Mr McFee has phoned his wife, Mrs Treasure. She's on her way to Mrs Hackle now,' said Furlong, not sure yet what to do with the newcomers, nor how to reconcile a death from natural causes with the deceased being an alleged kidnap victim.

The policeman was in his early thirties, a spare, energetic figure with a freckled forehead, lively, eager eyes, a tenor voice, and shoulders that moved backwards and forwards like a metronome as he spoke. 'If you'll excuse me a second, I need another word with the doctor,' he went on. 'Perhaps you'd all stay here in the hall? If you don't mind.'

'Nice young man, but a wee bit confused in the circumstances,' said McFee when Furlong was out of earshot.

'He's not the only one. This is dreadful news,' said Molly.

'If he died of heart failure, was it anything to do with the kidnapping?' asked Closter-Bennet.

'If he died of heart failure,' Treasure repeated, with emphasis on the first word. 'How did you find him, Hughie? Did you get this address from my secretary?'

'No, no. From Alison, my wife. But how did your secretary get it?' After Treasure briefly explained, McFee did the same: 'It happened Alison was in this building this afternoon. On a private visit. Total coincidence. She thought she saw Dermot's car parked in the basement. She told me as much when I got home. It was the number she remembered. Dermot and I took delivery of nearly identical cars on the same day last year. From the company dealer. The colours were the same. The registration numbers nearly so. All except for one digit. I told Alison she was most likely mistaken, but I had to check, you understand? There was no alternative.'

'And it was his car?' said Closter-Bennet.

'No question. Parked in the bay belonging to this flat. I thought of calling the police, but that would have been letting the cat out of the bag. With only a day or so before the SAE had promised to release the man, bringing in the police might have been unwise. Anyway, that's what I decided.' He gave a determined sniff. 'So in the end I came up here alone.'

'That could have been very dangerous,' Closter-Bennet put in. 'You should have rung one of us first.'

'And taken a worse risk if the line was tapped? I mean, we still don't know where we stand with these people. Whether their intelligence is as good as they said it was. If they'd found out we

133

knew their hideout they could have done anything. Lain in wait for us to come. Skipped with Dermot— '

'Or left him dead,' Molly interrupted with a shudder.

'Right. So I decided to play the innocent. See what happened when I rang the bell. Nothing did, so I went in search of the caretaker. A woman I met in the lift told me where I could find him. In a flat in the next block. I told him a friend of mine was staying in here and hadn't answered the phone for two days. That he'd missed a dinner date with me. I said my wife and I were worried about him. The man came over with a key. Reluctantly. Dermot was lying in there on the floor.'

Treasure looked about the quite large square hall which also served as a dining-room. There was an open door to the right into a kitchen. Opposite, on the left, was a lighted corridor with two doors leading off it. On the far side of the hall, across from the front door, was the double door into the living room that Furlong had just closed behind him.

The hall was furnished with reproduction pieces of middling quality. There was a sideboard and a linen chest in the Regency manner, with a circular inlaid table in the centre and four up-holstered Chippendale-style chairs around it, with two more set against the walls. But everything was starkly new, like the blue Wilton carpet that was still shedding fluff. It was a credit to the designer that with colourful modern prints on the white painted walls, some pretty lamps, and a liberal scatter of glass and china ornaments the place had been given an air of reasonable quality, if not exactly a lived-in look. Broadly the banker supposed that the steep rents quoted to Miss Gaunt for this and the other five flats would find some takers, though he wouldn't have expected a queue.

'Did it seem to you that Dermot was being kept prisoner here?' he asked McFee. 'I mean, was he bound or gagged? Were there signs of a struggle?'

'None at all. He was in a dressing gown. Just a dressing gown. His other clothes were in the bigger of the two bedrooms. That's the first door along this corridor. Not many clothes. Just what he'd been wearing, I suppose, and whatever he must have had in an overnight case.' He glanced at Molly, then away again to Treasure. 'The bed's in a turmoil. Pillows and bedclothes all over the place.'

'You don't imagine he'd just got up?' asked Molly.

McFee shrugged. 'He might have done. And been on his way back from taking a bath. Then collapsed.'

'In the living room,' said Treasure, only half questioning.

'Were there signs that *any* other people had been here?' asked Closter-Bennet.

'Difficult to say.' McFee had already decided to leave it to others to answer the last question – to determine whether more than one person had been in that bed, for instance. Nor was he volunteering why his wife had gone to the basement in the first place – and neither would she: they'd agreed that killing time was to be her excuse, if she was pressed. 'While we were waiting for the ambulance and police to get here, the caretaker and I had a quick look round. Very quick. The second bedroom looks as if it's never been used. It's laid out like the Ideal Homes Exhibition. That almost goes for the living room and kitchen too, except they're not quite so band-box.' He paused, hands thrust into the side pockets of his jacket, his feet set well apart in a characteristic stance, shoulders well back. His expression was solemn – while he remembered all those soiled towels in Hackle's bathroom. 'I didn't really take in the master bathroom. Bit of a jumble in there.' He was hedging again. 'Dermot's portable phone is in the living room, by the way. Battery's quite flat. Would be if it hasn't been charged since Sunday, of course.'

'Kitchen's fairly tidy,' confirmed Molly who had moved to stand in the doorway. 'Is there food in that fridge?'

'Plenty. According to the caretaker, the place was officially let for the very first time last Sunday, with food supplied as— '

'Let to whom?' Treasure cut in sharply.

McFee shook his head. 'He didn't know. The letting agents rang him on Friday, just to tell him there'd be someone here. He didn't pay much heed. You see, he's not the caretaker in the strict sense. A keyholder, that's all. For the six flats this company owns in the building. Three of the others are on this floor, by the way, and they're all empty just now. The company pays him a small retainer, that's all.'

'So he's not involved in servicing the flats?' said Molly.

'That's right. Nor his wife either. They wanted to be, he told me. They work where they live, in the bigger block next door. Nothing to do with this one which doesn't have a resident caretaker. They had time available. But the servicing of the six flats went to a specialist contractor.'

'Who wouldn't have been here since Saturday,' observed Treasure.

'How d'you know that?' asked his wife.

'The letting agent told Miss Gaunt the occupied flats are cleaned and serviced every Saturday.'

'So if the SAE intended using this place from Sunday till Friday they needn't have been seen by anyone?'

'But they'd have had to pick up a key from someone at least,' said Closter-Bennet. 'From the next door caretaker?'

'No. Normally from the letting agents. That's an estate agency along the road in Hammersmith,' Treasure supplied. 'I think we'll find Miss Greet did that, also that her company were the paid-up tenants for the week. So it seems they'd arranged the perfect hideout for the period.'

'Which was to end Friday. When they promised to release Dermot.' This was Closter-Bennet.

'Except the poor man died on them,' said Molly, with a sigh.

'But if Dermot was kept here against his will, why is there no sign of his . . . his jailors?' Closter-Bennet asked.

'That's a good question, sir,' said Detective Inspector Furlong who had just re-emerged from the sitting room, leaving the door ajar behind him. Treasure could see a number of figures through the opening, some in uniform, as the policeman continued: 'There's no sign of restraint on the body, and none of foul play either. Not in the living room, anyway. We'll be going over the rest of the flat shortly.'

'There was no physical injury at all?' This was Treasure.

'There's a small scratch on the back of the deceased's neck that could be significant, sir. They'll check that out at the autopsy. But at the moment the doctor still reckons on a straight case of heart failure. Anyone know what sort of age he was?'

'He was thirty-six,' said Closter-Bennet.

'Any history of heart disease?'

'Don't believe so.'

'But he was approaching the age for that, of course,' said McFee dourly. 'And he did lead a very stressful life.'

'We'll be taking the body to the hospital mortuary now,' said Furlong. He turned to Treasure. 'Mr McFee has explained it was a kidnap with a twist, sir. No ransom. But your directors had to sell their shares. And no one informed the police.' He looked hurt at that, as if he was about to deliver the obvious homily,

136

but Treasure's stare deterred him. 'The villains are assumed to be members of a group called Stop Animal Experiments.' He went on, looking down at the notebook in his hand. 'Krontag, the big Swiss company, being the only beneficiaries from the crime so far?'

'The grounds for that conclusion are circumstantial, Inspector. Also highly conjectural,' observed the banker pointedly. He was sorry that McFee had been so forthcoming. 'I don't believe anyone will be accusing Krontag of involvement in the kidnap. Not if they're wise, anyway. Nor in Dermot Hackle's death. Assuming it should turn out to be something more sinister than a heart attack.'

'Point taken, sir. Don't want to tread on any toes without reason. Not at this stage.' The policeman's shoulders were now moving backwards and forwards at an enthusiastic pace. 'So in your view Krontag won't be liable for anything that happened here?'

'Not knowingly, Inspector. I think you can count on that. International drug companies do a lot to stay competitive, but that doesn't involve crimes against the person. That's strictly for TV fiction. The SAE wouldn't have altered anything either. Although Krontag is the only apparent gainer over the share dealing, I think we'll find the relationship between them and the SAE was always intended to be what in chemistry they call a casual one.'

'You said the SAE *wouldn't* have altered anything, sir?'

'Yes. If it had actually existed. Except it never did. If we can find out who was responsible for the kidnap, we'll know who conned us into believing in the SAE. Krontag want to know that too.'

'Bit complicated, sir.'

'Yes, Inspector.'

And so far as the police were concerned, Treasure hoped it would stay that way for a little while yet.

Chapter Sixteen

'Proper turn-up it was,' said Bert Tanner, yawning loudly as he shuffled naked across the carpet, pulled back the sheet and got into the bed. It was eight fifteen on Thursday morning.

Bert was in urgent need of sleep, and feeling his age. Even the sight of Doris hooking up the new lacy black bra that matched her skimpy panties was quite failing to interest let alone arouse him.

Doris had been downstairs, dressed in a négligé, having breakfast when her husband had arrived home. He had been later than expected. She had warned him already that she was going to be late for the office. But she needn't have been concerned about his delaying her with amorous demands. He really preferred lovemaking first thing, and so far as Bert's body clock was concerned, this was the middle of the night. He'd scarcely had the energy to kiss her, let alone attempt anything bolder.

'From when I clocked on,' he recounted, his voice slurred, eyes half closed. 'From the first minute, it was nonstop. Not a break all shift.' He yawned loudly. 'Tell a lie. There was a lull around three. Short one. Rest of the time you'd have thought all Chiswick was one bloody great gas leak. Whole area about to blow up.' He leaned heavily on one elbow while rearranging his pillows.

'Real leaks were they, then?' She was wriggling into her dress.

'No. Equipment faults mostly.' He watched her, not so much dispassionately as resigned to inaction. 'The punters say there's leaks so you get there in a hurry. Emergency service. Don't fool nobody though.'

'That's dishonest. To say there's a leak if there isn't. Could be dangerous too. I mean if there's a real leak somewhere and no one left to go to it.'

'Yeah.' Bert yawned again. He wasn't affronted by the wiles of British Gas customers, just inured to them. 'Four hours' overtime, though, altogether. Really short-handed, the Chiswick depot.' The overtime was the compensation. He didn't earn as much as Doris when he worked normal hours. It was the overtime that levelled things. He smacked his lips as he watched her close the wardrobe.

The noise made her think he was changing his mind about getting her into bed. 'I can't— ' she began.

'Did I say who I saw?' he interrupted without realising it. 'From your office?' His eyes, nose and lips were tightly crunched together as he did a memory dredge. 'What's that director's name?'

'Mr Larden?'

'No.' He sighed, scratched his left crutch, and wished he hadn't started telling her. 'No,' he repeated. It seemed he had given up the effort of explaining further, until he said hoarsely: 'It was the one I did the installing job for. Heaters in stables. For cash. In the country. Village outside Maidenhead.'

'You mean Closter-Bennet?' She had moved to the dressing table to make up her face.

'Expect so.' His eyes were closed again, then they opened briefly. 'Yeah. I remember now. Same name as the company. They're the ones with all the money, you said.'

'That's right.'

He took a long breath through his nose, swallowed, then cleared his throat, making a noise like an overcharged blow-lamp.

'Bert, give over,' his wife exclaimed.

He made a sighing noise instead. 'In a Chiswick cut-price super-market, anyway. Half six on a Wednesday night. Not in the Closter-Bennet style. Slumming. That's what I thought,' he said.

'People shop around these days. After something special per-haps.' Or more like Mr Closter-Bennet had forgotten something his wife had told him to pick up, she thought, so he'd had to find a late shopping store: Chiswick was a bit out of the way for him of course. Perhaps he'd been to London. They said Mrs Closter-Bennet was a tartar at home, though she'd always been pleasant enough to Doris when they'd met. 'Anyway, Chiswick's not slumming,' Doris said aloud. 'Look at the cost of houses there. Mr Larden's wife is always decorating places in Chiswick. She's an interior designer. Often gets work there. He told me. Chiswick or Wapping. That's the other place that's come on.' She widened her lips at the mirror as she applied her lipstick. 'Mr Larden doesn't like her going to Wapping though. I can tell. Too far. The other side of London. Keeps her away from home too long, I expect. Of course, it used to be a terrible area, Wapping.'

139

She looked around as his broken breathing turned into heavy snoring.

'Watch it, Doris Tanner,' she said to herself. 'Your man's gone to sleep on you. Poor lamb.'

It wasn't until later that she was made to wonder more seriously what Giles Closter-Bennet could have been doing in Chiswick the night before.

It was nearly eight o'clock in the evening of the same day when Mark Treasure, showered, and changed into casual clothes, joined his wife for drinks before dinner in the first-floor drawing room of their house in Cheyne Walk. They had intended to be outside in the garden but the temperature had dropped unexpectedly and a chill wind was blowing.

'I went to Ealing to see Rosemary Hackle this afternoon,' said Molly from an armchair near the fireplace, closing the book on her lap. She had been on the telephone when the banker had got home, then, later, in the kitchen preparing their meal. This was their first chance to talk since breakfast. 'Rosemary's taking it all very well. Mary Ricini was there. She actually seemed more affected than Rosemary.'

'Tearful, you mean?' Treasure was pouring himself a whisky at the trolley near the door.

'Numb. She was going through the motions of being a help to Rosemary, but at moments it seemed to me the rôles were reversed.' Molly picked up her unsweetened tonic water laced with a token amount of gin. The drink still seemed raffish after a week on lemon juice. 'They went together to identify the body this morning. I don't know who was supporting whom then.'

'D'you suppose Mary was still emotionally involved with Dermot?'

'Of course she was. You could see that the night she came here. After the Savoy dinner. She hadn't come just to be bitchy about Jane Larden.'

'Surely she came to tell us that Dermot was making a play for Jane? That was after a lot of heart searching, as she said. She knew a liaison between those two could wreck Dermot's relations with Bob Larden, and with it the future of the company. I remember her words quite clearly. Bit ingenuous to think I could do anything about it, of course. She came here on impulse. Probably regretted it later. But I think her motives were right. Responsible too.'

140

'Nonsense,' said Molly. 'She admitted she and Dermot had just had an affair. She was obviously hoping you'd talk Dermot into letting Jane alone.'

'So he'd go back to his wife. His long-suffering wife. Mary made it plain enough it was because of Rosemary she'd broken with Dermot herself.'

'Also nonsense. I'm sure he broke with her. Mary simply wanted to get him back.'

'I think you're being uncharitable.'

'No, darling, just realistic.'

He came over with his drink, taking the chair opposite Molly, on the other side of the fireplace. 'I gather Mary really has been a pillar of strength to Rosemary and the children since Monday morning.'

'That's conscience probably. As for her theory about Jane, thinking back, it was perfectly obvious at dinner that night that it was Jane who was making off with Dermot, not the other way around. And that she must have been at it for some time before. I remember feeling vexed that Jane had been telling me the week before how attractive Dermot was to all the women at Closter. I wonder any of them got a look in with Jane on the prowl.'

Treasure stretched his long legs in front of him, crossing them at the ankles. 'I must live a very sheltered life,' he said, eyeing his shoes blankly.

'Just busy, I expect, darling. With no time for trivia,' said Molly tolerantly, before taking another sip of her drink. 'So tell me about today. Were you at the Closter factory?'

'No. At the Stock Exchange most of the time. Dealings in Closter shares have been suspended till Monday. Meantime, all transactions since last Tuesday are to be scrutinised.'

'That was quick.'

'Needed to be. On balance, this part of the business is another tragedy. Sort of episode that hangs over a company for ever. But it's unavoidable. The Stock Exchange Council and the Securities and Investments Board both accepted our evidence that the directors's shares were sold under duress.'

'So will all those sales be cancelled?'

'Yes. On the request of any seller. Any sale that was made at below a hundred and twenty-five pence a share.'

'That's Krontag's bid price?'

He nodded.

'But what about the people who *bought* Closter shares?'

'Their deals will be cancelled.'

'So can they buy again at the Krontag bid price?'

'A[.] the market price on Monday morning. That's likely to be a lot higher than a hundred and twenty-five pence. Effectively, of course, there was only one buyer this week.'

'Krontag?'

'Yes.'

'But other people besides Closter directors sold shares in a panic, too.'

'They can all have the sales cancelled. It'll be on the TV news tonight, probably. In the papers tomorrow, certainly. Krontag have turned Queen's Evidence, as it were. Through their London bankers. They've shopped Lybred and Greet in the process. Krontag have disclaimed all knowledge of the kidnap, and that's being presented as fact in the news announcement.'

'Will the disclaimer do for the police too?'

'Depends on whether the Fraud Squad decides to investigate. It's their pidgeon, not the ordinary CID's.'

'Even with Dermot dying?'

'Yes. Assuming it was a natural death. And nobody's suggested otherwise. The Fraud Squad probably won't be interested. Too busy with more complex things. It's an open and shut sort of case, with all financial losses about to be made good. Criminal proceedings against Lybred and Greet would involve complicated extraditions. Helga Greet is still in a coma. Her American partner Lybred can't be found. Skipped probably.' He waved a hand dismissively. 'Much better to forget the whole thing.'

'Better for Closter?'

'Especially for Closter.' He paused. 'And in view of the dead Dermot's somewhat enigmatic rôle.'

'Why enigmatic?'

'Because it's not clear if he was co-operating with the kidnappers. I think he must have been, but it's only a theory. He could have been bought over by them. After they took him.'

'You mean he wasn't a real prisoner in that flat? How d'you know that?'

'I don't. It's pure speculation, but it bothers me, along with a few other unfounded possibilities. But since they don't bother anyone else, much better to ignore them.' He took a handful of cashew nuts from a dish on a side table. 'In a sense it's a pity there's still life in the takeover. Krontag are surrendering claim to all the shares they've bought, except for their original holding. But they still want to take over Closter. That will almost certainly mean they'll have to increase their offer price.'

'Is that good or bad?'

'Depends on the price. And the attitude of a majority of the shareholders, of course. The Chairman of the Stock Exchange believes the Secretary of State was intending to refer the bid to the Monopolies Commission anyway. That's what he told me this evening.'

'Will that stop the bid?'

'It'll delay it certainly. For about six months. And stop it if the Monopolies Commission turns it down. That was always a possibility, of course.'

'Because Closter is a little company that needs protecting from Big Brother?'

Treasure chuckled. 'Not quite, but it's a nice thought. No. The Monopolies Commission would simply have to decide whether Krontag owning Closter would unduly increase Krontag's power to control a market. Krontag already have a large piece of the painkiller market, and that's also where Closter are strongest – and will be stronger still if Seromig succeeds. I'm anxious to have Stuart Bodlin's opinion on that one. Unfortunately he's gone missing. Since around four yesterday afternoon.'

'Disappeared?'

'Mmm. Nothing so unusual for Bodlin apparently, and nothing to get alarmed about either. Still, it's highly inconvenient after what's happened. Anyway, we need his input on the monopoly matter.'

'Is the Government bothered because Krontag is a foreign company?' Molly asked, just as there was a long ring on the front door bell.

'I'll get it,' said Treasure, heaving himself out of the chair. 'Funny time to call, whoever it is,' he complained as he left the room.

When he returned, Detective Inspector Furlong was with him.

'Sorry to disturb you, Mrs Treasure,' said the policeman.

'Not at all. Nice surprise,' Molly smiled. 'You look as if you might be thirsty. Sit down and join the drinking.'

'Thank you. A tonic water would be fine. Very kind.'

'Ice, Inspector?' asked Treasure from the trolley.

'Yes, thanks very much.' Furlong sat on the sofa close to Molly's chair – carefully, on the edge, and without leaning back to disturb the cushions. 'I'll try not to keep you too long.' His whole trunk had gone through a sharp forward and backward movement on the last words.

'So there's been a development over Hackle's death?' The banker put the glass and a dish of nuts on a table beside the other man.

'Several developments, as a matter of fact, sir. Mr Hackle died of drug poisoning. From ingesting a minute quantity of a veterinary anaesthetic made by Closter. It's called . . . er— ' Furlong was pulling out a notebook.

'Bovetormaz, I suppose,' Treasure supplied unexpectedly, spreading out the syllables. 'Poor chap. How simply awful. It's an injection. Used on farms and in zoos. For operations on large animals. It's lethal in humans. Even in the smallest quantity. I've never really understood how anything so dangerous is allowed at all.'

'Normally it's only used by vets, sir.'

'I know. Always with an antidote handy. And someone else to inject it, in case of accident. You still wouldn't catch me near any of it.' He moved back to his chair. 'Closter make the antidote too.'

'The cause of death wasn't clear till the post mortem. The indications were exactly like a cardiac arrest.'

'He was injected with the stuff?'

'No, sir. Scratched with something. Probably a hypodermic needle, with enough of the drug on it to kill him. But it wasn't a proper injection.'

'The scratch on the back of his neck that the doctor noticed?'

'That was it, Mrs Treasure.' Furlong rapidly pushed a hand through his curly fair hair. Then he did it again.

'Could he have done it himself?' Treasure asked.

'Not likely. Not in view of the position for a start. And we haven't found the needle. If he'd done it himself, accidentally or otherwise, the needle or whatever he'd used would have been near the body, or in the room at least.'

'Did he die immediately?'

'About thirty seconds after the scratch. Oh, and the time of death is estimated as between six forty and seven twenty.'

'So now you're treating it as— '

'Suspected murder, I'm afraid, sir. I rang you at your office earlier this evening but you'd just left. Mr Closter-Bennet wasn't in either.'

'Could Dermot have got hold of some Bova-whatever-it-is?' asked Molly.

'Yes, I suppose. Not that easily, though,' her husband replied. 'Closter directors must have access to the company products. For legitimate reasons. But I don't believe this stuff would be issued without stringent precautions.'

'The high-ups in most companies usually know how to get round regulations of that kind, sir. And it's not necessarily Mr Hackle who did the purloining in this instance, of course.'

Treasure debated for a moment. 'Unless he had some in a sample case. He was on a marketing trip after all. What if he'd had it hidden? Was about to use it on his captors and . . . and the strategy went wrong?'

'We've thought of that, sir. Bit fanciful. There was no sample case. No sign of a struggle— '

'The SAE of course,' Molly interrupted suddenly. 'Whether or not it exists as a proper group, wouldn't anyone involved in animal rights be involved with vets too? Might even be a vet?'

'That's possible, Mrs Treasure. Except' – he paused – 'the other important thing I have to tell you is Helga Greet regained consciousness at noon today. She was normal enough to be interviewed after the first hour. I've spoken twice to the Swiss police officer who's liaising with us. When they told her about Mr Hackle's death, Miss Greet confessed to a lot of things.'

'To the murder?' demanded Treasure.

'No. The opposite. She's scared stiff. Says the SAE was a stage army. Recruited by her for a demonstration in London, at the direction of Mr Hackle. Part of a plan he cooked up. He also leaked information to the *Evening Standard* ahead of a news conference.'

'We wondered who'd done that,' said Treasure.

'She says it was to make the demo there more credible. If that makes sense, sir?'

'It does, yes.'

'Anyway, she insists there was no real kidnap. That was also staged by Mr Hackle. The Irishman on the telephone was him all the time. Seems he was good at imitating accents.'

'Very good,' put in Molly.

'Hackle and Greet were setting up the situation that would get Closter Drug on the cheap for Krontag. Mr Hackle stood to

145

benefit to the tune of a million pounds if it worked. On a sort of commission paid by her company, Lybred and Greet. She swears the Krontag people weren't party to the plot.'

'Astute of her to swear to that,' said Treasure. 'If it were suggested they were party to it, there'd be criminal proceedings against them in Switzerland involving her as well as them. As it is, any court action looks like being in England. Extraditing her to this country might present difficulties.'

'Surely you can extradite easily for murder?' Molly questioned.

'Extradition's never easy, Mrs Treasure.' Furlong spoke feelingly, as though he had tried it and failed.

'And do you believe Miss Greet's story, Inspector?' asked Treasure.

The policeman rocked forwards and backwards making a pained face. 'Too pat, you mean, sir? Too easy to invent now Mr Hackle's dead? We hadn't bought it. Except' – he hesitated, glanced at Molly, then cleared his throat – 'we have other reasons for believing Mr Hackle wasn't exactly a prisoner.' He cleared his throat again. 'The pathologist's report says he'd had sexual intercourse with a woman shortly before he died.'

'That won't surprise too many people,' said Molly promptly, before an awkward silence could develop.

'I see,' said Furlong, though his expression suggested he might not have done. 'Has Mr Larden been in touch with you in the last hour, sir?'

'No. He was with me till around four. At a meeting at the Stock Exchange. He was called away from that.'

'I think it was his wife who called him. Two woman detectives interviewed Mrs Larden at her home around three thirty. She'd been in bed all day. Poorly. We needed to ask her to confirm or deny another part of Miss Greet's sworn testimony.'

'Involving Mr or Mrs Larden?'

'Mrs Larden, sir. Miss Greet alleged that Mrs Larden was Mr Hackle's local accomplice over the fake kidnap. That she suggested the flat as the hideout, and visited Mr Hackle there every day since Sunday, supplying him with food and er . . . and other things.'

'I find that difficult to credit,' said Molly quickly, in a tone more reactive than convinced. Her husband remained silent.

'Miss Greet said Mrs Larden had just finished decorating the flat for the owners,' the policeman went on. 'She knew it'd be available, and free of interference. Miss Greet made the reservation and picked up the key. That was on Sunday, she said. Later that day, she handed the key over to Mr Hackle.'

'What has Jane Larden said to all this, Inspector?' asked Treasure.

'At first she denied it, sir.'

'Had she been told how Hackle died?'

'She was told at the end of the interview. She still stuck to her denial, but later she called her husband. An hour ago, she came to Chiswick police station with her husband and their solicitor. She then made a voluntary statement.'

'Did that confirm Miss Greet's allegations?'

'It did, yes. Mrs Larden went further. She admitted she'd been with Mr Hackle yesterday from four thirty to six. When she left him he was alive and well. She said they were lovers. That the plot was to make it financially feasible for her to leave her husband for Mr Hackle.'

'Astonishing,' said Molly.

'Where's Mrs Larden now?' asked Treasure, in an overcasual tone.

'At home, I expect.' Furlong looked from one to the other. 'We haven't detained her, if that's what you meant. She mentioned you telephoned her yesterday evening, Mrs Treasure?'

'Yes. About some curtaining.'

'Do you remember the time of the call? It could be important.'

'I can see that.' Molly thought for a moment. 'It was straight after the radio news bulletin. The short one at seven. Must have been five past seven.'

'Thank you.' The policeman ticked something in his notebook.

'I called her at home. So she could hardly have been in Chiswick at six forty.'

'As a matter of fact she could have, Mrs Treasure,' said the policeman. 'But probably not after five to seven. The drive from Mereworth Court to her house can be done in five to ten minutes. Depending on traffic. The time of death is only approximate, of course.'

'Another drink, Inspector?'

'No thank you, sir. I'd better be going.'

'But not until you've told us why you came.' Treasure gave a shrewd smile. 'I mean, you haven't divulged all this fascinating information simply for our edification? Or as a trade for what my wife just told you, and which you probably expected.'

'Well there is one other thing, sir.' The hand went twice through his hair again, this time even more rapidly. 'You see, Mrs Larden also said Mr Hackle told her you knew about an arrangement to bring down the price of Closter shares last Tuesday. So that Krontag could buy the company. He said you'd arranged to be well away in America for that reason.'

'Indeed?' Treasure responded, poker-faced. 'Then I can only say, Inspector, that if you or Mrs Larden believe that, you'll believe anything.'

Chapter Seventeen

'So you think he told Jane you were involved just to make it all sound more . . . I don't know, respectable, perhaps?' Molly asked her husband.

'Respectable's a bit fanciful, but yes, I think that's possible. If he really did tell her such a brazen lie. If she didn't just make it up herself.' Treasure spooned into the depths of the orange Antiguan melon with more vigour than was necessary. The calumny was irritating deeply.

The Detective Inspector had left half an hour before. The Treasures were in the kitchen, finishing the informal dinner Molly had set out there earlier. They were at the round table in the window, with its cushioned banquette that seated two people in comfort and up to four with a squeeze.

'But why would Jane invent such a terrible thing to say?'

'Because she could be trying to make the kidnap and swindle seem more of a – let's say, a group activity.'

'In contrast to her affair with Dermot?' said Molly acidly. Then she shook her head. 'Even so, I still can't believe it was Jane on her own. Dermot *must* have told her.'

'But why did Bob let her repeat such a thing to the police?'

'He didn't know she was going to. In advance, I mean. The Inspector said it surprised Bob and the lawyer.'

'I must have missed that.' He spooned out some more of the melon, looking a little less disgruntled.

'And if Dermot really did pretend to her that you were party to bringing down the share price, didn't she have to admit it? Wouldn't she have been sort of on oath?'

Treasure pulled a face. 'In a manner of speaking, yes. But since the man's dead, it'll now be his word against mine for the rest of time.'

'No it won't be. You're dramatising.' Molly stretched a hand across the table to one of his. 'The Inspector obviously believed you.'

'Policemen work on hard evidence not blind faith. Furlong is deeper than he looks. Probably why he's so young for his rank.'

'No one's going to believe you were part of a swindle. And why should you have gone to Zürich like that if you had been? Forcing Krontag to own up. Exposing Helga Greet?'

'What if Hackle told Helga Greet the same lie as he told Jane Larden?' He frowned over this new awful possibility.

'Well he didn't. Because if he had she'd have told the Zürich police. When she was confessing all. Trying to excuse herself.'

'That's probably true.'

'I'm sure it is.' Molly smoothed an eyebrow. 'You know, I still can't help feeling dreadfully sorry for Bob Larden. To be done out of the company and his wife by his trusted lieutenant.'

Treasure looked at the time. 'I'll ring him again when we've finished.' He had called the Fulham number twice before they had started eating. There had been no reply, and the answering machine hadn't been switched on. 'Apart from Jane's bombshell about me, I must talk to Bob about the murder tonight.' His hand went out to his wine glass. 'I just hope Jane didn't do it.'

'You don't seriously think she could have?'

Treasure shrugged. 'She knew where he was. She admits being with him up to six. In terms of timing she had the opportunity, obviously.'

'But why would she— '

'Who knows? They could have quarrelled. They would both have been on edge. Perhaps Dermot had just been using her. Once he thought his million pounds was safe he could have told her he was dropping her for one of his other women. He might even have relented about taking her away from Bob.'

'Could she have got hold of the knock-out drug?'

'The Bovetormaz? Yes. Or at least she'd have had similar opportunities to everybody else to nick some.'

'Not such good opportunities as a Closter director?'

'Probably not. But Bob may keep samples of products at home.'

'Of lethal drugs?'

'Most drugs are lethal. Taken in large enough quantities,' he answered pedantically. 'But yes, I agree, it's unlikely he'd have had any of that one lying about. Maybe Dermot really did have some with him.'

150

'Well I don't believe Jane killed him,' said Molly flatly. 'Why couldn't it have been one of Helga Greet's lot? They knew where he was, too.'

'Getting rid of him to save on his million pound bonus? The police may want to think so. I believe members of the Greet brigade would have felt too vulnerable to have risked it.'

'The Inspector said Bob was standing by Jane.' Molly looked irritated as the doorbell sounded again as she stopped speaking. 'Oh no. Now who can that be?'

Treasure found Stuart Bodlin at the door – with a day's growth of beard which gave his normally pallid, sunken countenance a sinister dimension. He was dressed in a faded red T-shirt, jeans, and white sneakers.

'On the drive up I knew there was nowhere else I should go. No one else I should speak to. You understand? I'm sorry. It's urgent,' Bodlin was saying as Treasure showed him through to the kitchen.

The visitor seemed to be in a kind of daze, his voice devoid of expression. The excuse for his presence was probably meant to cover his appearance too. He stood irresolute in the centre of the kitchen, the legs of the shrunken jeans revealing that he was wearing odd socks – one dark blue, the other a patterned red. Wordlessly, he had acknowledged Molly with a dejected sort of bow.

'Do sit down, Stuart.' She moved up a little and patted the end of the banquette beside her. 'Would you like something to eat?'

He sat. 'Nothing, thank you.'

'Some coffee, perhaps? We were just reaching that stage,' said Treasure returning to the table himself. He had brought an extra coffee cup. 'We all wondered what had happened to you. No one at the factory knew where you were.' There was a touch of admonition in the voice.

'At a friend's cottage. In Dorset. I often go there at weekends. Or when I need to think.' If the need for thought wasn't sufficient to explain a day's absence from his laboratory, no other was being offered. 'The news on the radio at six said Dermot Hackle died of a heart attack. In the flat where he was held by kidnappers. As soon as I heard, I got in the car and drove up straight away.' The speaker's head was bent so low that he seemed to be addressing his feet beneath the table. Molly wondered if he would notice the socks. He had earlier taken off his spectacles.

'We were both at that flat shortly after Hughie McFee found the body,' said Treasure.

Bodlin's gaze came up. 'Hughie found him? They didn't say that. And both of you were there.' The last was a comment not a question. 'You must understand. There was no kidnap. That was a sham.' He looked down again, kneading his hands together.

Molly opened her mouth to say something, but was stayed by a glance from her husband as the scientist continued.

'You see, I was at Bob Larden's house yesterday. In the afternoon. After the meeting with Professor Garside. Something I heard then. When I was making a phone call. In the study. It seemed impossible. I didn't know what to do. Not till I knew Hackle was dead.' He drew in his breath sharply.

'What was it you heard?' asked Treasure.

'The tape of a phone conversation. Jane Larden talking to Hackle. Bob was having everything recorded. We'd all agreed to do that. In case the SAE called us at home. His wife couldn't have known it. Or she'd forgotten. Or thought she'd switched off the machine. Most likely it was that. The ordinary answering tape wasn't on. It's a complicated mechanism. Well slightly.' The speaker's frown deepened, as he drew the front of his right wrist across his brow. 'She called Hackle at lunchtime yesterday. I mean she knew the number. Where he was. I wouldn't have heard the tape, except I didn't want my call recorded. It was personal. Very personal.' The last phrase came out defiantly, as if he was expecting it to be challenged. 'I was checking the machine. To make sure I'd switched it off. When I recognised the voices, I had to hear the rest.' His voice was now reduced almost to a whisper. 'It was compulsive. I'm not ashamed of what I did.'

'Did either of them say where Dermot was?' Treasure asked.

Bodlin shook his head. 'She said she'd be with him after four thirty.'

'Did she say where she was phoning from?'

'No.'

'Then he probably assumed it was from her car.'

'He said he couldn't wait to see her. And . . . and what a pity he'd be setting himself free on Friday. That they'd miss their afternoons together. Except soon they'd be together for ever.' Bodlin paused. 'It was a very intimate conversation.'

'And it shocked you?' said Molly.

152

'Not because they spoke as lovers. Because they were conspirators . . . who'd tricked everyone . . . robbed us all. I couldn't believe it. The depth of it. You understand? I didn't know what to do. How I should tell Bob. You'll think that's weak, I know. But I couldn't just come out with it. Not cold.' He looked appealingly from Treasure to Molly.

'I understand,' said Molly. 'It was a terrible dilemma for you. Please go on.'

'It was then I heard Bob's wife. She was downstairs. Speaking to him.' Bodlin's nervousness had made him nearly breathless, and might also have been the cause of his suddenly running out of words.

'So what did you do, Stuart?' This was Treasure, in a lively, encouraging tone, while wishing Bodlin would get on with it. Nor did the banker share his wife's view on the terrible dilemma. The man's duty had been obvious.

Bodlin swallowed painfully. 'I left. I don't know what they thought. I didn't care.'

'You hadn't erased what was on the tape?'

'No.'

'So Bob could have played it himself later?'

'I thought he was bound to.'

'You preferred that to happen? As opposed to telling him?'

'Yes.'

'And after that?'

'I sat in my car. Up the street. I was too upset to drive. I knew they should be exposed. Hackle and Jane Larden. I nearly went back. But in the end I couldn't do it. I remember thinking the damage was done anyway. Then, before I left— ' He stopped, covering his face with his hands. He took several deep breaths before resuming despondently with: 'Anyway, what does any of it matter now? He's dead. They said it was his heart.'

'He was murdered,' said Molly.

'Murdered?' The hands parted. The eyes stared out between them in stark surprise. 'Are you sure?'

'Poisoned by Bovetormaz. Around seven last night,' Treasure added.

'Who did it?' The murder method seemed not to have impressed itself on the speaker.

'We don't know. Jane Larden's been to the police to say she didn't. She's confessed the kidnap was a hoax. The Irishman on

153

the telephone was Dermot doing an impersonation. It explains why both voices on the tapes opened the lock to your lab. We figured that as an outside possibility last night, after we checked the tapes. At the time it still seemed too bizarre to credit.'

'Was the Bovetormaz injected?' asked Bodlin.

'No, Hackle was just scratched with it.' The banker leaned back. 'So you'd remained undecided about what to do. Left for the country to make up your mind? Or hoping Bob would play that tape for himself?'

'Hoping he'd play it, yes.' But there had been hesitation before the reply.

'Did you have other ideas before that?'

There was a long pause. 'I thought I'd like to kill Hackle,' the scientist almost whispered.

'Did you kill him?' Treasure's tone was as impassive as a psychoanalyst's.

'No. If I'd known where he was . . . ' The words petered out. 'No, I didn't kill him.'

'You knew Jane was going to him. You didn't wait and then follow her?'

'No. I went home. I'm alone there. My . . . my friend's away. After a while I didn't want to stay in London. So I drove to Dorset.'

'To keep out of the way till the truth was exposed?'

This time there was no response to the question. Bodlin's gaze had dropped again.

'Of course, you couldn't rely on Bob playing the tape. So who else had you told?'

'No one.'

Molly had looked as surprised as Bodlin at the question.

'You confided in no one before you left?' Treasure pressed. 'Not to someone who happened along while you were sitting in the car near the Lardens' house?'

Bodlin's head came up rapidly, almost as though it had been tugged from behind. He looked confused. Both hands went to rubbing his thighs. 'No . . . no one.' His forehead was beading with sweat. 'Look, I came to tell you the kidnap was a hoax. I didn't know you knew that. I didn't know Hackle had been murdered.' He pulled his glasses from his shirt pocket and put them on. Suddenly his actions had become sharper, the expression in the eyes guarded. 'So I've nothing new to tell anyone. I should

154

have stayed out of it.' He rose from the table. 'I'm sorry. Sorry I came here. Sorry I disturbed you. It was all a mistake. I can find my own way out. Please don't bother . . . ' He was still muttering apologies as he reached the doorway.

Molly was about to call him back. Her husband's raised hand discouraged her.

'Is he a bit mad?' Molly asked as they heard the front door slam. She got up to clear the table.

'Eccentric and quite brilliant. I've told you before, he loathed Dermot.'

'Enough to kill him?'

'With the right provocation.'

'He didn't know where Dermot was. He said so.'

Treasure gave a dismissive grunt. 'He only had to follow Jane.'

'A lot of people could have done that. Bob himself. Even Mary Ricini as a matter of fact.'

'Oh? Why Mary?'

'Something Rosemary Hackle said. When we were alone. It didn't seem important. Not until just now.' Molly opened the dish-washer. 'Tim, that's the Hackles' little boy, told his mother last night that he saw his father with a ginger-haired woman on Sunday afternoon. At Heathrow.'

'He told her this after they knew Dermot was dead?'

'Mmm. Up to then, Tim had promised not to tell her. Promised his sister and Mary. It was to save Rosemary's feelings.'

'Mary knew though?'

'Yes. He told her yesterday afternoon, just before Rosemary got home with the daughter. Mary left soon after to go back to the office. Said she wouldn't be long. But it was after seven when she got back. Rosemary told me all this when we were just making conversation. Rather difficult conversation in the circumstances. She was saying what a help Mary had been all week, in so many ways. That she must have had to neglect her important work.'

'Except she went to make up for it between five and seven yesterday?' Treasure considered the two melon skins before dropping them in the waste bin.

'On the face of it, yes. But what if Mary had really gone to confront Jane at her house then? About her being with Dermot? When he was supposed to have been on his way to Nottingham.'

'Mary might have got a flea in her ear if she'd done that.

155

Helga Greet was also what you might call ginger. When she was Kirsty Welling she wore a black wig. So it could have been Greet or Jane who was with Dermot. More likely Greet. She was certainly with him some time on Sunday to give him the flat key. Furlong said so. Perhaps Dermot drove her to the airport to catch a plane to Zürich?'

'Should the police be told what Tim saw?'

'Doesn't have much significance now where Dermot was on Sunday. Or who he was with.'

'Except it might have had for Mary when the little boy told her yesterday. I still think it could have sent her to Jane to demand an explanation. And she could have run into Stuart outside Jane's house, then followed Jane.'

'Could have,' he repeated, but sounding unconvinced.

'Mary wouldn't have had trouble getting some of the knock-out drug. She even had time to go to the factory for it.'

'You're building a lot on a slim hypothesis.'

'Darling, you're very protective towards Mary. I think it's because you rather fancy her.' Molly gave an indulgent smile.

'Expect so,' he replied, as though the comment had hardly rated one. 'All right. If Stuart didn't follow Jane and then murder Dermot. If the murder wasn't done by one of Helga Greet's people— '

'And you don't believe it was.'

'That's right. In that case it could have been Bob who followed her, after hearing the tape before or immediately after she left. Or it could have been Mary after talking to Stuart. Or someone else who talked to Stuart.'

'You seem sure Stuart told someone what he knew.'

Treasure picked up the wine bottle to see that it was empty. 'I'm convinced he did. Then washed his hands of the whole thing. Like Pontius Pilate.'

'She's numb about it, I tell you. As if she's not involved. Not remotely.' Bob Larden looked up from the pewter tankard he was holding and stared out across the river, except his gaze was empty. The Managing Director of Closter Drug was grey faced. He seemed to have aged a generation since Treasure had last seen him.

'Jane's had a bad shock,' said the banker, who was standing beside the other man.

'She and I both have.'

156

'You might say we all have.'

The two were on the otherwise empty terrace of The Doves, the old waterside pub at Hammersmith. They had arranged to meet there after talking on the telephone. Jane Larden's sister was keeping her company for an hour: Larden had been glad of the excuse to get away briefly.

There was now a distinct chill in the night air but both men were dressed against it. The temperature was also ensuring their privacy: other customers were staying in the warmth of the bar.

'The husband is always the last to know about a wife's infidelities,' Larden went on. 'I suppose that's true this time?'

'I believe there'd been some talk. Nothing concrete.'

'Some talk. Oh God.' Larden leaned heavily on the rail over the river. 'I believe I did know. When she made me sell the shares. To protect Dermot. But subconsciously I thought at least I was buying her loyalty.' He grunted. 'How blind can you be? When you're besotted by someone.'

'And you're standing by her.'

'You think that's weak? She's nearly ruined me. Cost me a fortune, anyway. And she was leaving me for him. Now she's made it impossible for me to go on running Closter. But yes, as you say, I'm standing by her. You know why? Because I'm getting her back. That devious bastard's dead. I'm not in competition for her. Not any more. And I love her. To distraction.'

Treasure shifted his feet. Confessions always made him uncomfortable. 'Dermot had a curious fascination for women. Jane wasn't the only one to succumb to a . . . to a temporary aberration.' He was aware that the claims were wooden, and the comfort slim. 'I doubt they'd have lasted together,' he completed.

'You think that too?' said Larden, with a pathetic eagerness.

'I don't believe she'd have worn the dependency Dermot seemed to look for in women. Maybe even her design work wouldn't have fitted. Incidentally, Molly says she's good at that. Very good.' It was pleasing to have some leavening to add to the conversation.

'She is, you know.' The words were just as eager as before. 'Molly's not the only one. You know Jane's just starting on the Closter-Bennets' house?' The two men exchanged glances to acknowledge what an achievement that was. 'Except Barbara's always breaking dates because of sick animals. She did that yesterday.' His face had clouded again. 'It wouldn't have changed anything if she hadn't, I suppose.'

157

'Probably not. You're hardly ruined, you know.' Treasure swirled the beer in his tankard. 'And you don't have to write off your job.'

'Although my wife was party to a criminal conspiracy to hand the company to Krontag?'

'Your position is embarrassing but not necessarily untenable. I'm certainly not looking for your resignation.'

'Thank you, Mark.'

'I'm thinking of what's best for the company and the shareholders. Whether or not the Monopolies Commission give a thumbs down on a Swiss takeover, I've a strong suspicion there'll now be a counter bid from somewhere else.'

'Britain or America?'

'One or the other, yes.'

'Because Dermot's death accentuates our vulnerability?'

'Precisely. In any event, I'd like to have you running the place still if we have more important choices thrust upon us.'

'You think it makes more sense now for us to be taken over?'

Treasure thought for a moment before replying. 'Depends a good deal on how we come out of the present impasse. Put baldly, it partly depends on who murdered Dermot.'

'They should arrest Helga Greet, of course.'

'Not so easy, in the circumstances. Nor to prove she was involved in the murder.'

'Who else could have done it? Her or one of her minions?' When his companion didn't comment Larden went on awkwardly: 'Jane had nothing to do with it.'

'Good.' Except he was less convinced than he pretended.

'It was her own idea to go to the police.'

'What Helga Greet said about her was fairly damning, I gather.'

'Jane could have denied all that.'

'With her fingerprints all over the flat? Of course, since she'd just decorated the place, I suppose she could have said— '

'We both thought she should tell the truth,' Larden interrupted.

'Very wise. Even though it included Hackle's extraordinary charge about my knowing there was a plan to bring down the price of Closter shares.'

Larden straightened. 'The police told you that? Jane knew it was nonsense, and said so. They got it out of her when they cautioned her about leaving nothing out of her statement. She hadn't mentioned it to me or the solicitor first. The police attached no credence to it. They accepted it was one of the things Hackle said to make Jane feel easier.'

'Did they? They still came to see me about it. And they certainly didn't mention Jane had said it was nonsense.'

'I'm sorry, Mark. If I'd realised they were facing you with it I'd have warned you. I'm sure they were only checking it out for the book.'

'And I'm sure I'll survive it.' Having it in perspective helped. 'Tell me, did you play back a recording of the phone conversation Jane and Dermot had at lunchtime yesterday?'

Larden took some moments before replying. 'Has Stuart Bodlin been in touch with you?'

'Yes.'

'I've been trying to reach him. He played that tape didn't he? That's why he left yesterday in such a hurry?'

'When did you play it, Bob?'

'Well after Jane had left. More than an hour after.' He paused. 'I didn't follow her. I had no reason to. Not at the time. And later I had no idea where she was.'

'Laurence Stricton was coming to see you at the house at six. You rang him at five thirty to delay the meeting. You said you weren't through with Professor Garside. That wasn't true was it?'

'No it wasn't. After I heard the tape, I had to see Jane. You must understand that? I hoped she might be back shortly.'

'Stricton insisted it was still important you saw him last night. You agreed to meet at his club at seven. Did Jane return before you left for that?'

'No she didn't. In the end I realised it was pointless waiting. She'd known Stricton was coming. I'd told her he and I would be going out to dinner. There was no reason why she had to come back. I tried dialling her carphone, but it was on the blink yesterday. Anyway, there was no answer.'

'And you stayed in the house from the time she left it till when?'

'Until I left to meet Stricton. That was around five to seven. I missed Jane by minutes. I swear I was home the whole time before that. You believe me don't you?'

'Yes.' Treasure stood up from where he had been leaning. 'Do the police?'

'They haven't asked.'

'I think they will.'

Chapter Eighteen

Stuart Bodlin merely stirred at the first ring of the doorbell. He came more awake at the second ring, fumbled for his spectacles, put them on, but still had difficulty focusing on the digital bedside clock.

It was 5.47 a.m. Bodlin sighed heavily, swung his naked body out of the double bed, then reached for his short silk robe. The robe had been a Christmas present from Julian – whom Bodlin had no doubt was now standing at the front door.

Thirty-four year old Julian was appearing with a touring company. It wasn't much of a part, but then he wasn't much of an actor, and it was good for his self-esteem to get anything. The company was playing in Coventry this week.

Julian must have decided to get up early and drive home, just for the day. He had called Bodlin the night before, anxious about him. Julian was totally unselfish – not like the other caller, the earlier one, who really only wanted to know whether Bodlin had let on to anyone about what had happened in Fulham on Wednesday afternoon. Both callers had known how upset Bodlin had been, but only Julian had been concerned simply to proffer comfort and support.

But Julian was oblivious of time. Dear Julian: he had probably tried to open the door with his key, realised that it was bolted as well as locked, then rung the bell as though it were already mid-morning.

Bodlin always shot the bolts at night when he was alone.

He padded on to the landing of the little mews house in Hammersmith. It was time he bought them something grander. He could well afford it. But he and Julian had been happy enough here. He took off his glasses and rubbed his eyes before making unsteady progress down the steep stairs. He was still not completely awake, after sleeping only fitfully all night. There was too much on his mind – and more, not less, since his visit to the Treasures.

When he reached the front door he drew the upper bolt, then, out of habit, squinted through the peep-hole.

It wasn't Julian. Bodlin's heart sank when he saw who it was – in the driving seat of the car, one arm through the open window, and not bothering to get out until there were signs that Bodlin was in. That was the worst of living in a mews. People could drive right up to your front door and ring the bell with a lot less effort than it took you to answer it. He drew the lower bolt, and wrapped the robe more closely around him. Then he opened the door wide.

'Its early enough— ' he began, dazzled by the early sunlight outside. But he never finished the sentence.

The driver lifted the shotgun into view and fired one barrel at Bodlin's head.

At point blank range the result was devastating.

'Are you always here this early, Mrs Tanner?' Treasure asked as she handed him the coffee cup. It was eight twenty.

'If required. It's no hardship. We live just down the road. Is that enough sugar?'

'Plenty, thanks. You always make excellent coffee.'

'Mr Larden can't stand instant.'

'Well it's worth the extra effort to have the real thing.' He sipped appreciatively, continuing to stand in the centre of her office.

'Wouldn't you like to sit in Mr Larden's office?'

'In a minute. When the others arrive.' He had something he wanted to ask her.

'I don't know what's happened to Mr Larden, I'm sure.' She went back to unnecessary fiddling with the coffee things on the wall table behind her desk. She was not at all at ease. Mr Treasure was Chairman after all, and a City bigwig. This was the first time she had ever had to entertain him alone – so why did it have to be on this of all mornings? Not that he wasn't charm itself: a proper gentleman, and dishy with it. She tried telling herself she ought to be flattered he wanted to stay in here. 'Mr Larden's usually ahead of the time he says. So much on his plate today, of course. Well, you all have. I thought the takeover business was bad enough. But with Mr Hackle being kidnapped and then dying on top. Well, I don't know at all. So young, too. He'll be missed. Terrible thing.' In truth, she hadn't been much affected by Hackle's death. Bert seemed to have been more moved than she was: men were funny. 'It was the strain on his heart, I expect. The kidnap could explain that. Devils, whoever they were. I never dreamed it was that. His being away, I mean. We all thought it was odd, of course.' She always talked too much when she was nervous, and she knew it. She smoothed the top of the flower print dress and wished the skirt was slightly longer – not, she thought, that how much thigh Doris Tanner was showing or not showing would signify to a bloke with a wife like this one's.

'Dreadful thing to have happened. Awful for his family,' said Treasure neutrally. The news that Hackle had been murdered had not yet been made public, but he was surprised that it hadn't reached Larden's private secretary. Even so, it suited his purpose that she should stay uninformed for the moment. 'Doctor Ricini's done a marvellous job supporting Mrs Hackle, I gather.'

'She would do.' And she hadn't done a bad one supporting Mr Hackle in her time and all, Doris concluded cynically.

'That reminds me, were Doctor Ricini or Mr McFee in the office after hours the night before last, d'you remember? At sevenish, say? I know you often work late yourself.'

She shook her head. 'Wednesday I can't help. I was off early. Mr Larden said I could go at half three. My hubby works nights, you know? Chance for us to see each other for once.' And a fine sight we got too, one way and another, she mused. 'Was there a special reason you wanted to know, Mr Treasure?'

'It's not important,' he lied. 'I rang both of them on their direct office numbers from Zürich airport. There was no reply. I just wondered if I'd got the numbers right.'

'And their secretaries didn't answer either? Well they'd have gone too by then, of course. Mr Larden wasn't here, I know that. That's why he let me go early.'

'Yes, he went straight home after a meeting in London with Professor Garside.'

'Doctor Bodlin was with him. Now I know the doctor meant to come back here after seeing the Professor, but he didn't. His secretary, Mrs Edwards, she waited till quite late. He forgot to ring her. And about not being in yesterday.' She made a reproving face while taking a file from her desk to a cabinet. 'Doctor Bodlin's a bit forgetful at times. Comes of being extra brainy I expect,' she completed with her back to him.

'So brainy people like us all to think.' He smiled, drank some more coffee, and registered that she had nice legs.

She turned about. 'I've just remembered something. Mrs Edwards told me Doctor Ricini *was* here after office hours on Wednesday. She came back around five. Unexpectedly. I don't know whether she was still here at seven.'

'I may have called earlier than that.'

'Her secretary had gone already. Mrs Edwards offered to do any work she needed but there wasn't any. Mr McFee's often here after the others, of course. Leaves about half-past six usually. To avoid the traffic. Except he lives close enough.' She paused, a forefinger resting daintily on two prominent front teeth. 'If you'd been asking about Mr Closter-Bennet, I could have told you where he was at half six.'

'Oh? Where was that?'

'In Chiswick High Street. My husband saw him. It was a proper coincidence. Bert's not there usually, and I don't suppose Mr Closter-Bennet is either. Come to think, it was somewhere in Chiswick they found Mr Hackle, wasn't it? I'm not sure where . . . Excuse me.' She picked up the ringing telephone from her desk. 'Good morning, Mr . . . Yes, he's with me now.' She handed the receiver to Treasure. 'It's Mr Larden for you.'

'Good morning, Bob.' He listened for a moment, then his eyebrows lifted in astonishment. 'Good God. Point blank? This is terrible. How did you . . . You're at the police station now?' He let the other man speak again, this time at length, only making grunted acknowledgements to what he was being told. 'Bob, I can't credit they'll be able to hold her,' he said eventually, then went on: 'My dear chap, is there anything I can do? . . . Of course you must stay with her. Your lawyer's there already? . . . Leave that to me. Ring me here with any developments.'

'Jane Larden was taken in for questioning an hour ago,' Treasure was explaining, fifteen minutes later, to the group gathered in Larden's office.

'They can't think she murdered Stuart, surely? You said that only happened at six?' This was Giles Closter-Bennet, unaware that the second question did nothing to confirm the veracity of the first.

Closter-Bennet, Mary Ricini and Hugh McFee were seated with Treasure at the long table. They were four out of the six Closter directors expected at the meeting summoned the day before for this time. They were still digesting the unwholesome news that one of their missing number had been shot dead, while the wife of the second was being interrogated by the police.

'She hasn't been formally arrested yet. But Bob believes they're about to charge her with killing Dermot Hackle,' Treasure continued.

'Stuff and nonsense,' said McFee, producing his pipe and tobacco pouch from his pockets with aggravated movements.

'And probably with shooting Stuart Bodlin,' the banker completed.

'Not both, surely?' demanded Closter-Bennet. 'I mean, what kind of evidence can they have? The idea's preposterous. I mean . . . Well isn't it?' He looked around at the others. The final question made his outrage less credible than the Scotsman's.

'The police arrived at the Lardens' with a search warrant at seven this morning,' said Treasure. 'They found an empty package of Bovetormaz in a rubbish bin in the garden.'

'If you turn over garbage, that's exactly what you get. More garbage,' said McFee flatly.

'It sounds as if it was an outer pack they found,' Mary put in. It was her first contribution since the meeting had started. She had arrived before the others, and Treasure had told her of Bodlin's death first. In the minutes since then she had been fighting to compose herself. So far she had stoically avoided tears, but the shock had been visibly greater for her than for the men. She had been fond of Bodlin and had worked closely with him for several years. 'It could have been a sample outer Bob had at the house. With specimen packs of other products,' she went on, her voice flat and unemotional.

'I have plenty of sample outers at home. Couldn't tell you where. Or for which products. They just accumulate,' volunteered McFee, filling his pipe. 'If Jane had done in Dermot with Bovetormaz, she'd hardly have left the packaging lying about the place. I'll bet anyone the pack they've found never had a Bovetormaz phial inside. Not ever. Is that what Bob's said?'

'Not exactly, but you could be right,' said Treasure. 'He told me the bin was full of very old rubbish. It's hardly ever emptied.'

'And how can they link Jane with what's happened to poor Stuart?' McFee demanded.

'The police discovered one of Bob's shotguns is missing from its case in his study. The case was unlocked for some reason he can't account for. He explained he lent the gun two days ago to a cousin who's on a shoot somewhere in Scotland. He doesn't know where, and neither does the cousin's wife.'

'Pity,' McFee murmured.

'I agree. But there it is,' said Treasure. 'No doubt the point can be proved when the cousin comes back. Or gets in touch.'

'We'd better try to find him ourselves.' This was McFee again, while making a note on the pad in front of him.

'There's more, I'm afraid. When the police got to the house this morning, Jane's car was outside. They checked and found the engine was warm. The car had been used.'

There was silence for a moment after Treasure stopped speaking.

'No doubt there's a perfectly sound explanation for that,' McFee commented firmly, striking a match.

'There was, according to Jane,' said the banker. 'She woke early, couldn't get to sleep again, got up without waking Bob, and drove the car to Queens Club, Hammersmith where she jogged in the grounds.'

'So she must have seen someone there?' Mary questioned.

'Not that she remembers. It was very early. Around five thirty.'

There was another awkward silence until Closter-Bennet said: 'I'm sure Stuart's death has nothing to do with Dermot's. It's much more likely to be the result of a— ' He paused, evidently embarrassed, then cleared his throat. 'Well we all know about Stuart's sexual propensities.' He wiped his chin with his hand.

'That he was gay?' asked Mary stonily, but louder than before.

'Yes. And that he had a lot of homosexual friends.'

'A lot?' queried Mary. 'I know of one steady friend. The one who lived with him. An actor called Julian something. Sweet man. Wouldn't hurt a fly. He's away on tour at the moment. Stuart told me.'

'Yes, but there'll have been other friends?' Closter-Bennet was getting bolder. 'That kind can be insanely jealous. Dangerously so. One is always reading— '

'You're suggesting Stuart was shot in a gay lovers' quarrel?' Mary interrupted, anger bringing colour back to her face.

Closter-Bennet shook his head. 'I'm only suggesting that Stuart's lifestyle made him subject to that sort of risk, so his death is very possibly— '

'It may well be unrelated to the other. For a variety of reasons

165

we know nothing about. Including the possibility that he was shot by . . . by a would-be burglar, for instance,' said McFee, waving away the smoke from his pipe, and metaphorically the threat of an open clash because of Mary's loyalty to Bodlin and the Finance Director's evident prejudice.

'The murderer was in a car. It drove out of the mews immediately after the shots were fired. No one saw the car. Only heard it,' said the banker.

'If Jane was out at the critical time, I suppose there's no one to vouch that Bob wasn't out as well,' said Mary slowly.

'That's true probably. But if the engine of his car had been warm as well we'd have been told, I expect,' said McFee. 'And if Bob's a suspect, why not the rest of us? We may all have to account for ourselves at the time of the murders. Both murders.'

'Why?' Closter-Bennet challenged sharply. 'It's obvious his kidnapping cronies killed Dermot. And why should any of us have wanted Stuart dead?'

'Hughie's right, I'm afraid,' said Treasure. 'The police already seem to think there was only one murderer. And I'd say that's very likely true. Murder's not that common after all. Not at board room level, thank God.'

'Two killers on the same patch would be quite a coincidence,' McFee agreed. 'Well, I was with my wife at home between the times they say Dermot was done for. The same applies at six o'clock this morning. I hope a wife is an acceptable alibi.'

'And I was airborne between Zürich and London when Dermot was killed,' said Treasure, anxious to keep this particular ball rolling. 'Molly and I were asleep in bed at six today. And I think wives are admissible witnesses, Hughie. Even somnolent wives.'

There was silence for a moment until Mary volunteered: 'I have no alibi for either time.' She looked at the others in turn. 'I was devoted to Stuart. And . . . and Dermot too, of course,' she finished steadily, her gaze dropping to study the clasped hands in her lap.

'This is a lot of nonsense anyway,' said Closter-Bennet while staring accusingly at McFee who had started it. 'I was certainly asleep at six this morning. Barbara woke me as usual at seven when she came back from riding.'

'And you were here at the critical time on Wednesday, I expect, Giles? Until you came to meet me at the airport?' Treasure enquired carefully.

166

'Er, yes. I must have left my office about seven thirty.'

'And you were here till then?'

Closter-Bennet's expression showed some surprise at the banker's fresh enquiry. 'Yes, certainly.'

Treasure nodded, then shuffled the papers on the table in front of him. 'No doubt the news of Stuart's death has been released by now. Also that Dermot was murdered. As you know, the original purpose of this meeting was for the board to be brought up to date on the takeover situation. We'd better cover that briefly, but there's not much point without the Managing Director.' He fiddled with the pen he had picked up. 'How much additional damage the death of Stuart Bodlin will do us remains to be seen, of course.'

'His loss is irreparable,' put in Mary, voice choking at the end, eyes welling with tears. 'I'm so sorry. Please excuse me.'

She hurried from the room.

'I wondered how long she'd last. Poor child. She's hit harder than anybody,' said McFee.

'Not more than Rosemary Hackle,' Closter-Bennet countered bluntly.

In response, McFee simply pulled hard and noisily on his pipe.

'Will she be all right?' asked Treasure.

'I think I heard her go into Mrs Tanner's office,' said McFee.

'In answer to your question, Chairman, Stuart's death shouldn't affect the viability of Seromig. The drug is too far advanced for that.' This was Closter-Bennet. 'It could affect the other development drugs, of course.'

'It could,' said McFee. 'But I agree with Giles about Seromig. Of course, Stuart has very able senior assistants. There's no reason why they can't carry on with the other development work. And Mary Ricini is a first rate Medical Director.'

'If Bob should leave us for any reason,' Closter-Bennet put in, 'and I'm not saying he will, but if he should, a takeover by Krontag might make a lot more sense than before.'

'Why?' asked McFee. 'Why would Bob going make that any more attractive?' This was much more a challenge than an enquiry.

'For a start, he's never liked the idea of our becoming a subsidiary of a bigger company. Especially Krontag. But with the loss of three senior directors there'd be a lot to be said for our becoming the British arm of an international group, with a share of central management services. There are great economies of scale with that kind of set-up.'

'You mean because Closter is now light on line management?' said Treasure, leaning back in his chair, arms folded across his chest.

'More positively that our management expenses have been slimmed down a lot through the deaths of Dermot and Stuart. And could be slimmed even more.' This was another obvious reference to the departure of Larden. 'That's always attractive to the buyer in a takeover situation, of course. But we still have adequate management for a subsidiary company, and profitable on-going business, with a world-beating new product ready for market, and two more in the pipeline.'

'Sounds like just as good a scenario for staying independent, to me,' said McFee, being purposely contrary. In the past he had been neutral to the idea of the company's being taken over. He was now talking against Krontag because he objected to their recent machinations, even if they hadn't been directly involved in the kidnap. For the moment, he was also cussedly inclined to oppose anything that Closter-Bennet was favouring.

'I understand what you both mean,' said Treasure, surprised at the extent of Closter-Bennet's clearly well rehearsed appraisal. 'But this isn't going to be decision day. I don't think anyone should be contemplating Bob's disappearing from the scene either.' Privately he was more interested in Closter-Bennet's reason for suggesting that possibility than he was in the possibility itself. 'Look, I don't like no comment responses from company spokesmen, but today I think we should avoid public statements from Closter directors. That's till we have more on the Jane Larden situation. Is that agreed?'

The others nodded. 'I'll tell Mary later,' said McFee.

'If you would? Thanks. Now before you both arrived, I rang Penny Cordwright,' Treasure went on. 'She has all she needs to cope with the media for the moment. If she has problems she'll refer back to you, Hughie.'

'I'll make myself available too, Mark,' Closter-Bennet put in quickly.

'With Bob taken up with Jane's problems, I think we may need you for meetings at the bank, Giles. There's a lot to do yet to sort out those share deal cancellations. Could you call Laurence Stricton right away? Tell him you'll sit in for Bob?'

'Understood, Chairman.'

In Treasure's experience, Closter-Bennet had never before shown

168

such apparent keenness for his work or knowledge of the larger issues affecting it. From the start of the meeting it was almost as though he'd been programmed.

The banker stood up. 'Now I must go. I'll be in touch during the day.'

'I'll see you to your car,' said Closter-Bennet.

'Please don't. I need a word on the way with Mrs Tanner.'

Chapter Nineteen

It was twenty minutes later when Treasure emerged from the Tanners' semi-detached home in Longbrook. He had been driven there directly from the factory. Bert Tanner was not as sleepy as on the previous morning. He had come off a later shift and delayed going to bed after eating the light meal Doris had left for him. This was after she had called to tell him that Treasure was coming. She had also cautioned him to show the visitor into the living room not the kitchen, and to make sure it was tidy first.

'If I can help any other way, you only got to say,' Bert offered, not quite certain in what way he had helped already – or if he had. He held open the gate at the end of the short concrete drive up to the garage. The two dogs stayed obediently behind him.

'Sorry about the mix-up, Mr Treasure. I'm no good on directorships. That kind of thing. Nor shares neither. Closed book to me.'

'I'm very grateful. If we could just keep this conversation to ourselves for the moment? I'll be in touch if necessary,' said Treasure, while thinking that Tanner would more likely be hearing from the police. 'Those dogs are beauties.'

Bert watched the Rolls-Royce drive out of the birch-lined avenue, wondered what the neighbours had made of the visit, cast an eye over the budded roses in the little front garden, made up his mind to spray them for greenfly later, yawned, scratched his chest through his open shirt, and went inside with the dogs.

He was cheerfully unaware that with all his ignorance, he might just have put the finger on a double murderer.

'London or Maidenhead, sir?' asked Henry Pink as he halted the car at the junction with the main road.

'Sorry, Henry. Maidenhead.' Treasure had been uncertain before his talk with Bert Tanner. 'I think I can direct you from there.'

'We've been to the house before, sir.'

170

'I'd forgotten.'

Earlier, Treasure had thought it likely that one or both of the Tanners had made a mistake. Now it was all clearer to him – if none the more palatable for that.

He had been sure from the start that Helga Greet had not been involved in Hackle's murder. The connection was too easily traced. Of course, that connection would never have come out in full if Hackle hadn't died. Since he had died, Greet and her collaborators simply didn't rate as prime suspects. They weren't even genuine kidnappers – only parties to an outrageous corporate scam that with a touch more luck might have worked. But they were industrial swindlers, not murderers. The police now seemed to have accepted that conclusion firmly enough. It was a pity they hadn't applied similar logic to eliminating Jane Larden from the suspect list.

Jane just might have killed Hackle – from jealousy, or slight. You could only guess at a reason. And you could never set limits on the behaviour of an oversexed, spectacularly beautiful, and very neurotic woman. The thing was possible, even allowing that Jane would have known that her professional connection with Mereworth Court would come out later, and that her affair with Hackle was known to some already. But Treasure was sure that she couldn't have killed Bodlin as well. The weapon used was witness to that, when compared with the subtle method he imagined she might have used to dispose of Hackle – taloned fingernails scoring the back of the victim's neck during a passionate embrace, disguising the prick of the skin with the Bovetormaz needle. But the same Jane Larden could never have felled Bodlin with a highly unsubtle barrelful of buckshot. It was out of the question.

Treasure was sure there had been only one murderer – someone connected with Closter who had planned Hackle's death, and who had most probably been panicked into killing Bodlin for a reason that ought to be more obvious than it was proving. And the identity of the killer needed disclosing fast. Apart from the harm being done to the unfairly implicated, the damage to the already beleaguered company was getting close to irreparable.

Because if the police let Jane Larden go, as Treasure was sure they would, there were plenty of others they could put in her place.

As a spurned lover, Mary Ricini had a reason to hurt Hackle – if she had known where to find him. She had left the Hackle house after learning from Tim that his father had been with a ginger-haired woman on Sunday afternoon. Had she gone to the Larden home assuming the redhead had been Jane? – and intending to discover if Jane knew something about Hackle's whereabouts? If so, had she run into Bodlin outside? And had he told her about what he had heard on the tape? And had she then waited to follow Jane when she left to meet their shared lover?

But this was another scenario that failed to account for Bodlin's murder. Death by Bovetormaz at the hands of a dextrous woman doctor seemed plausible enough, but Mary Ricini and a shotgun killing didn't go together – apart from the sheer unlikelihood of her doing harm to Bodlin in any circumstances. Her admiration for him as a scientist was clearly total.

Was it significant, Treasure wondered next, that Mary Ricini had just implied that Bob Larden had the opportunity at least to kill Bodlin?

Certainly Larden could have murdered Hackle, despite what he said to Treasure in the pub the night before. He could have played the tape without Jane knowing, before she left the house, perhaps when she was making the tea. He might have realised that something in the study had upset Bodlin. Then he could have followed Jane – spurred by a personal reason for wanting Hackle destroyed that transcended anybody else's.

But even in those circumstances, it made no sense for Larden to have gone on to kill Bodlin. He could only have done so *after* he knew that Bodlin had told Treasure about the tape, disclosing that Larden had also had the chance to hear it in time to do the killing. In other respects too, Larden could hardly have wanted to harm Bodlin who had been the key figure in Larden's own commercial future. All this was blindingly obvious – unless Larden had been desperate: unless murdering Bodlin threw suspicion for Hackle's death away from Larden and on to someone else.

While he was still debating whether it was right to dismiss Larden as a potential murderer, Treasure registered that the car was on the outskirts of Maidenhead – where the McFees lived.

It was Alison McFee who had discovered where Hackle was, allegedly by chance, and later disclosed the fact to her husband. But what if she had come upon more than Hackle's car parked in the Mereworth Court basement?

What if Alison had seen Jane's car in the basement too, or watched Jane driving in? Could she even have seen Jane and Hackle together? And would she have avoided disclosing this to anyone to protect Jane. Or could she have murdered Hackle herself, leaving Jane to be implicated for the crime? In fact, would it have taken more than a knowledge of Hackle's fresh infamy to rekindle the loathing Alison must have previously harboured for her daughter's seducer?

And if it was still too fanciful to imagine that Alison had been touring West London with a phial of poison ready to extinguish enemies on impulse, would her husband have done so in a premeditated way, once she had told him what she knew?

McFee had a triple motive for killing Hackle – outrage over the kidnap scam, retribution for the seduction of the McFee daughter, and finally the prospect of his eventually becoming Managing Director of Closter Drug if Hackle was removed. There was only his word for it, too, that the Scotsman had been with his wife at the time of Hackle's death – something no doubt Alison could have been warned to confirm.

And Treasure was almost sure that McFee had figured Hackle to have been the Irish voice on the telephone long before anyone else. He was nearly certain that McFee had begun to say so when he returned to the meeting in Larden's office, after testing the tape, on Tuesday evening. That the Scotsman hadn't finished what he had started to say then was capable of several interpretations – the most charitable being that he had been interrupted.

But it was again the death of Bodlin that saved McFee from being an evident suspect now. As with Larden, he hadn't lacked the opportunity to kill the scientist, but it seemed illogical that he should want to harm him at all, unless Treasure had overlooked something important.

Closter-Bennet's position was different.

The Finance Director had seemed to dislike Hackle almost as keenly as Bodlin had done. And if keenness was not his usual forte, he was still as outraged as both Bodlin and McFee at Hackle's duplicity over the kidnap – and more than anyone else over the way Hackle had leaked the confidential reports on Seromig: he had called that the essence of perfidy – strong words for Closter-Bennet. He also had a larger personal expectancy about becoming a future Closter managing director than either of his two colleagues, if with less justification. For that reason, he might have been readier than McFee not to baulk at wasting Bodlin with a shotgun if it was essential. He might also have had time to drive to Bodlin's place and back this morning while his wife was out riding.

Added to all of which, Closter-Bennet had just been the one to insist that Hackle must have been murdered by his fellow kidnap conspirators, and that Bodlin had been shot by a boyfriend.

Except: Closter-Bennet had a witness to his being at the factory at the time Hackle was killed. Mrs Edwards, Bodlin's secretary, had told Doris Tanner that she was sure she saw him at ten to seven on Wednesday evening, just as she was leaving. Doris had dutifully reported this to Treasure after the meeting this morning, although both she and the banker had been puzzled by the information. It had even gone through Treasure's mind, after leaving Doris Tanner, to question if Closter-Bennet and Mrs Edwards might be special intimates, or even lovers, which was a choice bit of misdirected lateral thinking: Mrs Edwards, whom Treasure had never met, was a grandmotherly sixty-two, and the worthy Convenor of her local Methodist Sisterhood.

Bert Tanner had proved to know the lady well.

Which left only one person.

'We're here, sir. Mr Closter-Bennet's house.' Henry Pink was holding the rear door open for Treasure to get out.

'Thanks. I shouldn't be long.' He had hardly been aware of their covering the three miles between Maidenhead and Later Burnlow. The weathered brick house was on the edge of the village, its substantial grounds bordering open farmland.

'Mark, what a delightful surprise.'

But Barbara Closter-Bennet's welcome had a note of question in it too. She had appeared not at the front door but from the far side of the gravelled drive, advancing with lively steps from the direction of the stables. A tired-looking spaniel was plodding at her heels. Barbara's almost boyish figure was clothed in a brown shirt, fawn trousers and green gumboots. She had a shotgun tucked in to the crook of one arm, with a large canvas game bag slung over the opposite shoulder. The head of a dead rabbit stared balefully from under the flap of the bag.

'I came on the off chance,' the banker explained. 'I rang from the car earlier, but there was no reply.'

'I've been out keeping down the vermin, as you can see. Did you expect to see Giles? I'm afraid he isn't here.'

'I know. I've come from the factory. He was just leaving for a meeting at the bank. It's you I've come to see.'

'I'm flattered. Sorry I'm not dressed for the occasion. D'you want to go inside? It's such a pretty morning the garden might be nicer.'

'Much nicer. Your roses are well advanced.' They moved along the wide paved pathway around the house to the terrace.

'Everything in the garden's early this year. After that mild winter.' She touched a rosebud in passing. 'How's Molly? Back at work?'

'No, still resting.'

'I remember now she told me. Do her good. Give her my love, won't you? Want some coffee? It won't take a minute.' They were moving towards chairs set near the lawn. There was a massive copper beech close to the eastern flank of the house here. It was throwing morning shadows over the York flagstones. Barbara dropped the bag at her feet and leaned the double-barrelled gun against the table at her side.

'No coffee, thanks.' He frowned. 'I don't know whether you've heard. Stuart Bodlin's been killed. Murdered.'

'Good Lord. No I hadn't. We only heard late last night about how Hackle really died. But how ghastly. When did this happen?' She moved a chair so that when she sat it was with her back to the sun. The dog settled beside her.

'This morning, around six. He was shot in the head.'

'Do they know who did it?' She was sitting very upright, her back and arms not touching the chair.

'The police think they do. They're on the point of arresting Jane Larden.'

'Oh no. I can't believe Jane could do such a thing. I mean, she's sunk to the bottom of everyone's estimation, but a murderess? No.'

'I'm glad you think so too.'

She crossed her legs. 'Is Bodlin's death linked to the other?'

'To Dermot's? It seems inevitable, yes.'

'And they're accusing Jane of both?'

'They're about to.' He raised a hand, then stroked the back of his head with it. 'Do you see much of her?'

'Not that much, no. And it'll be considerably less in the future, I can tell you. Even if Bob takes her back. More fool him if he does. Cigarette?' She offered the packet she had taken from her shirt pocket.

'No thanks. I gather Jane's doing some work for you here?'

175

'She was,' came out bluntly, as the speaker lit her cigarette. 'Making estimates to do over two of the rooms.'

'Bob told me you had a meeting arranged at their house on Wednesday morning.'

'To look at some fabrics, yes. I had to cancel it.'

'Because of trouble with a horse?'

'That's right. I had Parkes, the local vet, here.'

'What was the problem?'

'My grey stallion Fernando. He had a twisted gut, poor old boy. Needed a nasty little operation.'

'Is he all right now?'

'Yes, thanks. He's a tough old thing.'

'Did the operation involve a full anaesthetic?'

'Yes.' She blinked quickly several times after replying.

'Did the vet use Bovetormaz?'

Her forehead creased. 'He may have done. D'you know I'm not sure?' She blew smoke from her nostrils, while holding the cigarette between the very straight fingers of a hand held at eye level, to one side, and well away from her body. 'There are several anaesthetics of that type. All much of a muchness, I imagine.'

'And all equally dangerous?'

'To humans? Probably. One is so used to handling these things though.'

'Did you assist in the operation?'

'Assist? I mucked in, yes. Owners do, you know. It was fairly straightforward.'

'Was there anyone else present? Did the vet bring an assistant?'

She smiled. 'He doesn't have one. There was only me. Why?'

'Were you in charge of the antidote? In case the vet got any anaesthetic on his skin?'

'Yes, but Reggie Parkes is very careful. Old, but very careful.'

'But he had the antidote handy, and showed you what to do in an emergency?'

'It was there, yes. One knows what to do. I've been around horses a long time. I don't understand— '

'What happened to the syringe afterwards? The disposable syringe with the anaesthetic in it?'

'It went into Reggie's sharp box.'

'Sharp box?'

'Little plastic bins vets carry around with them. For things destined for the incinerator. Doctors use them too.'

'So who put the syringe in the sharp box – you or the vet?'

'Reggie, I expect.' She inhaled deeply on the cigarette.

'You expect?'

'Does it matter?'

'Perhaps not. And he took the sharp box away with him?'

She shifted in her chair. The spaniel looked up nervously. 'As a matter of fact he didn't. It was full of used bits. He always forgets to get rid of his boxes. Left it for me to incinerate.'

'You have an incinerator here?'

'No. There's one at the hospital. I'm often there. On voluntary work. Lady Bountiful stuff.'

'Did you go on the same day?'

'Probably. That or the next day.'

'Yesterday?'

'No, it was Wednesday. The hospital's on the route to practically anywhere from this house. Look, Mark, if you're suggesting that syringe had something to do with Dermot's death, forget it. The box would have been locked in my car boot till it went for burning.'

'And you went to London later on Wednesday?'

'Yes. In the afternoon. To my dentist. Bloody inconvenient as it happened, but I didn't want to cancel that appointment. Not unless I absolutely had to. It's so difficult to get another these days. I got a girl from the local livery stable to sit with Fernando.'

'And you incinerated the vet's sharp box on the way up or the way back?'

She hesitated. 'On the way up to London.'

'I see. And on the way home you dropped in at the Lardens'?'

She jerked forward. 'I didn't say that.' Her eyes squinted at the cigarette as she stubbed it out in the large glass ashtray on the table.

'Let's just say you did go there, all the same. Hoping to catch Jane. To see the fabrics after all.'

'But I did no such thing.'

'Only because you ran into Bodlin outside the house. A confused, jibbering Bodlin. You wouldn't be his natural confidant, but he was desperate to unburden on someone. And what he told you made you see red. About the tape he'd just heard. Of a conversation between Jane and Dermot. That made it very plain there'd been no kidnap. So they'd tricked everyone into selling their Closter shares. It also proved that Jane and Dermot were lovers, with a meeting planned for four thirty. And I imagine all that made you angrier than you'd ever been in your life.'

Her shoulders lifted and dropped again. 'I'm sure I don't know what you're talking about.'

'I think you do. You followed Jane, and told Bodlin you were going to. He wouldn't have done the same, of course. Or gone with you. Not his style. You found out which flat she was in by checking the bays in the basement at Mereworth Court. Then waited for Jane to leave. You knew she'd be a while, of course, which is why you had time to go shopping. At a guess, for some strong household gloves? Something you didn't have with you, but which in view of the plan you'd concocted you knew you'd be needing? For handling something dangerous? They'd also ensure you left no fingerprints in the flat.'

'Really, Mark, is this a game? I was never in— '

'You were seen leaving the supermarket. By a reliable witness who followed you.' He paused for a moment. Barbara stayed silent. 'You got Dermot to open the door of the flat immediately after you saw Jane leave,' he continued. 'Probably because he thought you were Jane coming back for something. You took him by surprise. Was he trying to slam the door on you as you stabbed at him with the syringe? And did he know what you'd done to him? I don't think he did. Not till it was too late.'

'You're quite mad.'

'No, but you were. When you cut him with that needle.'

'Leaving Bodlin to tell everyone I'd gone there, I suppose?'

'I'm afraid that's just what he did eventually.'

'But he's dead.' She glanced to one side, directly at the gun.

'I'm afraid he told people before he died.'

'You're lying. He promised me— ' She stopped in mid-sentence.

'Promised you he'd tell no one?' He watched her carefully. 'But he went away to think about it. Last night he came to see Molly and me. At home.'

'Oh? At what time was that?'

'After dinner. About nine.' He noted the relief on her face. 'Did he phone you after that? And did he swear he'd kept his word to you? To that point? But from the way he talked, did you have serious doubts he'd stay the course? And in the end did you figure you'd have to silence him? That it wasn't too late to do it this morning? Well you were wrong about

178

that. After he'd spoken to you he had a call from his actor friend.'

'You couldn't know that. You're lying again.'

She was right, of course, but her eyes showed doubt.

'You can risk thinking that if you want,' Treasure replied. 'But there are other witnesses to what I've said.' He looked at the gun. 'Incidentally, it'd be pointless trying to shoot me too. Even if you were quick enough on the draw. You'd have to do for my chauffeur afterwards, and my office knows where we are.'

She gave a snort. 'The gun isn't loaded.'

'Then you won't mind my taking charge of it.' He rose, picked up the gun, and opened the breech. Both barrels were empty. He went back to his seat, placing the open weapon beside it. 'So, going back to Chiswick on Wednesday evening.'

'I wasn't in Chiswick on Wednesday evening.' She rubbed the dog's head: it had sat up expectantly when Treasure moved the gun.

'I've told you someone will swear to seeing you there. Leaving the supermarket. And going into Mereworth Court.' The last claim wasn't true, but it hit home because the first one had been. 'And once the police know about that, you can be sure they'll find other witnesses. Someone who saw you with Bodlin near the Larden house. Someone who'll remember you driving into or out of that mews this morning. Once they have a strong lead to follow the police are very dogged. Their enquiries take time, but they have plenty of that. You haven't. Not before they come to arrest you. And I imagine they'll be doing that quite soon. As soon as they've interviewed Bodlin's friend Julian. I'm deadly serious.'

For the first time in several minutes there was a prolonged silence between the two.

Eventually, when the woman lifted her gaze to meet his, there was resolution, not panic or even surrender, in her eyes. She breathed in and out several times, deeply and slowly, before speaking. 'Bodlin was the risk, of course,' she said slowly. 'Either way. Yes, I was mad when I went after Hackle. I don't regret what happened to him.' She looked away defiantly, across the lawn. 'Bodlin was different. He was so bloody weak and wet. He only had to promise he'd keep his mouth shut. Permanently. He couldn't do that. Couldn't stop quibbling. No guts, that kind.'

'Or in his case too much, perhaps?'

Her eyebrows lifted. 'I hadn't thought of it that way.' Her

gaze was strangely remote as she turned to Treasure again and added, 'Honestly, I didn't want to kill Bodlin. But what else could I do?'

The spaniel's head lifted. The animal looked up pleadingly at its mistress, wiggled its rump, then let out a whimper.

Chapter Twenty

'My grandfather started the company. He was very successful. I think I've always known my father deserved to lose control of it,' Barbara Closter-Bennet was relating in a monotone. She seemed oblivious to time and her plight. 'It was still humiliating when Daddy sold out. For so little. If only I'd been a man. I'd have gone into the business. With proper training, who knows? I might have stopped the collapse.' She shook her head gently. 'Daddy didn't believe in education for daughters. Even a daughter who was an only child. I didn't complain, of course. Not at the time. I was only interested in horses.'

'And Giles?' Treasure put in.

'Was Daddy's choice of a husband. I'd just begun dimly to realise something had to be done about Closter Drug. Giles was in the company. Daddy said he was going to make him Managing Director eventually. It never happened, of course. Anyway, it seemed only right I should marry him. Support for the old firm, as it were.'

'But he wasn't destined to save Closter either.'

'He was never offered a proper chance,' she came back with more feeling than before, though her gaze stayed on the hands clasped in front of her. 'Because others didn't believe he was up to it. In the end the chance went to Larden and Hackle. And see what's happened as a result? One of them swindles us all, abetted by the other's wife. It's so wrong.'

'And you thought getting rid of Dermot would put Giles on top again?'

She hesitated for a moment before answering. 'In the end I was mad enough with Dermot to destroy him whatever the consequences. For his perfidy. He disgusted me. Still does. But I didn't set out to kill him. Just to frighten the bloody life out of him. With the syringe. If I could get him seated. Then rush him.' She

181

shrugged dismissively. 'I don't know. I imagined holding the thing over him. While I made him confess everything to Bob Larden on the phone. That's roughly what I planned. While I waited for Jane to come out.'

'You didn't try to catch them together?'

'No chance. They'd never have let me in. You were right, as soon as she'd left, I pretended to be her so he'd open the door. And when he did, he panicked as soon as he saw me. Fought to shut me out again. We struggled. I'm much stronger than I look. He never saw the syringe. It was under the flap of my handbag. I wasn't certain I'd caught his skin with the needle. Not quite certain. In the end he pushed me back into the hall and slammed the door on me.'

'And you didn't send for anyone?'

'I was going to call Giles. Or Bob Larden. As soon as I found a phone box. To tell everything. What Bodlin couldn't bring himself to do. Do you see that? He'd been sitting in his car till I came along, still not really crediting what he'd heard on that tape. And if Jane had since wiped the tape, nothing could have been proved. I realised that. It's why I followed her in the first place.'

'But after the struggle with Dermot, you still didn't phone anyone?'

'No. When I got to a phone box it dawned on me I might have killed him. All right, probably had killed him. In which case I knew there was a chance I'd get away with it. I did the incinerating on the way home.'

'You realised that someone else would be blamed for the murder?'

'Certainly not. Death from Bovetormaz looks the same as a cardiac arrest. Heart failure. Giles told me that years ago. I've never forgotten it.'

'But an autopsy— '

'Wouldn't necessarily have proved anything different. If they hadn't got all conscientious about the scratch on his neck they mightn't have looked for another cause of death. And don't tell me they're more thorough than that, because I know that often they're not. Depends on who does the autopsy. I was just unlucky.'

'Which left your future in Bodlin's hands? You know he still believed that Dermot had died from a heart attack?'

She looked up at Treasure. 'Until you told him differently. Then he put two and two together. On the phone last night he

182

swore he hadn't told anyone he'd seen me. Or that I'd followed Jane.'

'So why— '

'He hadn't told anyone up till then, that is,' she interrupted. 'And when he promised not to he was hedging. I simply couldn't believe he'd hold to it. Not once he was sure it was I who'd killed Hackle. His conscience was worrying him already. Can you credit, he had a conscience about the bugger who'd swindled him out of millions?' She took another deep breath. 'I came to the conclusion I couldn't live with my freedom dependent on Bodlin's conscience. Why should I when my own was clear? I woke up early this morning knowing I had to silence him. It was him or me. Or that's the way I saw it in the small hours. All right, it was selfish as well as brutal. And I know he was an important scientist. But he brought it on himself all the same. For being so bloody wet.'

'How much does your husband know of all this?' Treasure asked woodenly.

'Nothing. Absolutely nothing.' She made the words sound the most convincing she had spoken. 'He was asleep when I left this morning. I had to wake him when I got back. He assumed I'd been riding as usual.'

'At the meeting this morning he was unusually bullish and confident. Seemed to be trying to take command. Almost as though he'd been programmed.'

'Good. In a way he had been programmed. I'd told him he had to stake his claim to be the next MD. With Hackle dead and Bob Larden probably having to resign over his wife's behaviour. I've ended Giles's chances now, of course.' But her tone still suggested there might be some doubt in the matter. 'Look, before you turn me in, can I ask a favour?'

'Naturally. In any case I'd rather you turned yourself in.'

'Glad you made it, darling. It's really great fun,' Molly Treasure enthused. 'Bit crowded. More so this afternoon, for the Highland Games. Junior Highland Games really. More like a school sports day, but still very Scottish. You should have seen them tossing the caber. Weather's been idyllic, of course. They say it's the start of a heatwave. I gave out some of the prizes at the end. Tonight is just the dancing and a barbecue. Very superior barbecue.' She slipped an arm under her husband's as they weaved through the crowd.

183

'Come and look at the river. It's rather romantic. The food and drink are down there too.'

It was nearly eight o'clock on the day following Treasure's confrontation with Barbara Closter-Bennet. He and Molly had arrived separately at the Scottish Festival in Maidenhead, she several hours before this as the McFees' special guest. The event was being staged on a big river meadow next to the McFees' house, north of the town. There was a canvas pavilion with a bandstand and dance floor. The Treasures, who had just found each other, had been watching from outside. The tent sides had been removed because of the warm weather. It had been dry and sunny in the afternoon, then balmy as the evening lengthened.

A seemingly endless eightsome reel was being performed, expertly, by a troupe of swarthy young men in kilts, and lithe young women in white dresses with tartan sashes, all to the accompaniment of Scottish pipes.

'Would you believe, the dancers are from Basingstoke, and the pipers from Milton Keynes? Rather incongruous but perfectly genuine,' said Molly as the two moved away.

'More national barriers tumbling before the onward march of the European Market,' Treasure observed dourly. 'They'll be offering haggis on the Champs-Élysées soon, I expect. And welcome to it. Sorry I was so late.'

'Poor you.' She squeezed his arm. 'You've worked the whole day.'

'And not the only one. Though the City's pleasantly empty on Saturdays.'

'Your dedicated secretary got here about an hour ago. She's over there somewhere, decked out like a mature Flora Macdonald, and dying to dance when the demonstration stuff is over. The McFees have been treating me like royalty. There aren't so many Closter people here. Not the ones I know, anyway.'

Treasure glanced about, failing to recognise anyone. 'Miss Gaunt left the office around five,' he said. 'It was the police who delayed me at the end. Detective Inspector Furlong turned up just as I was leaving. Wasn't awfully pleased. Can't blame him, I suppose. Except the case was as good as wrapped up for him.'

'Had the Closter-Bennets' solicitor called the police?'

'As promised. As soon as he had the confirmation that Barbara's plane had landed.'

'And the solicitor told them she'd followed Jane to the flat on Wednesday?'

'And confronted Dermot there.'

'And that was all?'

'That was the deal I made with Barbara. The police were also told that she went abroad yesterday afternoon and doesn't intend to return. Ever.'

'And that was enough?'

'Enough for them since to have released Jane.'

'So they know Barbara did the murders?'

'That circumstances indicate she did, yes. They still need to prove it if they want. But they've stopped treating other people as suspects.'

'Even though there's been no actual confession? Not to them?'

'That's true. But they now have the same evidence I had.'

'Which wasn't much, you said.'

'Because I had to bluff Barbara a good deal of the time. The only really damning fact was Bert Tanner seeing her in Chiswick.'

'Which you dismissed at first?'

'Only because Mrs Tanner said it was Giles Closter-Bennet he'd seen, not Barbara. And I knew he couldn't have. The Tanners had misunderstood each other. Anyway, the police now know Barbara was there. They also have the Closter-Bennet shotgun.'

'Can they prove it was the gun that killed poor Stuart Bodlin?'

'Not for certain, apparently. It seems that kind of identification works with a pistol or a rifle, but not a shotgun. Especially if the gun's been used again later.'

'Do you suppose Barbara knew that? Purposely went rabbit shooting?'

'It's possible. Even so, the police still have enough material to start building a case. And Barbara certainly knew that.'

'You didn't tell Mr Furlong that she'd admitted anything more to you?'

'No. That was also part of the deal.' His serious expression deepened. 'I didn't see it as my task to send the guilty to jail. Only to keep the innocent out of it.'

'And to lift the cloud from Closter Drug?'

'That too, of course. The rest really is up to the police.'

'They can extradite Barbara from Argentina can't they?'

'They can try, but they'll have problems. Without a confession, and with a case still largely based on deduction. Most justice departments, including ours, need pretty strong indications of guilt before authorising an extradition. Remember, Barbara has dual nationality.'

'Because her mother was Argentinian?'

'That's right. Very well-to-do Argentinian. Barbara has a lot of influential connections out there.'

'More than Scotland Yard perhaps. So what about Giles?'

'The police have already had him in for questioning, and let him go again.'

'But he won't be staying with the company?'

'No. He gave me his resignation this morning.'

'And you've settled the future of Closter Drug?'

'Hardly that. But we've made some decisions today. I shan't be giving up the chairmanship, and Bob Larden will carry on as MD. We're going to oppose takeover bids from whatever quarter, unless someone offers a lot more than we think is the company's present worth. I have a solid group of institutional shareholders supporting that view. Effectively they make a majority.'

'But you're still saying Closter Drug is going to be taken over by somebody? Eventually?'

'That's up to the shareholders to decide. What's important immediately is for the company to get back its credibility. Its dignity, if you like.'

'Which is why you didn't want a murder trial?'

'Mmm. To further muddy the waters. Seromig is the key, of course. If we're first with a migraine cure the price of the company could double. Otherwise it'll still be valuable for its other interests, only it may not be able to develop them on its own. You're right, this is very peaceful,' he ended.

The two had wandered to a point on the river bank away from both the pavilion and the barbecue area, and where the music was very much only in the background. There was gentle activity on the water appropriate to the hour and the temperature. Two swans glided past parallel with the reedy bank where a family of ducks was exploring. Pleasure craft – crews idling, engines muted, lights diffused by the gloaming but reflected in the darkening water – were slipping past, making down river to Windsor or up it to Henley.

Molly was watching the ducks. 'And as part of un-muddying the waters,' she said, 'have the Closter-Bennets really given away their Closter shares to the Hackles?'

186

'Yes. Giles transferred them into a trust for Rosemary and the two children this morning. The trust will be administered by the bank.'

'And that was part of your deal with Barbara? For letting her fly away yesterday afternoon?'

'It was the key part of the deal. I honestly believe it's the fairest outcome for the Hackles. Having Barbara Closter-Bennet tried and imprisoned would have provided nothing for those children.' He ruminated for several seconds. 'It was a horse trade of a particularly uncomfortable kind, of course. I hope it proves the right decision.' But there was more heaviness than uncertainty in his voice. 'Giles had to agree to the transfer, of course. The shares were in his name.'

'Well that's to his credit.'

'I thought so.' But the tone was less than magnanimous.

'Will he join his wife in Buenos Aires?'

'That's the intention. They'll have to rub along on what's left of her capital. The sale of the Later Burnlow house should fetch quite a bit, I suppose. But they won't be as comfortable as they were in this country.'

'Well they don't deserve to be, either. She doesn't anyway.' Molly was deep down disquieted that justice hadn't been properly served. Like her husband, though, she saw what was happening as the best solution for the Hackle family – and one that would not have been achieved if Barbara Closter-Bennet had been brought to trial. 'Of course, Barbara's certainly not in the clear. And she'll have to live with her conscience for the rest of her life,' Molly ruminated aloud.

'I'm not sure she'll find that too hard,' Treasure commented. 'Her crimes were motivated by ambition and revenge. And according to her own very twisted logic they were justified.'

'The ambition being for herself?'

'No, for Giles. And Closter Drug. The revenge was against her father. For failing her.'

'And how does Giles feel about being married to a murderess?'

'It's something he'll choose permanently to ignore, I should think. He's always been totally dependent on her. His only true career aspirations were the ones she forced on him. He'll be happy to drop out of the business scene now. He has no proper regard for his own industrial acumen – and that's an opinion he shares with many others, including me.' Treasure's tone had remained sombre.

Molly wrapped both arms around one of his and began steering him towards the bar. 'So altogether you've made the best of an appalling situation.'

'That's a charitable way of putting it.'

'And you richly deserve a large Scotch. Followed by a slice of whatever it is they're roasting on that spit, before we recklessly plunge into a round of the Gay Gordons at . . . at nine forty.' Molly had checked the time and her programme.

Treasure sniffed, then stared around defensively. 'I'm not sure that bagpipes don't sometimes give me migraine,' he said in an overly self-protecting way.

'Good for trade,' his wife answered firmly, and with enthusiasm.